The Hot One

by Lauren Blakely

Also By Lauren Blakely

The Caught Up in Love Series (Each book in this series follows a different couple so each book can be read separately, or enjoyed as a series since characters crossover)

Caught Up In Us
Pretending He's Mine
Trophy Husband
Stars in Their Eyes

Standalone Novels
BIG ROCK
Mister O
Well Hung
The Sexy One
Full Package
The Hot One
Joy Stick (May 2017)
Most Valuable Playboy (July 2017)
The Wild One (August 2017)
Happy Trail (November 2017)
Far Too Tempting
21 Stolen Kisses
Playing With Her Heart

The No Regrets Series
The Thrill of It
The Start of Us
Every Second With You

The Seductive Nights Series

First Night (Julia and Clay, prequel novella)

Night After Night (Julia and Clay, book one)

After This Night (Julia and Clay, book two)

One More Night (Julia and Clay, book three)

A Wildly Seductive Night (Julia and Clay novella, book 3.5)

Nights With Him (A standalone novel about Michelle and Jack)

Forbidden Nights (A standalone novel about Nate and Casey)

The Sinful Nights Series

Sweet Sinful Nights

Sinful Desire

Sinful Longing

Sinful Love

The Fighting Fire Series

Burn For Me (Smith and Jamie)

Melt for Him (Megan and Becker)

Consumed By You (Travis and Cara)

The Jewel Series

A two-book sexy contemporary romance series

The Sapphire Affair

The Sapphire Heist

ABOUT

At first glance, stripping naked at my ex-girlfriend's place of work might not seem like the brightest way to win her back.

But trust me on this count - she always liked me best without any clothes on. And sometimes you've got to play to your strengths when you're fighting an uphill battle. I'm prepared to fight for her...and to fight hard. I might have let her slip through my fingers the last time, but no way will that happen twice.

He's the one who got away...

The nerve of Tyler Nichols to reappear like that, stripping at my job, showing off his rock hard body that drove me wild far too many nights. That man with his knowing grin and mischievous eyes is nothing but a cocky, arrogant jerk to saunter back into my life. Except, what if he's not a jerk . . .? He's the one I've tried like hell to forget but just can't. Maybe I'm cursed to remember him. My money is on him being the same guy he always was, but what's the harm in giving him a week to prove he's a new man? I won't fall for him again.

But how do you resist the hot one...

Dedication

To Karen. For one note that mattered so much.

His Prologue

Technically, I didn't drop my drawers the first time I saw her again. Just my balls.

The ones in my hands. *Juggling balls.*

Here's how it went down. Picture a Sunday morning in Central Park. A perfect summer day. The grass was green, the breeze was warm, and I'd just spent the last few hours getting acquainted with turtles and frogs at the children's zoo because I'm an awesome uncle. And Carly's one cool seven-year-old.

The kid loves all creatures, but especially the ones that jump and crawl, so I took her to the enchanted forest part of the zoo. When we finished, she tugged on my shirt sleeve, batted her hazel eyes, and asked ever so sweetly for an ice cream cone.

Like I stood a chance at resisting her. *C'mon.* She's my cousin's kid, and clearly she gets her charm from our side of the family.

With her hand in mine, we strolled across the grass near the running path, hunting for the nearest ice cream dealer.

And then Carly did that thing little kids do.

She shrieked for what seemed like absolutely no reason. Next, she pointed to an impossibly tall dude wearing a beret while juggling two Rubik's Cubes, two orange balls, and a small green beanbag.

"He can do five, Uncle Tyler!" Carly shouted, her eyes going wide.

"Five isn't too shabby," I said with a shrug.

She turned to me with a questioning stare. "I've never seen *you* do five."

"That's because I haven't shown you all my tricks yet."

"Can you really juggle five balls?"

I scoffed. "Please, I can do that with my eyes closed."

I didn't put myself through law school juggling for nothing.

Just kidding.

You can't put yourself through law school juggling anything but insane class schedules and lack of sleep.

Carly arched an eyebrow. So did the juggler, as he kept up the cascade of his quintet. *Show-off.*

"I want to see. Show me," Carly urged.

Yeah, Carly's a chip off the old block. She's all about challenging me, and I'm all about rising to the challenge.

The stick-thin guy with the beret raised his chin. "Have at it, man."

With clockwork precision, he let the balls fall out of orbit and into his palm. Next, the Rubik's Cubes. Then the beanbag. He stepped closer, handed me the objects, and flashed a crooked, put-your-money-where-your-mouth-is grin.

Game on.

Packs of runners jogged along, cyclists wheeled over the black asphalt, and rollerbladers whizzed by on the concrete. With my feet parked hip's width apart, I stood at the edge of the grass getting a feel for the items, weighing them, and then one, two, three, four, five, I whisked each one up into the air in a high oval arc. Round and round, in a perfect five-ball cascade.

Carly clapped, then demanded more. "Yes, now close your eyes!"

I groaned. What was I thinking? Juggling with eyes closed is fucking hard. But I could pull it off for a couple seconds. My special skill. I obliged my niece's request, pulling off a few quick blind ovals. Five seconds later, after I'd shown off that particular party trick, I opened my eyes.

And I saw a vision from my past.

A blond beauty, with long legs, a lovely round ass, and a high ponytail swishing back and forth across her shoulders. She ran along the path in tiny orange let-me-peel-them-off-with-my-teeth-pretty-please running shorts. And that face. Dear Lord, the stunning face of an angel. High cheekbones. Deep brown eyes that saw me like no one ever had. Those red lips, shaped like a bow. Fuck me, the things she could do with those lips. The things I taught her to do with that sinful mouth.

Delaney sure as hell knew how to use it, and I don't just mean in the bedroom. We used to talk about anything and everything when we were together in college. Days with her. Nights with her. Best time of my life. That woman was full of spark. Full of fire. So damn passionate. And look at her now.

Jesus Christ.

It had to be illegal to be that smoking hot.

She wasn't alone. She ran with two other chicks and a couple dogs.

As for me? Mister fast on his feet, quick with a word, never met a situation he can't talk his way out of? Scratch all that right then and there. Because I dropped the cubes. I dropped the beanbag. And I dropped the orange balls in a pile of wreckage at my feet.

My jaw fell, too.

But the best part? All that came out of my mouth was a muffled *Hey.*

Yep. Eight years later and I could only utter a monosyllable.

Height of my mother-fucking unbrilliance.

She rolled her eyes and shook her head as she trotted past me. Over her shoulder, she called out, "How's the juggling working out for you now, Tyler?"

Oh, zinger, how you slay me.

The lady won.

The lady killed it.

"Great. I kept it up," I shouted.

She gave herself away for a sliver of a second, and if I were in court, I'd have known then I had her. She let her gaze linger far too long. Giving me that patented you-were-in-my-fantasies-last-night look I knew so well, her eyes roaming down my face, my chest, and yeah, there, right fucking there, to her favorite part.

She *loved* that part.

But this wasn't a courtroom battle.

Because when she cast her pretty brown eyes to my niece, I saw Delaney adding up the years and computing possibilities. "Looks like you sure did," she said, deadpan all the way.

She snapped her gaze from me, zeroed in on the path in front of her, and sprinted.

With her friends and the dogs flanking her, she tore past and left me in the dust with my balls, my jaw, and my composure lying in the dirt at my feet.

To say I'd been thinking of her every day for the last eight years would be a lie. To say I'd gone those eight years without ever once thinking of her would be an even bigger fib.

But I sure as hell didn't expect to run into her one fine Sunday morning in the park. I wasn't prepared. I wasn't ready. And my first thought was to catch up and explain that I hadn't ditched her to have a kid. Closing the distance would have been easy. I can run like the wind. I can put one foot in front of the other and hoof it. But I had my favorite person with me, and no way was I going to drag Carly in a chase after a girl I once loved like the sun.

Still, I tried.

I grabbed Carly's hand and yelled. "Delaney!"

She didn't even turn around, and soon she was a speck rounding the bend.

I suppose, in retrospect, the last words out of my mouth when I dumped her shouldn't have been, "It's too hard to juggle classes and you."

Her Prologue

I'm cursed.

There's no other explanation for this *thing* that happens to me every time I get close.

I'm not talking about horseshoes close, either.

I mean every single time I take the rabbit out for a ride.

The bunny makes it clear it needs a certain stallion to get over the hump.

Do bunnies even like horses?

I don't know, but it pisses me off that my traitorous body seems to need one man, and one man only, to fly off the cliff.

I don't ask for this kind of sexual haunting. Hell, I don't even believe in ghosts. But the ghost of boyfriends past has been inhabiting my fantasies for years. I try like hell to rely on Henry Cavill, Chris Hemsworth, or Michael Fassbender. I mean, really. *Michael Fassbender.* And we all know what he's packing.

But nope.

My brain won't bend to his Fass.

I've learned to stop fighting it. I just go with it when my ex pops into my solo flights. I grit my teeth and bear it, and let him join Bunny to take me to the magic land. Then I turn off the pink toy, tuck it into the drawer, and drift asleep, satisfied, but also not.

That's been my life for the last year and a half. The biggest and littlest Os come with double-A assistance. So Bunny and I have gotten a lot closer. Sometimes, we make it a double.

And in the mornings, I pretend I didn't get off to Tyler Fucking Nichols.

That man.

That cocky jerk who broke my heart.

But even if he inhabits my naughty imagination, I do take some solace in knowing I'm over Tyler. I'm so over the way he ended things eight years ago. I've moved on, thank you very much. This is purely a physical possession, nothing more. Hell, it's not really a surprise that my mind wanders to his particular talents, given the way he owned my body when we were younger. But I sure do wish he'd stop crashing my BYOB— that's bring your own batteries—parties.

One Sunday morning, I stumbled upon the key to exorcising him.

Here's how it all went down.

I popped out of bed, washed my face, brushed my teeth, pulled my hair into a ponytail, and tugged on my running shorts.

A little later, I met up with my good friends Penny and Nicole at the entrance to Central Park, and we began our training run for a 10K race we're doing in a few weeks. I figured it would be just another morning jog, followed by a plate of two eggs, any style, with a strong mug of green tea at my favorite sidewalk café, The Charming Breakfast Spot.

Instead, I saw *him*.

Juggling.

Of all things, the man was juggling.

The spitting image of irony.

At the edge of the grass by the running path, he spun five objects in an oblong blur with the most adorable little brown-haired girl by his side. *Who looked just like him.*

And in the blink of an eye, I seethed.

I ached.

As I ran, I broiled. I went from zero to sixty miles per hour of hurt in mere seconds. All I could think was the bastard had found a way to juggle in the end. I couldn't believe he'd moved on so easily after me. And he didn't just rebound to another girlfriend. He leveled all the way up to fatherhood.

The worst part? The absolutely, completely, horrifically unfair part? He was still so goddamn handsome, with that chestnut hair I wanted to run my hands through, that square jawline I could have touched all night, those lips made for kissing me everywhere.

In last night's unbidden appearance in my mind, he sure as hell had. He'd been my first in that department; he was still the best.

At that, and at everything.

Look, any woman who says she doesn't rate her lovers is a liar. She might not have a whiteboard with a numbered list or a diary with rankings. But we all know who rocked our world and claimed our bodies.

He was the one for me. Top of the list. End of the line.

But no more.

Tonight, I'd kick him out of my head, no matter what it took.

"Look," I hissed to my girls. "It's Tyler 'the Juggler' Nichols."

Penny's amber eyes went round as moons as her mouth fell open. She jerked her head to Tyler. "Holy smokes, he is hot," she whispered, as she ran with her little Chihuahua trotting beside her.

I could have tripped her for that. But I loved her too much, and her little dog, too.

"He's not hot," I muttered, as I breathed hard from our pace.

But Tyler Nichols was indeed a specimen, just like he'd been when we were in college. From the day we met in an advanced poli-sci seminar, the man hooked me, he lined me, he sinkered me. He was my best friend, my boyfriend, my most fearsome competitor, my greatest ally, and my first love.

Then he broke my heart, and a few weeks after that, my ego shattered when he finished me off at a debate tournament.

That was devastating . . . and yet, at the same time, it wasn't. But before I could linger on the ways my future shifted during the tumultuous end of my senior year of college, the present shifted, too. When Tyler opened his eyes and met mine, the expression in his was priceless. He blinked, then recognition flashed in those dark-brown irises.

He was clearly shocked to see me, and yet, he also seemed excited. Like he was gazing upon his favorite work of art. The way he stared at me almost made me think I was a regular attendee at his private one-man shows.

And if that was the case, the man could eat his heart out.

This time, I was going to have the words. All of them. All the hurt and sadness morphed into something beautiful and wholly necessary—the right words at the right time. "How's the juggling working out for you now, Tyler?"

As I ran past him, he uttered a strangled string of words. "Great. I kept it up."

"Evidently," I said, locking my stare briefly with his pretty little girl.

I looked away, and I thanked the lucky stars that I finally had all I needed to eject him from the driver's seat of my fantasy life. Even as he called my name, I kept running.

Leaving him far behind, where he belonged.

If I had to go on a Tyler starvation diet, I'd sign up right then. Because no way, no how, was I getting off anymore to a man who'd fathered someone else's baby.

Good-bye, Tyler Nichols curse.

It ended today.

CHAPTER ONE

Delaney

I sink into the wooden chair at the mint-green table at our favorite sidewalk café and turn to my two closest friends —dark-haired Penny and redheaded Nicole. Penny leashes her little dog, Shortcake, to the leg of her chair, while Nicole ties up her Irish setter mix, Ruby.

"I can't believe he has a kid," I say, still in shock that Tyler had turned down the procreation path so quickly.

Penny shakes her head, surprise registering in her eyes. "He's so young to have one, too."

Nicole laughs as a busboy delivers a pitcher of water and four glasses. We're regulars, and he knows our drill. Nicole thanks him as he pours. She offers a glass to her dog sprawled at her feet under the table. "Right," Nicole says, her voice thick with sarcasm, as Ruby laps up the drink with loud slurps. "Because age has so much to do with his ability to deliver sperm to a waiting egg during one of the numerous times he let some loose from his body."

She's right, of course, and now I want to know all the details. "I wonder if he met her right after me? The kid looked, what, six? Seven? And we split eight years ago. Do you think it happened right away? After college? Before he went to law school? He barely even waited after he split up with me," I say, dragging a hand through my ponytail as the questions tumble free in a rush. "I haven't seen him or talked to him since we split. I didn't even know he was in Manhattan."

"And is he married now?" Penny asks. "I'm dying to know, since I saw the way he looked at you."

I latch on to her words. "How did he look at me?"

She wiggles her eyebrows. "Like he liked your running shorts," she says, in a salacious little whisper.

"Like he wanted to take them off," Nicole adds, with a wink.

I wish their comments didn't stir something inside me. Like my treasonous libido. I remind myself I can't go there. I hold up both hands as stop signs. "He could be married, like Penny said."

"Did you see a ring on his finger?" she asks.

"My X-ray vision is on the fritz these days," I say, though I'm not sure how I can joke. A part of me is still embarrassed at the role he's played in my nightlife. A part of me is furious, too. The man cast me aside clinically, claiming he needed to focus on law school, like I was simply a growth to slice off instead of a woman he wanted to find a way, come hell or high water, to stay with. Then, it turns out he found someone else and knocked her up. "Maybe the truth was he didn't want to juggle *me*." I swallow harshly. "Maybe I simply wasn't the woman for him. Maybe I never meant to him what he meant to me." I hate that my voice breaks the slightest bit. Tyler and I were in love. I shouldn't feel a damn thing for him now, and I shouldn't care that he's created a life for himself that's perfectly reasonable. Even though we had talked about a life together. We were hoping to have one after law school.

I draw a deep breath, needing to find my lost zen. This is what I encourage my clients to do—focus on the things they can control. Let go of the stresses in their days and find their happy place.

"We need to find out everything." Penny jumps into her Nancy Drew role. She tucks her dark hair behind her ears and sits up straight. All-business Penny. "Let's look him up on Facebook," she says, counting off on one finger. "Find out who he married." Another finger. "Figure out where he's working." One more. "And make voodoo dolls of him."

If they only knew I was the one who needed to be voodooed.

"Look," Nicole says, crossing her legs as she picks up a menu. "I know he looked at our girl like he wanted to have her for breakfast, but how about we order actual breakfast? How about we focus on eggs and coffee, instead of eggs and sperm? Besides, you love the eggs here, Delaney. You roll your eyes in happiness every time you eat them."

"Of course, she loves them," Penny says. "They're so good I'm convinced they're hatched from magic chickens who lay enchanted eggs."

A chuckle bursts forth from my throat. I can't help it.

"You really do think they have magic yard birds out back?" Penny asks playfully, pointing to the swinging screen door of The Charming Breakfast Spot, as a waitress saunters inside.

I nod. "Absolutely, a whole shed full of charmed creatures serving up food for us," I say, since I don't want to explain that this makes me think of my naughty nicknames for Tyler. His cock was magic and his tongue was beyond enchanted.

"So, what do you say?" Penny continues. "Should we look him up?"

Nicole answers before I can, gesturing at me like I'm exhibit A. "It's not like she's been pining away for him all this time." She sets her green-eyed gaze on me. "You haven't even mentioned him in ages. Who cares that he has a kid? Who cares if he's married? You don't care about him anymore." She bangs a fist on the table to make her point. Her dog Ruby raises her snout in alarm and Nicole gently strokes the animal's long nose as she talks. "You've moved on. So let's focus on the opportunities in front of you. Like breakfast."

That's Nicole for you. The woman never dwells on the past. She has a saying that exes are exes for a reason, and they should stay that way.

"Or," Penny suggests, "we could focus on breakfast and encouraging Delaney to date again."

Nicole beams at the mention of dating. "Yes, that too."

I shake my head. "Please. You know the last time I tried dating—it was a parade of mama's boys, players, and far too many unsolicited dick pics, and I wasn't even on a dating site." I cringed at the memory of the collection of appendage imagery that appeared on my cell phone. "I can't go there again."

"Nonsense. There are plenty of good men in the city." Nicole slaps the menu on the table. "And plenty of men who have been trained not to send dick pics without permission." She leans in closer and lowers her voice. "But admit it. A cock shot can be nice from the right man."

I roll my eyes. "Nicole, is that the topic of your next column? Nice Cock Shots and How to Score Them?"

Nicole wiggles her eyebrows. "But of course. It's a critical skill for the modern woman navigating the minefield of online dating."

Nicole writes a dating column, but it's more like a humor column, and it runs on several prominent women-centric lifestyle sites. She covers key topics for today's single ladies, from whether to go full bush, landing strip, or bare as a baby's bottom, to how to pen the ideal breakup letter, especially one you don't accidentally send from a secret ghost account you use to spy on the men you're dating from the same online site. That happened to one of her readers, and Nicole guided the distraught woman to not only remedy the error but actually patch up with the guy.

She's a dating guru.

Penny scoops her Chihuahua mix into her lap. "Look, dating might be Crazylandia, but we can help you through it," she offers. Penny's happily engaged, and Nicole is single and just plain . . . happy.

"What better day to get back in the saddle than when you see your college boyfriend?" Nicole adds.

I roll my eyes. "Nicole, if only the world could be as cool and calm as you when it comes to exes."

She stabs her finger against the menu. "But you can. If you really cared about his situation, you'd have looked him up a year ago, a month ago, a week ago. You only mildly care because you saw him out of the blue." She pats my hand. "Find the will to resist looking him up."

I furrow my brow. "In theory, that makes perfect sense. In reality, I'm all about expunging toxins from the body, and that man is some kind of toxin."

Nicole tosses her hair back and laughs. "Oh, you win." She mimes rubbing a pair of shoulders. "Maybe you need to massage him out of your system, too."

"Let's not go that far," I say. Though I am a big believer in confronting the knots in your muscles, since I'm a massage therapist by trade. That mantra is also how I like to approach life—don't avoid problems; work through them.

"If you need to look him up before you start dating again, then by all means, let's purge him."

Penny grabs her mobile device from her pocket, sets it on the table, and clicks on the Facebook app. She hovers her finger above her screen. "Are you ready to go down this rabbit hole, Delaney? You want to find out what he's up to?"

I nod. I need to know. I need to shut the door permanently on Tyler Nichols. Now that I've bumped into him, I want to get him out of my system once and for all.

"Like a cleanse," Penny mutters as she taps his name into the search bar.

"Exactly. I'm going to the juice bar of Facebook to begin my detox," I say, feeling strangely good about this plan. My girls are right. Time to move on. Time to try again.

After a few quick searches, Penny looks up and declares, "Got him!"

She turns the screen to me and I brace myself, expecting a mélange of casual shots of that gorgeous devil of a man.

But his profile photo is . . . not him at all. It's a cartoon cat shooting rainbows from his eyes into a bowl of cereal.

I point, barely able to make words. "What the hell is that?"

Curiosity seizes me, and I click on it, but there isn't any info about the laser-eyed tabby. I toggle around his profile page for his relationship status.

Single.

I gulp, but then I remind myself he could be a single father. His status only proves he's not with the mother of his child now. I click on a few more images, and quickly realization dawns on me. Against all my better judgment, I smile. I smirk. I grin. For some odd reason, I find myself ridiculously happy that I jumped to a big fat conclusion.

"She's his cousin's kid," I admit softly, the smile tugging my lips higher. Why does this fact make my shoulders feel light? Make a butterfly or two try to flutter around inside me?

Penny claps. "Yes! That is great news!"

Nicole gives her the evil eye. "Why are you clapping? Because he didn't impregnate someone?" She grips my shoulders protectively. "That doesn't mean we can let our girl ride that ride again."

I push aside that little flurry of happiness. Ignore it. Shove it back down. So what if he hangs out with his cousin's kid? Doesn't mean I should be all smiles and giggles.

"That's right. No rides will occur whatsoever," I say, adopting a stern expression.

Penny stares at Nicole, and my two best friends volley like tennis players. Apparently, I'm the tennis ball. Or rather, my love life is. "Why is that such a bad thing to get together with an ex? I reconnected with Gabriel," Penny says, since her fiancé is a man she met ten years ago then lost touch with until they reunited recently.

"Different," Nicole says crisply. "You and Gabriel were star-crossed lovers, classic missed-connection style. You were destined to reconnect under the stars." She turns to me and arches an eyebrow. "Correct me if I'm wrong, but isn't Tyler the reason you didn't go to law school? Something about a debate competition?"

The fresh, sharp memory of that last debate with him grapples me by the waist, yanking me to the ground. I'd made my choice shortly before then, but that competition was the nail in the coffin of law school for me.

"Not really." I wave off this moot discussion. "Guys, I'm not getting together with Tyler. That's not even in the cards. I simply wanted to know if he was single, a father, or something else. Now I know, and it all helps with closure. I'm not even thinking about him anymore."

The waitress comes by and we order. When she leaves, I clasp my hands together resolutely. "Let's do this. It's time for me to start dating again." If I'm ending this one-way thing my mind has had for Tyler, it'll be far easier if I'm back in the saddle.

Nicole thrusts her arms in the air. "Victory! And I have someone to start with right away. This guy I work with. His name is Trevor, and he's kind of a hottie, and he's also quite smart," she says, then rattles off a list of traits, pointing out that Trevor and I have a lot in common. Penny chimes in with a suggestion that I go out with her fiancé's business partner, and soon enough my girls are deeply enmeshed in matchmaking games.

As they chat about my romantic fate, my phone buzzes, and I grab it. A Facebook message icon flashes on the screen. My heart beats faster, and it's the oddest sensation. Like a wish against my better judgment.

I swipe and discover a message from him.

Chapter Two

Tyler

When you went out with someone for a year, spent nearly every night with them, attended college hockey games together, grabbed late-night snacks at Josiah Carberry's, watched reruns of CSI under the covers, pelted each other with snowballs on the quad, and then fucked her in the dorms, in the showers, behind the stacks, in your car, in a cab, in your buddy's dorm, under the covers after CSI, in her roommate's closet, and once in the history lecture hall when you snuck in after hours, you get to know someone.

And I don't just mean physically. I don't *only* know the roadmap of Delaney's body. I know *her.* I know she loves her mom and her brother, fairy tales, and shoes, lilacs, and 90s hair bands, her nod to retro. Poison, Guns N' Roses, and Aerosmith were her guilty pleasures. She used to joke about how she wanted to marry Axl Rose someday, especially since she loved his long hair. She'd say that as she ran a hand through my short hair.

I know that she never met a vegetable she didn't fall in love with, that she liked to argue—thoughtfully—with our history and poli-sci professors, that she was terrified of getting in trouble and always tried to please people, and that was because her father was rarely happy with her, nor with her mother. Which is why the dickhead walked out on them when she and her little brother were teenagers. But she also believes in the power to change, that true friends are worth their weight in diamonds, and that you can do anything you put your mind to.

There's something else I know about her, too. I once rocked her world.

Look, I'm not being cocky, just honest. We were the night sky and the stars, loud thunder and crackling lightning, a Stratocaster and a kickass amp.

Seeing her earlier today sparked all those memories, sent them rocketing back to the surface in seconds.

That's why when I drop Carly at her home a little later that morning, I give my niece a quick hug good-bye, and as she runs off to play with her mom and their dog, I make a beeline for the door. I need to track down Delaney and set the record straight. I don't want her to think something about me, us, or the way we split that's untrue.

"In a mad rush to ditch me?"

Clay strides across the hardwoods in the foyer of his Greenwich Village home. He's my cousin, my mentor, and my business partner. Well, he's the senior partner. I joined his firm a few years ago, and together we kick unholy ass as one helluva pair of entertainment lawyers. Our client list is sick, and I've worked my ass off to nab some of the best ones.

"Nah, just have some things to do," I say, keeping it casual as I point toward the door.

He strokes his chin, narrowing his brown eyes at me. "Yeah? Well, thanks for taking Carly to the park. She loves hanging out with you. Hope she didn't cramp your single-man style," he teases.

He doesn't know the half of it. But I could never fault that sweet girl for the misunderstanding that was clear in Delaney's eyes. I wave off his comment. "Never. Your daughter is my style. Love her like crazy."

Clay claps me on the back. "Join the club. We have jackets."

I laugh, but I'm bouncing on the heels of my sneakers, ready to bolt. The need to find Delaney is like a buzzing in my brain saying *do it now.*

"Had a little too much caffeine today?"

"No. I saw Delaney, and I need to find her," I say, because I'm not one to hide shit from my cousin.

His mouth forms an O. "The one and only?"

I nod. Clay knows the score. He's well aware of what went down eight years ago, even though he wasn't entirely on my side when I ended things. "How was that?"

"Illuminating. You ever feel like something just hits you out of the blue? Bam." I slam my palm against my forehead.

"Like seeing your ex and regretting not being with her?" he asks, his tone full of the wisdom that happily married dudes seem to have.

I bristle at that word. "I wouldn't call it *regret*." I'm thirty and single, and even if my last few hookups felt more meaningless than I would like, that doesn't mean I'm experiencing the Great Remorse of 2017.

More just like a need.

A desire.

A want.

And I'm all about taking chances.

"Yeah? What would you call this intense need to see the girl you were madly in love with in college?"

The way he puts that makes it sound like we're scripting the romance movie version of my life. I downplay his comment. "Curiosity," I say with confidence. "I didn't realize she was here in New York. And that she looked . . ." I pause. It's not that I don't have the words. I'm just not sure I want to say them out loud.

"Like heaven?" Clay supplies, remembering what I'd called her.

Guess I don't have to say them. "Yeah, exactly."

Clay taps his finger to his lips. "Hmm."

I tilt my head. "Hmm, what?"

He parks his hand on the doorway. "Let me go out on a limb. Feel free to call me crazy if this sounds the slightest bit off-character," he says drily.

I roll my eyes. "What is it?"

"You're going to do that thing right now. That thing you do when you jump headfirst into something, damn the consequences, and don't even bother with a parachute, right?"

Like I'm playing charades, I act out diving from a plane. Or really, falling off a cliff. "I believe you've called me Bungee Jump Tyler for a reason."

"And you think you're gonna bungee jump right back into her life? Like you did with the *Powder* deal earlier this year?" he asks, mentioning a show we worked on. I took the lead and pushed hard in the negotiations. It was one of the riskiest deals we ever attempted, but with a laser attention to loopholes, and making them work in our favor, we nabbed a big new client, and got the client what he wanted.

"And if memory serves, my full-speed-ahead approach worked like a charm, did it not?" I tilt my head, waiting for his acknowledgment that my aggressive strategy sometimes is the perfect counterbalance to his more circumspect one.

Clay shakes his head. "No. Your aggressive approach combined with your eagle-eyed focus on details did it. The perfect combo. That was precisely what the client needed." He shrugs with one shoulder. "But with a woman? Is this strategy going to solve your regret?"

"Not regret," I correct. "Curiosity."

"Right, of course. You're a cat, and you simply can't resist pouncing into the empty cardboard box to see what's inside. Just like any cat would do."

"Exactly." And like a cat, I'll land on my feet.

Clay claps me on the back. "Good luck."

I arch a brow. "What's that supposed to mean?"

He grips my shoulder. "It means . . . good luck."

"No, it doesn't, counselor. It means something else. Just say it, man. Dispense all the wisdom."

"It means, good luck parachuting into her life without a plan."

"Fine. You think I need a plan?"

"I fucking do," he says, laughing.

"Why?"

He sets his hands on his hips. "Women aren't empty cardboard boxes for kitty cats to play in. They're complicated, beautiful, sophisticated creatures with amazing bullshit detectors. And since you broke her heart years ago, you might want to consider applying a little finesse to your plan."

I huff. "Then I'll come up with the finesse in the elevator."

"Hope you land safely," he says with a quirk of his lips. "I'll see you tomorrow after you meet with LGO about *After Dark*."

I salute him. "Full-speed-ahead on that one, too." I tap my watch. "Time is ticking."

I saw the look on Delaney's face. She thinks I have a kid, that I rebounded from her in seconds flat. I can't let her think that. I say good-bye to Clay and head down the hall. The second the elevator doors close, I look her up online. I wonder where she's practicing. Hell, I'm not even sure where she wound up going to law school. When we broke up, we broke all the way up. I went cold turkey and didn't look back. It was the only way to do it. The only way I would be able to achieve my dreams, no matter what our make-believe fantasy for our future might have been. I was twenty-two, and yeah, I *wanted* to have it all. But that shit isn't possible. I focused on one thing and one thing only—my career. She was driven as hell, too, just as determined to ace law school, and I've no doubt she did. That woman was the fiercest competitor I've ever gone up against in a debate tournament.

She was fiery in bed, too, but that's also where she lowered her guard the most. Where she let me in. When our clothes came off, she truly gave herself to me, and I greedily consumed her, every time.

Afterward, we'd had some of our best talks. We'd lie in bed, tangled in sheets, and that's when Delaney would share her hopes and dreams, her sadness and her disappointment. Sometimes, it felt like pulling teeth to get her to open up to me, and my God, I wanted to know all of her. She still held pieces of herself back, but I knew the key to unlocking her. Kiss her. Touch her. Please her.

That's when she most felt like mine.

It doesn't take long to find her. When I click on her Facebook profile and see her occupation, I blink. I grab hold of the brass handrail in the elevator to steady myself. Never would I have pegged Delaney Stewart, one-time aspiring barrister, as the owner of Nirvana, a rejuvenation spa on the Upper West Side.

Sure, the woman gave one hell of a shoulder rub. She worked the kinks out of my neck from being bent over studying at my desk. She ran her hands through my hair and whispered sweet nothings of relaxation as she massaged my scalp.

But I never imagined she'd turn those talented hands into a career. Not when she was so damn good at law. For the flicker of a second, a dark notion swoops down from the sky. This isn't because of how I went into the last debate like a boxer, fighting to win . . .

I was merciless in that competition. Was that what drove her away from law school? Shit . . . I hope to hell I wasn't that much of a dick that I destroyed her dreams in one debate.

I dropkick that thought away.

The elevator dings at the lobby. I step outside and walk to the doors, clicking on some of her pictures. That smile. That hair. That face.

My body reacts instantly, giving her photos a full salute.

"Settle down, champ," I mutter. My dick remembers her quite fondly. No surprise. My cock loved her, and she loved my cock. She had all sorts of names for all of her favorite parts of me.

I scroll through her recent pictures, checking out Delaney and her friends at some sort of event full of dogs and people in the park. In one, she's toasting with martinis at what looks like a Girls' Night Out. In another, she lounges in a yellow bikini under the bright blue sky with the same women she ran with today.

I add up the evidence. All roads to Delaney seem to lead through her friends. They're in nearly every picture. Like a pack. And like a pack, I bet they protect their own.

I type out a message.

"Hey, Delaney. Great seeing you this morning, and your friends. The dogs were cute, too. I see you're doing massage now? How's that going?"

But before I hit send, I look at the note.

Fuck it.

This isn't what I want to say. This isn't who I am. I want to see her. Talk to her. Catch up with her. I don't want stupid bullshit. I've had enough of that. I've had plenty of meaningless dates and pointless conversations.

This woman was *never* pointless.

She was everything, and that's exactly why I'd had to slice her out of my life once upon a time.

I hit the delete key and start over.

I ignore Clay's advice. I'm going to parachute into this from the back hatch of the speeding plane. That's the only way I know how to do things. Full speed ahead.

Hey, Delaney . . . seeing you this morning was a complete and utter shock. In case the look of surprise on my face didn't make that apparent, I figured I'd put it in writing. I spent the morning at the zoo and the park with the girl I consider my niece—that sweet little lady who was watching me juggle. You may remember my cousin Clay. He has a daughter now, and I try to spend as much time with Carly as possible. I sure as hell didn't expect to see you this morning, but I'm grateful I did. You're as stunning as you always were, and as fierce and fiery. Glad to see you're in New York City and enjoying life with good friends. I'd love to take you out for a drink and catch up. There's a lot to say. Are you free this week?

I hit send.

CHAPTER THREE

Delaney

Dear Tyler,

How interesting to see you, too! My, how the years have flown. I'm doing great, thanks for asking. Yes, life is wonderful. So glad you inquired about that, too. I'm also single, but you didn't ask that. You just assumed. Which makes me think you're just the same guy you were before. In your note, you went straight for what you want, without thinking of what I might need to hear from you. And isn't that what you did at the end? You put yourself first. You didn't even ask what happened to law school. Did I go? Did I win another scholarship? You didn't care, did you?

The thing is I wouldn't mind having a drink with you. I used to love chatting with you. I adored our talks that spiraled well past midnight, drifting from politics to history to your beloved Los Angeles Dodgers, to what would make the world become a better place, and even whether ham or bacon was more abhorrent to this vegetarian girl. So, you're right. There is a lot to say. But how do I know you want to hear it?

Delaney

* * *

The next morning, I stare at my phone and the draft of the message on the screen. I read it over for the seven hundred sixty-second time as I swipe on some blush in front of the bathroom mirror.

Fact is, I don't blame him for my change in career. How could I? Tyler might have stepped on my law school dreams, but I'd made my choice before that final debate. I've got another man to thank for the change of heart. Dear old dad.

Just thinking of my father stirs up far too many mixed emotions—the bitter and the sweet. Funny, in an ironic way, how one phone call with him my senior year of college could change the course of my future. But that's how it goes. Sometimes we just know when it's time to make a change.

I'm so much happier in my chosen field than I ever would have been as an attorney.

But hell if Tyler knows that. The man didn't even ask. Not one single question about what I'm doing, and that's how he behaved the last week we were together. Distant, cold, focused solely on himself. That's probably why I never even told him the details from that call with my dad, and the things my father said that made me rethink my future.

One little call.

One offhand remark from the man who left my mother, brother, and me. My dad called to congratulate me on being accepted to law school, even though he was wrong about the timing. Letters hadn't been sent out yet. Then he said, "You'll be a great lawyer, Delaney."

"You think so?" I asked eagerly. I couldn't help myself. I still wanted his support. I hadn't had it for years.

"Absolutely," he said, with the kind of certainty only a father can give his daughter.

"Why do you say that?" I was hungry for his praise. So damn desperate.

"You're just like me. You love to argue. Like I did with your mom."

I froze, the phone like a brick against my ear. I didn't want to be like him. I didn't want to be the way he was with my mom. I had no interest in that kind of fighting future.

After he hung up, I sank onto my mattress and I contemplated *everything* about my career choice. I didn't decide immediately. Instead, I told myself I would do the final debate, and see how I felt in the competition. Would I still enjoy debating? Would I like arguing a point as much as I had before?

Or had my father's words colored everything I thought I wanted for my future?

The debate would be my final test, and it told me all I needed to know about how to be happy.

Now here I am – happy – but the memory of those moments on the phone with my dad tightens my spine like a high-tension wire as I do my makeup.

Except, I didn't enter the massage therapy business to let myself be consumed by piss and vinegar. I went into it because I didn't want to be surrounded by the kind of world I grew up in. I wanted to work in harmony, not discord.

I loosen my pincer grip on the blush brush.

Let the past rest. Let the future unfold. Let the present be a gift.

I can't send a note to Tyler with that kind of ire attached to it. And it's been nearly twenty-four hours, so at the very least I should respond to Tyler's invitation.

A drink with him sounds intoxicating.

But far too dangerous. Given the way he's invaded my mind for years, I can only imagine what sitting down to have a drink with him would do to my efforts to kick the addiction. Last night, I went on the wagon. I blocked him from my brain. Successfully. I earned my first-day sober chip. And I can't risk falling back.

I set down the brush, pull my hair into a ponytail, and tap out a new note on my phone.

Dear Tyler,

Thank you. Your niece is lovely! Such a little doll. What a surprise to see you, too. Thank you for the invitation to drinks, but I have a packed schedule. Hope you're well!

Best,
Delaney

I copy and paste the note into Messenger. My finger hovers on the screen like it's resisting me. But this is the right approach. I believe that wholeheartedly, even though my stomach nosedives the closer my finger gets to the send button. Nerves swirl like a tempest, trying to trick me into seeing him. Trying to fool me into spending a few minutes with him at a bar.

I won't give in.

I hit send.

I don't look at my phone as I head into work. I don't take a peek the rest of the morning to see if he writes back. Fine, I have back-to-back-to-back clients, and that helps.

Still, progress is progress, and I can beat this desire by focusing all my energy elsewhere.

Like on others.

With a groan, one of my regular gals flops down on the massage table in the Rainfall Room. Faint sounds of ocean waves lapping the shore drift from the sound system. The scent of lavender wafts through the dimly lit room. Relaxation is always the goal, but for some it's tougher than others, and Violet needs the full effect.

"I'm addicted to my tablet in bed," my raven-haired client mutters as she face-plants into the headrest. She says her words like a confession.

As I adjust the sheet on her lower back, I tsk at her gently. "I've told you before, Vi. We need to break the nighttime tablet habit. It's bad for your wing," I say, then run my fingers lightly over her bare shoulder.

"I know, I know," she says, guilt in her voice. "My shoulder is killing me. I can't help myself, though. I lie awake in bed at night, reading the news. I hate the news, but I can't stop. And then my arm is extended the whole time, which makes my shoulder yelp in pain."

I reach for the lightly scented oil and drizzle some in my palm. "Can you make bedtime an iPad-free zone? What if you tried it for a week?"

"I don't know if I can do it."

"They say the first day is the hardest," I tell her. "And it's true. I'm trying to break the habit of thinking about my ex-boyfriend, and I was successful last night. If I can do it, you can do it."

Her face sinks deeper into the face rest. "I'll try," she says, and I can hear a soft smile in her voice. "Was it hard?"

"Like catching a taxi in the rain. But then when you hail one . . ."

"It feels like the biggest victory in the world," she says, finishing the thought.

"Exactly. And it was completely rewarding. And that's why I know you can do it. It's what your body needs. Treat your body like a temple and it'll treat you with reverence," I say, then she sighs deeply as I work on her shoulder and the rest of her knotted-up muscles for an hour.

My next two clients keep me equally busy. One is waylaid with regular headaches, so we work on her neck, and the next suffers from sciatic nerve pain. "Sitting is the new smoking," he grumbles, as I try to give him some relief from the chronic aches that shoot down the back of his leg.

"Then massage is the new ibuprofen," I say with a cheery smile. "Let's see if we can get you feeling better."

Ninety minutes later, he says he feels human again.

And I feel proud that I barely thought about Tyler the entire morning. When I slip out for a quick lunch break at my favorite salad bar around the corner, I check my phone for the first time in hours as I walk down the block.

My shoulders sag.

There's no reply from him, and I try to fight off a kernel of disappointment that takes root as I go inside.

As I spoon arugula and jicama into a Tupperware dish I brought with me, I tell myself there's no need to feel the slightest bit empty. I'm not at all bummed over the absence of a response. Since I said no to his offer, why on earth would I even think he'd write back?

Except, I knew him as a man who fought relentlessly for what he wanted, who dug in like a Rottweiler with a bone. His tenacity was limitless. So if a guy like him didn't reply, then clearly my toned-down rhetoric in my more tactful note was strong enough to ward off even his won't-back-down approach.

I smile to myself, pleased that I still have it in me to win a battle or two.

I show the cashier my salad, and she weighs it, then subtracts a quarter since I brought my own container, though that's not why I do it. It's the same reason I fill my own water bottle from the tap—I don't want to add more waste to the landfill after every meal.

I grab a table and dive into my salad with gusto, enjoying the crunch of the fresh green beans. As I spear a cherry tomato, I open a new email to send my mom a cute shot of Nicole, Penny, and me from the other day. My mom is my rock, and she loves seeing pictures of my friends and me.

When the phone bleats a second later, I swear it's not me who nearly knocks her water bottle over in a mad rush to see who's calling. That's my evil twin sister sliding open the screen, cheering like a Sweet Valley High teen to see the number is a New York cell.

"Hey, this is Delaney."

"Hey, you."

And that damn stomach of mine? It flips like a flapjack in the skillet. "Hey there. I'm eating a salad."

I'm eating a salad? Why the hell did I just announce my lunch menu? So much for winning at words.

Tyler laughs, a deep, throaty chuckle. "Can I take from that you still won't eat anything with a face?"

A tiny smile tugs at the corner of my mouth. "Me and green beans, we're as tight as we've ever been."

"Excellent. The lady still loves carrots. I'm taking notes. And does bacon still win for the meat you'd least want to eat?"

I shake my head as a bespectacled woman at the table next to mine barks into her phone at a million miles an hour about who's picking up the laundry. "Ham, actually," I say, glad my conversation sounds more fun than hers. "It overtook bacon in a long, but well-fought, race."

"Poor ham," he says wistfully.

I scoff. "Poor pig."

"For the record, bacon is way better. Anything wrapped in bacon is pretty much a perfect food," he says, and I laugh.

We used to tease each other mercilessly about my devotion to a vegetarian lifestyle and his to a carnivorous one. I don't believe in eating animals; he prays at the church of the almighty barbecue.

"And does your affection for snack food still remain strong? Pretzels and peanuts for the win?" I ask.

"Always. But only as long as there's beer," he says, and I remember he used to joke that beer warded off hiccups, and he was one of those unlucky people who was prone to them.

Wait.

I turn down the volume on the memories. I'm not supposed to be talking, or joking, or laughing with him. This is far too easy. I slipped into old habits with him in a heartbeat, like we were pre-lubed and ready to go.

"Anyway," I say, resuming my all-business tone as I pick up my fork. "How did you get my cell? It's not on Facebook."

"I tracked it down."

"How? Is that hard to do?"

"It's not like splitting the atom hard, but when you're a determined bastard, you get stuff done," he says, and I hate that I love that he worked for my number.

Almost as much as I abhor that I adore that he remembers I don't eat anything with a face. I take a quick bite of a garbanzo bean. "So, how are you?"

"I'm great, but I was better before I got your note this morning."

I sigh. "Tyler . . . I'm busy," I say because I can't give in. I clench a fist, trying to hold tight to my advice to Violet a few hours earlier. *Completely rewarding. Biggest victory. Catching a taxi in a storm.*

"No time to catch up with an old friend?"

I set down the fork. "You're hardly just a friend," I say because what's the point in pretending? We were boyfriend and girlfriend, madly in love, college seniors who couldn't keep their hands off each other. There was nothing remotely friendly about how he touched me.

"But I have the ability to become friendly," he says, pressing on. "Did you know I've been lauded for my friendship skills?"

I roll my eyes. "Yeah, what are those?"

"Let me take you out for a drink, and I'll show you. I'll show you that I can be an amazing friend."

My phone buzzes. My alarm. I bolt up out of the chair. "I have a massage in fifteen minutes. I need to go."

"Think about it," he says, in a firm but hopeful voice. "Promise me you'll think about it."

As I gather up my salad remains and pop the plastic top onto the bowl to save for later, I press the phone harder against my ear. "Why? It's been years since we've talked. Why now? I saw you in the park for five seconds, and now you want me to think about a drink?"

"Yes, Delaney," he says, his voice smooth and certain. "I do want you to think about having a drink with me. I want you to think about it a lot. So much you say yes."

His persistence reminds me of the man I fell for in college. The guy who was dogged in his pursuit of me then, sending me texts and messages, chatting me up after classes, finding me in Josiah Carberry's late at night and telling me I was going to fall for him if I'd just give him a chance.

I'd relented, giving him all the chances, and all my heart.

Then he broke it, and derailed my plans, too.

Fine, plans might change, even for the better. But people? I'm not sure they do. Not when he sounds like the same cocky guy. "I'll think about it," I say as I leave the salad bar and hang up.

I try hard *not* to think about the ease of our three-minute conversation as I return to Nirvana and work my way through the afternoon.

That evening I hunker down in the tiny office in the back of the spa and take care of my online banking, then answer some work emails. I hit refresh once more on the inbox before I close out. For a few days I've been waiting for a particular email, hoping to hear from a guy I hired to track down information about someone I once loved. I'm eager, even antsy, but as I scan my inbox I'll have to live with those emotions a little longer. There's no word yet. I try to put the possibility out of my mind. I shut down my email and pore over bills and invoices, happily paying all of them—because I believe bills should be paid with a smile, since it means I'm fortunate enough to own a business that makes money—until the receptionist raps on my door.

"Hey Jasmine," I say to the pretty girl who handles the phones. Yoga pants with a butterfly pattern hug her hips, and silver bracelets adorn her wrists. A nose piercing glints in the evening light.

"Look what we have! A gift for you," she says. Jasmine loves gifts. She loves that working the front desk means she's the one to sign for flowers and packages, even if they're intended for others. She simply likes delivering them, like she fancies herself one of Santa's elves.

She hands me a potted plant, bursting with light purple blooms.

A tiny lilac bush.

She rubs her hands together. “Who’s it from? It smells so good. Someone must know lilacs are your favorite flowers.”

My stomach pirouettes this time, like it’s excited. Like *I’m* excited. But I’m not. I swear I’m not.

I swallow but don’t answer right away. He does know they’re my favorite. But he was never a big gift-giver before. So these can’t be from him. I can’t get my hopes up.

A notecard hangs on the side of the pot. I flip it open and read: *Don’t think. Just say yes.*

Two, three, four pirouettes.

I bend my nose to the plant and inhale my favorite scent in the world.

Motherfucker.

CHAPTER FOUR

Tyler

I suppose Delaney could have turned into a bitch. It's possible she might bore me to tears. There's a chance we'd have nothing to say to each other.

But I'm a betting man, and I'm not putting my money on any of those options.

"I won't give up until I have a chance to talk to her again," I say to my buddy Simon when I shoot hoops with him the next morning.

After he sinks a layup, he gives me a doubtful stare. "*Talk* to her? You're trying to make me believe you simply want to *talk* to her?"

I nod, resolute and then some. "Hell yeah."

"And what is it you want to talk to her about? The stock market? The weather? The latest movie you're dying to see?"

"No, asshole. I want to talk to her about . . ." I trail off, remembering how easy our phone call was. I shrug and hold my hands out wide. "Anything. Just anything."

"All this from five seconds of you juggling in the park?"

He dribbles then passes the ball to me. I grab it and throw, watching it catch nothing but net. "That, and a phone call yesterday," I add as he grabs the rebound.

"A two-minute call?"

"Oh, ye of little faith. It was three or four minutes, and we reconnected like that," I say, snapping my fingers. "She also sent me a thank you note for the lilacs, I'll have you know. You're not the only one who has game when it comes to the ladies," I point out, since Simon recently wooed and won a very special woman.

"What did her note say? Was it demonstrative of her deep and undying affection for you? Like, say, *Thanks for the lilacs*?"

"Yes," I admit, annoyed he totally nailed it. "And she said they were still her favorite flowers."

"Well," my friend says, raising the ball above his head. "That's all the proof you need that she wants you to win her back."

"Hundred bucks says you miss and I'm not wrong. I know the two of us can be good together again."

Simon laughs as he shoots. "Man, you kill me. Not only are you an entertainment lawyer, but you're entertaining."

I'm also damn determined to get her to say yes, no matter what Simon thinks. Especially since he misses the next shot.

The next day, my morning starts bright and early when I meet the top lawyer and an executive at LGO, a premium network that's been giving HBO a run for its money with its equally aggressive online and on-air approach to programming. Even though Craig Buckley, the dark-haired and famously risk-taking network head, has home-field advantage, since the meeting's at his office, I win four out of the six deal points I want for my client, the creator of a new sexy show, *After Dark*.

I thank Craig with a handshake, and his attorney grumbles that he'll call me soon.

I leave the high-rise building in Times Square, emboldened that I can wrap up the rest of the thorny issues in the deal over the next several days. As I weave through the morning crowds and tourists, heading toward the relatively quieter route up Eighth Avenue to return to the office, I call my client, Jay Benator, a brilliant artist who is poised for breakout success. I update him on the developments.

"That's great. But what about the final points?" he asks, in a reedy voice, nerves getting the better of him. "I haven't slept at all since this has been going on."

"Relax, Jay. Working with me is like an Ambien. I'll get you there, and you'll have sweet dreams, too. I promise."

"You sure?" he asks, his voice wobbling.

"Trust me. I've got your back. We'll seal this up soon," I say, then reassure him some more as I walk toward Columbus Circle. Sometimes with clients, my job is being their shark, their shield, their lubricant, their hawk, their watchdog, and their therapist. Jay seems to need all of the above, but especially my psychotherapy skills today. Mostly, I manage those by steering him to a heated debate about which NBA team is having the best season so far.

I say good-bye when I reach my building, telling him I won't even bill him for the head-shrinking.

"Thanks, man. And the Lakers suck."

"Ouch," I say, but I'm glad he seems to feel good enough to trash-talk.

Once inside the offices of Nichols & Nichols, I say hello to Holly, our perky new receptionist, who's studying at night to become a paralegal.

"How's it going, Holly? Any messages for me?" I ask as I stretch my neck from side to side. Too much time reading contracts makes it stiff. "Need me to quiz you on anything?"

She smiles and shakes her head. "No to both, but maybe later?"

I bang my fists on the edge of the high desk, then point at her. "Count on it."

"Oh, quiz me now, Tyler. Please, please, quiz me now on intellectual property."

The deep British voice mocks me as I turn to Oliver, our newest associate, who loves to give me a hard time. Especially since he thinks I flirt with Holly. But I don't. I respect her—the woman is working her ass off trying to advance her career, and all I want to do is help her.

He walks into the reception area, debonair as always in his suit. The accent helps, obviously.

"Here's a question for you, Edgecombe," I say, using his last name as I give my tall, dark-haired colleague a stern look. "If my last name's on the sign, would that make it *my* property or yours?"

Oliver clasps his hands to his chest, like I've shot him. "Oh, the wound. The intellectual wound. It hurts so very much."

I wave him off as I head down the hall. "Get back to work on your IP deals."

A second later, he pops into my office. "By the way, great advice on the Newton deal. The studio loved it, and so did the client."

I park myself in a chair. "Excellent news. I guess we'll keep you on staff, in spite of your surly attitude."

Oliver flashes a huge smile. "So surly." He blows me a kiss, then whispers, "Behave around Holly."

I roll my eyes. "You don't have to worry about that, Edgecombe."

After he leaves I settle in at my desk and track down the salad bar next to Delaney's spa.

An hour later, her lunch is delivered to Nirvana, courtesy of me, and her meal is full of all her favorite things.

Two hours later, I'm rewarded with a Facebook ding and a message. When I open it, I grin proudly. She sent me a GIF of a dancing carrot.

I take that as a cue to call her. "So, is it safe to assume you don't have a boyfriend?" I say as I kick my feet up on my desk and lean back in the leather chair. Might as well get the possible hurdles out of the way.

She laughs. "I wouldn't have accepted the lilacs or the salad if I did."

"Didn't think you would, but I do like to confirm important details like that. Oh, and while we're on the topic, I'm one hundred percent single, too, so feel free to say yes to drinks."

Another laugh lands softly on my ears. "Yes, Tyler. The salad was delicious. Thank you so much for sending it to me."

I smile. "Fine. Tell me all about that salad before you say yes to the drinks," I say, with a hint of a dirty tone of voice. "Was it crunchy? Was it healthy?"

She answers in an equally flirty tone. "You know little excites me more than a crisp green salad. It was all of the above, and it had the best Green Goddess dressing in all of a ten-block radius."

"What more can you ask for when it comes to lunch?"

"Only that it turn into a bowl of cereal," she says wistfully. "Hey, speaking of cereal, I keep meaning to ask what's up with your profile picture on Facebook?"

"You like the laser-eyes feline?"

"It's cute and completely bizarre. Naturally, I love it."

"It's a cartoon from one of my clients. Nick Hammer. Creator of *The Adventures of Mister Orgasm* and—"

"*Naughty Puppet Theater Presents Dirty Girl Mechanic.* I love his new show. It's hilarious, and I've seen every single episode."

"I'll let him know you're a fan. He loves hearing that." I set my feet on the floor and spin lazily in my office chair. "Did I ever tell you the story of how I met Nick?"

"I don't think so," she says curiously. "He didn't go to Brown with us did, he?"

"No, he was an RISD guy. That's where I met him. I saw him drawing at the RISD museum when I was there for a class one day—an art history elective. He was sketching a caricature of a Jackson Pollock."

"Um," she says, deadpan. "How do you caricature a Pollock?"

"Excellent question. Here's how. He said he liked to pretend Pollock's abstract paintings were representations of everyday things. Pickle jars, brooms, cereal . . . So, Nick was drawing a cereal bowl with a cat shooting lasers into it."

She laughs. "That's kind of crazy and genius at the same time."

"Anyway, we chatted for a few minutes and wound up becoming buddies."

"And then he became your client later on," she adds.

"We stayed in touch after college." I stop talking as a morsel of guilt crawls through me from wherever it had been lurking. I feel like shit for my choices—I kept in contact with my friends, but I didn't stay in touch with the girl I loved. But I couldn't. It was too hard. Too fucking tempting. If I'd stayed in touch with her, I never would have gone after my dreams. "He became my first client," I say, focusing on the topic, rather than dwelling on things I couldn't change.

"So the cat cartoon is like a memento of your friendship?"

I adjust the knot in my tie. "In a way, but it's also a new show concept he's sketching. A cat with magical superpowers. His name is Cat Crazypants, the Great Illusionist."

"I want to see that show . . . *tonight*. You had me at 'cat with superpowers.' I've been hoping to adopt a cat someday soon."

"A cat with superpowers?"

She laughs. "If that's an option, sure. I'd also like him to have six toes."

I laugh. "Like the Hemingway cats?"

"Yes, but I learned all the details from an author I like who has several of these cats—Tawna Fenske. They're called polydactyl. The coolest thing is their extra toe is kind of like a thumb," she tells me, her voice rising with excitement.

"Can they open doors and such with these thumbs?"

"Of course. Drawers and cans, too. Tawna even gave me an early copy of her next book—the heroine inherits a B&B that's now a sanctuary for polydactyl cats, so I'm even more hooked on them now. You should tell your client he can give his cat a real superpower with an extra toe."

I sit up straighter, sensing an opening, and try once more to win a date with her. "I could tell you more about the cartoon cat over a drink."

"Ooh. Bribery now."

"You call it bribery. I call it giving the woman what she wants. You want a kitty cat with powers. I can deliver. Over drinks." My tone is full of confidence, but my chest is tight with nerves.

I want her to say yes so fucking badly.

My suggestion is met with silence then a heavy sigh. Before she even speaks, the lightness of the conversation seeps away. Her quiet is nothing but a preface to a no.

"I don't know if that's a good idea, Tyler," she says softly.

It's not a no, but it sure as hell isn't any closer to a yes.

"Why? We're chatting. We're getting along." I push, like I would in a business negotiation. "How could it be bad to have one drink with me?"

"Because it's too easy with you," she says.

"What?" I furrow my brow. "That makes no sense. What's too easy?"

"Talking to you. Chatting. It's all too easy."

"You say that like it's a bad thing."

"It might be a bad thing," she says, her tone soft.

"We were always good at talking, Delaney."

"I know," she says softly, but with a hint of longing I latch onto.

"We were good at a lot of things," I say, low and husky. "Remember that time in the library?"

"Which one?" Her tone turns a little breathy, and that sound encourages me. We're not at *no* after all, and I've got to keep trying.

"Every time," I say, my mind awash in a deliciously dirty image of her backed up against the shelves, her cheeks flushed, her lips parted in an O, her hair wild. She bit my neck to muffle the noise as she came hard. "But especially that afternoon when you wore that little red skirt, and we got to know exactly how sturdy the books on the French Revolution were."

A small whimper seems to escape her. But then, just as quickly, she seems to reel it in, cloaking her weak moment with a quip and a light laugh. "The barricades of books all came tumbling down." Her voice shifts to pragmatic. "But still, I'm not sure—"

I'm not resting my case so easily. I've got plenty of evidence to present to her.

"How about the afternoon in the English lecture hall? The professor left, and it was just you and me in the back row. We loved being sneaky, loved those stolen moments," I say, and a flash of images pops before my eyes. Delaney's hand slipping inside my jeans, those wild eyes lit with desire, her mouth finding my ear, begging to do it right then and there. "We were damn good at all of that, too."

"Tyler," she says with a sigh. "Why are you doing this? We both know we couldn't keep our hands off each other. That's not up for debate. We don't need to go tripping back in time."

"Why am I doing this?" I repeat. "Because I know we were good together. But do *you* know we were good together?" I turn the question back to her, like the counselor I am.

She relents a touch. "Yes, we were good together."

"Then have a drink with me."

"Why? For old time's sake?" Her tone is softer now, inviting. Maybe I've knocked a brick free from her wall.

This is as much of an opening as I'm going to get, so I grab hold of it. "For old times and new times. C'mon. Say yes. You know you want to."

She scoffs. "Are you kidding me?"

I furrow my brow, wondering what I'd said. "No. I'm deadly serious."

"*You know you want to*? You are un-freaking-believable," she says with a laugh, but not the good kind of laugh.

I groan, dropping my forehead into my palm. Just when I thought I was getting close with her. "Sure sounded like you wanted to," I mumble.

She huffs. "Maybe I did. But then you act all cocky and pushy, saying you know what I want."

"I'm not being cocky."

"You were. You always were so sure of yourself. As if I can't possibly have any other opinion than wanting to have a drink with you."

"You are more than welcome to have another opinion. But I'm not going to apologize for wanting that opinion to be yes. I want to see you. How hard is that to understand?"

"We don't always get what we want, Tyler. How hard is *that* to understand?"

"It's not hard. And even if you're pissed at me, I still want you to say yes."

"Why? So you can win this one, too? Is this your latest debate with me? Do you think I'll say yes if you remind me how good we were in bed? That you rocked my world in the sheets, and in the stacks, and in the back row of English class? Did you think you'd just strip for me and all my brain cells would evaporate when you showed me your magic cock?"

"No. But would that work?"

She laughs, and I can't tell if it's a "you're ridiculous" snort, or a "just try me" chuckle. "I bet you'd like to know." Then she's no longer laughing. Instead, she sighs, and her words are laced with sadness. "You haven't even said you were sorry for the way you hurt me. We had plans, Tyler. *Plans*. You upended all of that. Every last thing."

"I'm sorry," I say, desperately earnest. "I swear, I'm sorry."

"It's a little late, isn't it? Maybe you should have said that eight years ago."

"Maybe I should have. But maybe if you see me in person I can say it properly, and you'll believe it."

"I'm not really sure why you think saying it *properly* is the key." She tosses my words back at me. "Meaning it is what matters."

* * *

Later, I meet Simon for a drink at Speakeasy. This time, I don't serve up the situation with my usual bravado. I simply tell him what went down. He's smart, and he also has a reputation for being upfront and honest. He has a young daughter, and he recently fell in love with his daughter's nanny. She's madly in love with him, too. If anyone knows women, it's this guy.

"Give me your advice. What do I do?"

He takes a drink of his beer then sets it down. "She's telling you that you need a grand gesture to get back in the game."

I nod. "Got it. I'm at the plate. I need to swing for the fences."

He laughs and shakes his head. "Sorry, man. You don't even have a ticket to the game now. You're wandering around the parking lot, begging scalpers, and even they won't sell to you. You need a grand gesture just to get into the ballpark. Something to get her to notice you. Something to remind her why she once loved you."

I flash back to the phone call from earlier. To what Delaney might want from me.

I grab my beer, knock back a thirsty gulp, and slap the glass onto the bar. "You're right. Go big or go home."

And in an instant, I know what to do.

CHAPTER FIVE

Delaney

Nicole was right.

Trevor is a hottie.

And a smartypants.

And he's interesting to talk to.

After work on Wednesday evening, we meet outside Central Park, grab some kabobs at a food truck called Skewered just inside the park entrance, then stroll and chat.

Trevor is a former brewmaster who now hosts a popular online video series about beer, mostly the craft kind. He travels around the country, visits different breweries, and taste tests the beer.

"Toughest part of the job?" I ask.

He takes a bite of a chicken kabab then answers. "The spitting. Honestly, I'd have to say it's the constant spitting after the tasting."

I laugh. "Do you have to carry a bucket with you? Or do you prefer an old-fashioned spittoon?"

He holds up a finger. "Actually, I'm quite advanced. I have a custom mug that says 'When in doubt, spit it out.'" His smile lights up his handsome face and his light blue eyes.

I arch an eyebrow. "Do you really have a mug?"

He laughs, shaking his head. "Nah. The truth is far less glamorous. I just spit into a glass."

"Ever wish you could swallow?" I ask, then nibble on the grilled eggplant on a stick that I ordered.

He cracks up. "I can say with confidence that I do not want to swallow. Or spit. If you know what I mean," he says, and I nod playfully, letting him know I sure do. "When the brew is delicious, I've been known to go into mourning over not being able to consume it. But I can't spend every day drunk, so spitting it is." He finishes his chicken and tosses the stick into a trashcan. "What about you, Delaney? What do you like most about your work in massage?"

He meets my eyes, and everything about Trevor seems earnest, upfront, and truthful. I can honestly say this is one of the better dates I've been on in a long time. Usually, I can pick up in the first hour the warning signs that the guy will lie, sleep around, or bug the ever-loving hell out of me. Trevor seems like . . . the real deal. And he's easy on the eyes, too, with his dark blond hair, his lean frame, and his baby blues.

Which means he's got to be hiding one hell of a skeleton in his closet. Surely something will go wrong any second. I've never had a date this comfortable.

"What I like most is that I can effect change, often immediately. Someone comes into the massage room, puts their stress, or pain, or discomfort in my hands, and I'm able to help heal them."

He nods. "I like that answer. You're something of a fix-it woman."

"Maybe in some ways I am," I say as we reach the edge of the path.

Then we both stop at the same moment and bend down at the same time. We've got the same damn target in our crosshairs. "You want to call dibs on the plastic bag pickup or should I?"

His smile spreads across his face. "I'll do it. You get the next one. Deal?"

"Deal," I say, and Trevor doubles back to toss the plastic bag in the trash can.

A burst of excitement spreads inside me. Nicole called it at the café. She said we had a lot in common, and I rarely meet guys who pick up trash in the park, like I do. It's a little thing, but it's part of my contribution to the planet.

We wander through the paths some more, enjoying the warm summer air, chatting about work and friends, and when we leave the oasis in the middle of Manhattan, Trevor tells me he wants to see me again.

"I'd love to see you, too," I say.

He strokes his chin. "The thing is," he says, and I tense, figuring this is when I learn he has a secret meth lab in his apartment or an estranged wife who's hunting him down. "I have to go out of town for a week. I'm leaving Sunday."

And the answer is none of the above. Which means Trevor might live a skeleton-free existence.

I shrug happily. "Just let me know when you want to get together again. Text me when you return?" I'm all about no pressure at this stage of the game.

He taps his finger to his lips. "I'd love to see you before I go. I have a business dinner on Friday. Any chance you're free tomorrow or Saturday?"

Well, we've got an eager beaver here. "I work late on Thursday, and Saturday night is Girls' Night Out."

"Girls' Night Out is a holy day," he says, and I smile since he totally gets it.

"It's sacred. It's protected in the Constitutional Girl Code." I don't miss Girls' Night Out for anyone. My friends are my rock, my family away from home.

"Then let's get together when I return from the beer festival. I'm the emcee and a judge."

"Sounds like fun. Just don't make the contestants cry with your withering commentary," I tease.

"I promise to be the non-dickhead judge." He returns to the issue of scheduling. "How about the Monday night after I return next Sunday?"

Wow. This guy is raring to go. What a nice treat. "Sounds perfect, Trevor."

He pumps a fist happily. "Excellent. I had such a great time with you, Delaney." His smile grows big and wide. "I truly can't wait to see you again. Can I give you a good-bye kiss?" he asks with a cute quirk of his lips.

And he's polite, too, as well as adorable, even though he's more gung-ho than I'm used to. But it's a welcome change not to play games.

"Sure," I say, pressing my lips together in anticipation. I hope he's a good kisser. I hope he gives me one of those trip-the-light-fantastic kisses. The kind that's barely there, just a promise of what's to come. The kind that sets off sparklers in your chest as you long for more.

I rise up on tiptoe the slightest bit. Ready for a kiss. As early evening traffic whips by on Central Park West, he lowers his face to me, and I wait.

Then he presses his lips to my forehead.

Okkkkaaaaaay.

Nothing wrong with a little forehead action, I suppose.

"Until the next time," he whispers.

As we head our separate directions, I wait for the butterflies to take flight.

My belly is pretty much butterfly-free, but I'm sure that's because it was a forehead kiss.

Besides, you can't really tell about chemistry on the first date.

Surely sizzles and sparks are a second or third date phenomenon.

As I walk home, I send myself a note. *Ask Nicole and Penny when butterflies make their damn appearance.*

That'll be a good topic for our night out.

* * *

As I get ready for bed, I crank up the music on my phone, blasting my favorite band, Guns N' Roses. As Axl croons about eyes of the bluest sky, I replay parts of my date. Scrubbing off my makeup, I flash back to the ease of the conversation, to Trevor's interest in my work, to that little moment with the plastic bag.

I weigh what those might mean and if they harbor any insight into what the next date will be like.

But as I sink into bed, the day washed off, I spot an email and my mind switches to a whole new topic. In a split second, I turn off the music. I can't listen to the hair bands I love while I read this note. I straighten, my nerves snapping tight as I slide open the message in silence.

Dear Ms. Stewart,

Hope you're having a good week. I expect to have some information for you soon on the whereabouts of your father. Hang tight.

Best,
Joe Thomas, PI

My stomach roils as I read the note. It's been more than eight years since I've talked to my father—courtesy of that pivotal "congratulations on law school" phone call—and sixteen years since I've seen him. The last time I set eyes on the man was the afternoon he shut the door behind him.

He kept in touch—if you can even call it that—with emails on holidays and birthdays. So thoughtful, I know. But that contact dwindled after college. The last I heard, he'd moved to Oregon and shacked up with a new woman. Then he married her and didn't invite us to his wedding. I would have been the worst flower girl anyway, considering I'm no fan of the groom, so that wasn't a huge loss in the scheme of things.

The loss, though, was the end of contact with my father.

I don't know if he's in Oregon, or if he and his new bride decided to, say, set sail across the seven seas. Move to Peru to build homes. Escape to Canada.

I've no clue.

But since I'm turning thirty in a few more weeks, I decided now was as good a time as any to find out what had become of the man who gave me his last name. Watching someone who's supposed to love you to the moon and back slam the door on his family can give you a warped sense of, well, of everything. My recent dating woes surely cast their lines back to the day that I heard the screech of his tires backing out of the driveway.

I don't wonder if he's dead or alive. If he'd died, news would have traveled back to me.

That's not why I'm on the hunt.

I'm searching now because I want to know what happened to the man who left. Maybe then I can better understand what to make of the moment with the plastic bag and Trevor.

Not to mention the salad and the lilacs from Tyler.

CHAPTER SIX

Tyler

Details are my friends.

Loopholes are my bedfellows.

And detours are often the way I get where I want to go.

I've mastered all three for work. While my cousin has often said I charge out of the gate when it comes to work, he's also acknowledged that I'm in love with details, and they counterbalance my relentless pursuit of unconventional deals.

All those tools are in my arsenal on Thursday morning.

I dress for work. Charcoal gray slacks. A black leather belt. A crisp white shirt. And a forest green tie. It's too warm to wear a jacket, and who needs one these days anyway?

I grab my phone and wallet and leave my apartment, sliding on my sunglasses, since the big yellow orb in the sky is shining brightly. I take that as a good sign as I walk across town, passing the usual neighborhood haunts—the bodega on the corner, the dry cleaners, the organic café.

All around me, New Yorkers are talking, walking, moving. I was born and raised in Los Angeles, but this city energizes me like no place else as I put one foot after the other on the pavement. I'm not a car person; I'm a man who gets around by foot, quickly and with purpose.

Today's goal is singular.

Some might call it a Hail Mary.

Some might say it's a leap off a cliff.

I say it's a strategic bid for a second chance. The past week on the phone with Delaney—however brief—has only cemented this desire. I loved her like crazy in college, and when we talk now, I can still hear the parts of her that I fell for. The way we connect pulses with its own energy.

The chemistry is still there. I just need her to know I'm sorry.

So it's time to say it like I mean it.

When I reach my destination, I yank open the door and walk inside. Nirvana Spa is the opposite of the crisp, quick, do-it-now-ness that pervades my law offices, and that makes it perfect for a spa. It's soothing from the second I enter. Lotions and potions perch on shelves. Lavender eye pillows flank them, along with yoga mats, a tray of jewelry made from recycled glass and metal—there's a sign that says so—and greeting cards featuring photos of faraway island enclaves, snow-capped mountains, or sandy beaches.

I check in at the front desk. The receptionist peers at the screen, her nose-piercing shining in the morning light that filters through the windows. She looks up and smiles. "Mr. Pollock," she says. That's the first detail—the name I gave when I booked my appointment. "Welcome to Nirvana. Delaney is finishing with someone else right now, but she should be with you shortly."

"Excellent."

"Have you been to Nirvana before?"

Considering Nirvana is a synonym for heaven, a perfect place, or one's happy zone, I'd have to say yes. "In some ways. But not this spa. I hear it's the best."

The woman nods happily. "Would you like to change into a robe? We have a relaxation zone in the back. You can wait there and have a mug of tea or some cucumber water."

I hold my hands out wide. "How can you go wrong with cucumber water?"

"You just can't. It's the best. I'll have Felipe take you back," she says, and a few seconds later a slim young guy with kind brown eyes and fully inked arms strides into the reception area.

"Welcome to Nirvana," he tells me, then holds open a wooden door, and I follow him into the rest of the spa.

That's another detail. Knowing the terrain. Mapping out a strategy.

I called earlier in the week and asked a few casual questions about the whole massage protocol here so I could plan properly. The woman on the phone walked me through the details, and that's what I need to navigate next as Felipe escorts me to the robe portion of the plan.

"So glad to have you here today, Mr. Pollock," Felipe says. I canvas the hallway while we walk. A heavy man walks ahead of us, and a lady with purple hair darts into the women's room. There's no sign of Delaney popping out early from her current appointment, and I'm glad of that.

When we enter a locker room that's more like a quiet sanctuary, Felipe hands me a white robe, pats a locker, and gives me a key for it.

"These robes are amazing. So soft and comfy," he says, like he's cooing at the clothing item.

Well, then. "You don't say? I probably won't want to take it off now."

He smiles and laughs, then tells me he'll be back shortly to "fetch" me and take me to the Rainfall Room. He points a finger at me and adopts a playful grin. "With your robe on, Mr. Pollock."

"Ten-four. I just need to hit the little boys' room first," I say, since that'll buy some time.

Now it's time for the loophole. Because once he leaves, I've got my window.

He exits, and I briefly stare at the robe in my hands. I don't really see the point of one. A robe to me represents a lack of commitment—you're either naked, or you're dressed, plain and simple.

I set the material on the bench, and now I'm ready for the detour.

I push open the door, poke my head into the hall, and scan up and down. Coast is clear. I step into the hall, find the Rainfall Room, and hope.

This is the part that could trip me up. I'm assuming she won't be using the same room for her client before me, but that was a detail I couldn't procure. So, I'm winging it.

My shoulders tense as I turn the knob, and I breathe a sigh of relief that the room is empty. I wouldn't want to walk in on someone else's rubdown.

With a soft whoosh, I push the door so it's barely ajar. I toe off my shoes, pull off my socks, and then I unknot my tie.

I work open the top buttons on my shirt when I hear the footsteps. A flurry of nerves spreads inside me. Partly because I hope to hell Felipe's not coming in here, hunting me down like the Robe Police.

Mostly, though, I'm nervous because I'm flying blind from here on out.

I've no clue how Delaney is going to respond. But the woman made the path to forgiveness crystal clear. *Say you're sorry. Make it believable. Mean it.*

The evidence from our calls in the past week points to our rekindled chemistry—so I need to lean on that for my apology.

I slide another button out of its hole.

A soft rap sounds on the door, then someone pushes it open wider, and soft feet pad into the tiled room.

"Hi Mr. Pollock, so glad you—"

"I'm sorry," I say, meeting her brown-eyed gaze. She frowns.

I slide open another button. "I'm sorry for the callous way I ended things." I reach the hem of my shirt. "I'm sorry for the juggling comment. That was cold and cruel."

Her lips purse, like she's trying to ask a question. As I move to the tie and unknot it fully, leaving it undone around my neck, I keep up the words—I've always loved words, and shaping them into just the right argument to make a point. Now, I need all the letters of the alphabet to let this woman know I want her to look beyond the idiot I was eight years ago. She prizes honesty, so I give her more of the bare truth. "I was a stupid, twenty-two-year-old cocky, conceited jerk."

She blinks as I pull my shirt from the waistband of my slacks. "What on earth are you doing here?" She waves wildly at my unbuttoned shirt, like I'm a brainteaser about two trains in opposite directions entering a one-way tunnel at twelve o'clock.

"I'm your ten a.m. massage, and I'm here to say I'm sorry."

"You booked a massage?" she asks, like that statement makes the train puzzler even more confusing.

I nod. "I sure did. A massage and an apology for the way I cut you out of my life."

She runs a hand through her hair, still processing the riddle of me. And, for the record, two trains *can* enter that one-way tunnel without colliding—one goes in at noon, the other at midnight.

She parks her hands on her hips. "You know, Tyler. That *really* hurt," she says, and I can hear the pain in her voice. The sound of it hooks into my heart.

I nod. "I understand why it would, and it was something I thought I had to do. But I can see now that I could have handled it a lot differently. In so many ways." I hope she can hear the honesty in my voice as I pull the loose tie from around my neck. Her eyes follow my every move, drifting down to the green silk in my hands. She nibbles her lip, a tell if I ever saw one. "Your favorite color. I wore it for you," I say, trying to get our flirt on again.

"I love ties." Her words tell me one thing, but her delivery says another. She bites out each word like they cost her something. "And I can't believe you had the audacity to wear my favorite color."

I raise my eyebrows. "Audacity is my middle name. Besides, why would I wear anything but your favorite color?"

She snaps her gaze away from me. "I can't even look at that tie right now."

I shrug and toss the tie on the stool in the corner of the room. "Out of sight. Out of mind."

Slowly, she turns back to me. "Good." She crosses her arms over her chest. "It's out of my mind, too."

Time to put something else in her mind then.

And so, I undress for her. Because sometimes you've got to give it your all. Show a woman you're willing to bare your heart for her.

And, let's be honest, your body.

Look, you've got to play to your strengths when you're negotiating. You need to know what your opponent wants. And sometimes you need to give them what they can't resist. I'm in excellent shape, fit as a fucking fiddle, and I work out hard. Delaney used my body as her playground once upon a time. She loved getting naked with me.

Let's do this.

Off goes one sleeve, then the next. I toss it behind me. My hands reach for my belt.

"Tyler," she says, but her voice hardly sounds like a protest. She sounds half turned on, half pissed.

I focus on the first half. Glass half full and all. "And I listened to you. You said I needed to do it properly and to mean it. So, I'm taking a chance, like I did when we met in college and I kept asking you to go out with me," I say, unhooking the belt buckle.

She arches a brow. "Like that time you showed up at the snack bar, plopped down next to me, and asked what it would take to get me to finally go out with you?"

"And you said, 'An ice cream sundae with chocolate sprinkles.' The snack bar didn't carry sprinkles, so I went out and found some. And then you said yes."

She shakes her head, like she's all discombobulated. "That was different than *this*," she says, waving her hand up and down my body.

"But do you want me to stop? I could get chocolate sprinkles this time, too, if that helps." I yank the belt from the loops and let the leather fall to the tiled floor.

Her lips part, and she stares—simply stares at my hands poised above my zipper. No answer comes, so I trust she wants me to do the opposite of stop—she wants me to keep it up.

I slide open the button on my pants.

She inhales sharply. "What are you doing?"

"Showing you I'm sorry. Meaning it. And asking you out one more time."

Her eyebrows knit together. A tiny smile tugs at her lips. But then she erases it, pointing at me. "You can't just come in here and strip."

"But isn't that what I'm supposed to do before a massage?" I tilt my head like I'm trying to remember. "I'm pretty sure fully clothed is not the proper attire."

"You know damn well that fully clothed isn't the proper attire. But you also know stripping isn't how it's done, either."

I furrow my brow again. "How else would I get down to the appropriate state of undress then?" I ask, tossing the question back at her.

She heaves a frustrated sigh. "Mr. Pollock. You're completely ridiculous."

"Yes, I am. But I was a persistent bastard in college, and I got you to go out with me. I'm hoping it will do the trick again."

And the rest goes quickly. I unzip my pants, push them to my hips then down, and her eyes pop wide.

"What. The. Hell?"

I shrug casually, then shove the pants to my ankles and step out, leaving them on the floor.

She squeezes her eyes shut for a second, opens them and lets her gaze drift down to my boxer briefs. Black and snug. I'm not sporting a raging boner. *C'mon.* I'm apologizing. It'd be a little tacky if I was pointing in her direction. Not right away, at least. But she is fine as sin, and as sexy as she's ever been in those black yoga pants and a black V-neck T-shirt. A thin silver chain with a turtle charm hangs around her neck, and her blond hair is pulled into a ponytail. A tremor of lust rattles me as I remember how she liked me to pull her hair.

And the one-quarter in my shorts turns into a semi.

Her eyes stray to my chest, like she's taking me in.

Good.

I'm not saying relationships should be built on the physical. But it can be one hell of a fantastic foundation. The way she looks at me tells me she likes what she sees. And I like the way she stares with heat in her dark eyes.

"You're so fucking gorgeous," I say, because I can't not.

Her hands flutter and seem to dust across her breasts. They're not big. They're small but firm and perfect. Perky, too. "Thank you," she answers, but she's not giving in yet. So I keep going.

"And you said I need to mean it. Here goes. I'm stripping for you, but I don't want your brain cells to evaporate. I just want you to say yes."

I strip off my boxers, let them fall to the floor, and stand naked in front of her. Her tongue darts out, wetting her lips. She looks at me, and yeah, I do have a hard-on now. No semi anywhere—the full monty deserves a full monty. Her chest rises and falls, and I love that I can tell she's fighting with herself.

She purses her lips, then she brings her fingers to her forehead like she's shocked I did this. Like she can't even process it. "I don't know what to say," she says, taking time with each word. "You're naked at my work, and I can't even think."

"I'm supposed to be naked."

She lifts her head and points wildly to the massage table. "You're supposed to be naked *under* the sheets, not standing here at full mast, showing off your rock hard body and perfect dick. I can't think straight when you look like this."

I rein in a grin.

She inhales sharply. "I mean it. I can't think at all." She turns on her flip-flopped foot, yanks open the door, and strides in the hall.

Oops.

That wasn't part of the plan. Time to improvise, since I've got no choice but to follow her. I don't want her to get away from me again.

"Give me a chance, Delaney," I say firmly. I won't beg. But I will speak my mind. I cup a hand over my dick and walk into the hall.

Double fucking oops.

This time the coast isn't clear. It's stuffed with people, who all catch a glimpse of my Garden of Eden attire, my hand mimicking Adam's fig leaf.

A short, muscular, forty-something woman wanders out of the ladies' room and snaps her head toward me, her eyes widening.

A masseuse sporting a long braid down her back steps out of a massage room, calling over her shoulder, "Yes, come see me again tomorrow." Then she sees me and asks, "Are you my ten a.m.?"

I'm about to answer with a no when Felipe rounds the corner and halts in his tracks. His eyebrows rise, and he clasps his hand over his mouth gasping, "Oh my."

I raise my other hand in a casual wave. "Like I said, not a fan of robes."

As his eyes roam my body, he utters, "I'm not a fan of robes anymore, either."

The muscular woman waves her hand, like she's calling for attention in class. "Honey—" The woman levels a sharp gaze at Delaney. "You need to give that man a chance."

Delaney smiles tightly, nodding a thanks that I'm sure is hard as hell for her to give. Especially since I have more supporters.

The masseuse with the braid pipes in. "If not, I'll take your chance."

With her jaw set hard, Delaney gives a quick, "thanks for the feedback" wave, then spins around, smoke seeming to billow from her nose. She sets a hand on my chest and pushes me back into the Rainfall Room.

She slams the door behind her.

Chapter Seven

Delaney

This stunt.

This crazy, ridiculous, over-the-top stunt.

This goddamn parade of flesh.

I just . . . can't even.

Can't even stand how ballsy he is.

Can't even comprehend what the hell I'm supposed to think, feel, or do.

He waltzed out naked in front of my employees and customers.

And now he's nude here with me.

I stand in the massage room, my arms crossed over my chest as I lock my gaze with Tyler's.

Let me state this for the record—I didn't drag him back in this room because of that body. I'm not that shallow. But it's impossible not to notice his finer features.

His shoulders are deliciously broad, his arms are muscular, and his chest operates like a magnet for my hands. I cross my arms tighter to resist the force of attraction.

Don't even get me started on those magazine-spread abs. A six-pack is my shrine. I want to touch it, lick it, and rub my head against it like a cat rolling in catnip. Meow, indeed.

I dig in my heels. Push my toes against the soles of my shoes, like I'm holding firm with my feet alone.

And let's not forget his legs. His thighs are toned and look powerful. His calves are strong. He even has seductive knees, and hell if I know how that's possible. Knees aren't so sexy, but connecting *those* thighs to *those* calves, they are a mild aphrodisiac. My mouth waters as I take him in, and sadly I can't even see his ass.

That's what is so freaking unfair. I meant it when I said I can't think straight. How could I? He's *naked.* N-A-K-E-D. In front of me. Asking for a second chance.

This is the definition of "rock and a hard place."

Because it's him.

Tyler Nichols is more than the opening act, the closing act, and the main attraction of my dirty dreams. He's the one who got away. He's the guy I loved more than sprinkles. He's the man who made me feel beautiful, adored, and cherished.

Speaking of all his parts . . .

Even though my eyes are locked with his, I got more than a peek of his cock. The man has a magnificent dick. Long, thick, proud, with just the perfect left hook to it.

It looks great soft. It looks glorious when it's unapologetically hard.

But none of this would matter without the face. His eyes are like chocolate, his cheekbones could be carved by sculptors, and his lips are so damn kissable. His brown hair is thick, soft, and a little bit in need of a cut. The slightly unkempt style makes me want to drag my fingers through it.

And yes, my ode to his body might sound like I'm obsessed with the surface. But what I can't get out of my head is that he pulled this off. He wanted to apologize properly so much that he stripped to his full birthday suit here at my spa, giving a preview of most of his parts to my staff and customers in the hallway.

And I honestly don't know whether to slap him or grind my body against him.

I can't be completely mad because it's just so over the top, and that's what I used to love about him.

Even so, the pissed-off part jostles its way to the front of the line, pointing out the insanity of him strutting around as naked as the statue of David. I narrow my eyes, uncross my arms, and push my hands to his chest. "Are you crazy?"

He nods and wiggles his eyebrows. "I might be."

"You think after eight years, you can just wander in here, do a little Magic Mike mea culpa, and that's it? That's all it takes to get me back?"

"I'm not asking you for a shot. I'm asking you to have a drink."

I push harder at his chest, so his butt hits the edge of the massage table. "I know that, Tyler Nichols. I'm clear on what you're asking. And what is really driving me crazy now is one thing."

"Is it the sheer amount of naked skin in front of you?" he asks gesturing to his body. "I don't like robes, sweetheart. You know that."

An image of him in college, walking down the dorm hall covered by nothing but a white towel cinched around his tight waist flashes before my eyes. I'd stayed in his room the night before, and he joined me in the shower the next morning. He washed my hair, lathered it up, and then gave me one hell of an amazing scalp massage. I believe I purred the whole time. Then, after he rinsed the shampoo from my hair, his hands mapped a winding path down my body, over my breasts, across my belly, and between my legs. As the water beat down, he slipped his fingers across me, then inside, then there, right there, as he stoked the fire in me, making me pant and moan and bite his shoulder when I came. After the shower, I scurried down the hall ahead of him. When I reached the door to his room, I glanced behind me and all I could think was how unbearably hot he was with that towel hanging low on his hips, his skin glistening post-shower.

He walked with swagger.

With confidence.

With ridiculous sexiness. And he was mine. Every part of him—that body, that face, his bold, daring mouth—and his mind, too. When he reached his room, I wiggled my eyebrows. "I'm so glad you don't wear a robe."

"Yeah, why is that?"

"So I can ogle you as you strut down the hall in nothing but that towel." I pressed my teeth into my lips, savoring the sight of him. "Do you have any idea how sexy you are?"

He shook his head, cupped my cheek, and brought his nose to mine. "No. Why don't you show me?"

It's a wonder we ever made it to class with the way we couldn't stop touching each other.

But yet, we somehow juggled it all.

I'm not sure if it's the past or the present, the memory of that morning shower or the moment right now with him in the nude. I don't know which one compels me more, or if both drive me. But my hand is on his chest, and my heart is in my throat, and my body crackles.

I push hard on his pec. He stays rooted to his spot. I push again, though there's nowhere for him to go. He stands stock-still. Then I grab his nipple and I pinch.

He lets out a small yelp.

"I seriously can't believe you." I do it again.

He winces, but maintains his ground. "Believe me."

"What are you thinking, coming to my business naked? Have you lost your mind?"

"I'm completely sane," he says, and I twist his nipple once more for good measure.

He grabs my hand, covering it with his bigger one, tugging me even closer. I gasp. The feel of his hand on mine sends a charge through me. I'm not just touching him now. We're touching each other, and all at once, the drive to hurt him melts away. Fact is, I never wanted to hurt him. I only wanted to have him. And now that I've sorted out my shock, my annoyance, my frustration, my I-can't-believe-you-had-the-nerve-ness, I'm simply done with it.

With his hand on mine, I give in.

"You're crazy," I say, but it's hardly a protest as I spread my hand wider, no longer pushing him away. Instead, I dig in. I press. And then I drag my fingers down over the hard wall of his pecs.

He feels like coming home.

I wanted to shut him out to protect myself. It's a natural human response. We are programmed to fight for survival, and he represented pain, a threat to my well-being, the spiked bat that would hurt me.

But I've been trained to look at both sides of a situation. To handle either aspect of a debate. To argue the pros or the cons. Those skills rise up in me once more as I consider the other side of his stunt. Yes, he might have embarrassed me. But on the other hand, he's the one who let down his guard and showed me, in his own very Tyler way, how vulnerable he could be.

Baring all took away the threat of pain. I can no longer see him as a Molotov cocktail for my heart when he's willing to chase me down the hall without even his skivvies on.

I don't keep the light on red. I turn it to yellow and proceed with caution.

My fingers travel to his abs, and I trace the top row of his six-pack. My breath hitches. My skin flares with heat.

I have to fight the urge to bend and run my tongue over the grooves. Instead, my fingers do the walking. Down the middle, over the muscles, and to his waist. I don't look in his eyes. I can't. I won't venture further south, either, even though I'm keenly aware of his hard cock, thick and pulsing mere inches from me. A weapon of mass pleasure.

I want to kiss him so badly. Want to touch him everywhere. I want to smash into him and reconnect with this frustrating, brilliant, vexing man I once loved—falling in love with him was like floating in the water under a clear sunlit sky. He warmed me all over.

But there are things to say. "It's not you being naked that drives me crazy," I say in a whisper.

He tucks his finger under my chin and lifts my face. "Tell me what drives you crazy," he says. His voice is an invitation, like my answer matters. Like I matter. And although I felt like I didn't mean a thing to him when he cut me from his life, I can tell I mean something to him now.

As the pitter-patter of gently falling rain sounds on the speakers and the room nearly hums with this electric energy, I part my lips. "What drives me nuts is that I might seem like a hard-ass."

He recoils and shoots me a stare like I'm crazy. "Seriously?"

I nod. "Here you are, naked, and gorgeous, and contrite, and asking for one date, and if I say no, I'm the total hard-ass."

"To who?"

"To anyone." I point my thumb at the door. "To everyone who said to give you a chance."

"They're not here right now. It's you and me."

"But I feel like I can hear people saying, 'Give him a chance. It's one drink. He's naked in front of you. Just go out with him.'"

The corner of his smile lifts. "They probably are saying that. But what do you say? Do *you* say 'you should give him a chance'?"

A tiny grin tugs on my lips, too. "Maybe . . ." I tease as I drag my nails down his chest once more, and this time I'm rewarded with a groan. A low, dirty groan that sends a wild thrill through me. He inches closer, his thick hard-on pressing against my yoga pants. I fight back every carnal instinct telling me to slide my body against his. To wrap my arms around his neck. To crush my mouth to his.

I don't know if he's changed.

But more than that, I don't know if I have.

All I know is this: he's more than earned a drink, and that's not simply because he's aroused me like no one ever has. "But right now I say you're getting the hardest deep tissue massage of your life, and you better leave me a great tip," I say playfully. Then I swat his ass.

Oh, my.

That's one firm cheek if I ever felt one.

And I want to get a full-on view. Not to mention a hands-on one, too.

I pat the massage table. "Hop on, Mr. Pollock."

He smiles, doing as told. And there he is, facedown, ass-up on my massage table. The verdict is in. He is the proud owner of a perfect, round bubble-butt—hard, sculpted, and totally squeezable.

I could objectify him all day long.

But I've done enough of that. For the next fifty minutes, I focus on my job. Covering him up to the top of his cheeks, I run a hand down his back. A sexy growl rewards me as he shifts his body, adjusting to being facedown on the table.

I step away, reaching for the bottle of vanilla massage oil on the counter and drizzling some into my palm. I press my hands on his shoulders, and I begin there. For nearly an hour, I dig into his muscles. I unknot the tension I find in his right shoulder, above his hip, and along his spine. He sighs, he murmurs, he even drifts off to sleep at one point. I can tell from his even breathing. With him in dreamland under my hands, the rainfall our aural companion, I let myself relax, too, and reflect on the past week.

I didn't expect to bump into him in the park, obviously.

I didn't think he'd track me down online, determined to set the record straight.

And I certainly didn't anticipate he'd send me a salad, deliver a potted plant of lilacs, and chat with me on the phone.

But above all, *this* is the unexpected. And I find I like it.

More than I thought I would when he strutted into the hall, his hand covering his package.

I might have some explaining to do to my employees. But I don't have anything to explain to myself. I want to know what happens next.

When I finish and he rouses from his slumber, his voice is gravelly and morning-husky. "I think I dozed off."

"You did, sleeping beauty."

He stretches and flips over, enjoying a deep inhale. "Wow. You're fucking amazing, Delaney. I feel like a brand new man."

The metaphor is not lost on me, but only time will tell if that's true.

"That's my goal." There's something about having had my hands on him in this capacity that feels even better. Not a sexual touch, but a healing one, where I work the kinks from muscles, and he lets me be the caretaker for his body.

I lift my chin and ask him a question. "Mr. Pollock. Tell me something."

"Anything."

"What time do you want to meet for that drink?"

His eyes sparkle, and he says eight tonight.

I shake my head. "I'm busy. Tomorrow?"

"Done." He sits up, and I can't help but wonder if we'll kiss, or touch or anything. If he'll drop his lips to my forehead. The tingles racing down my spine make me want to sing "Kiss the Girl." But the past, the present, and the unknown future tell me that now's not the time.

"I have another appointment," I say. "Be sure to drink a lot of water. We released a lot of toxins from your body, and you want to flush them out. Have some water, a piece of fruit, and sleep well tonight."

He nods, and I point to his clothes. "I'll leave you now so you can get dressed." I turn toward the door, then halt, and set my hand on his shoulder. "And Tyler?"

"Yeah?"

"Thanks for being my ten a.m."

"Thank you for putting your hands all over me."

As I leave, softly closing the door behind me and giving him his privacy, I find myself unexpectedly delighted.

Especially since the butterflies in my belly are flying high.

CHAPTER EIGHT

Delaney

"And you didn't touch it?"

Penny stares at me through narrowed eyes, asking me once more the question that has evidently bedeviled her since we met at Blue Suede a few minutes ago in this hastily called shoe-shopping session with my girls. Minus one—Nicole isn't here.

"No, I didn't touch *it*," I say, emphasizing the last syllable as I turn away to scan the white cubes in this shoe boutique on Columbus Avenue.

I eye some tan suede pumps with a silver stripe along the side. Pretty, but too monotone for a date night. I spot a pair of black leather Mary Janes with two straps over the instep. Promising.

I arch an eyebrow at Penny and point at the shoes. "Too sassy or just right?"

"Try them on. They have *totes* potential."

My eyes land on a pair of red beauties next—fire-engine-red peep-toes with a sling back and a cardboard placard that says "Made in the USA."

I crane my neck heavenward. "Dear God, please let these red shoes come in my size, feel like soft pillows, and make me look like a sexy angel."

Because I love made in the USA products. For many reasons. Not only am I a big fan of making goods right here in the homeland, but also because that means less waste, less transport and shipping. A total win-win.

That is, if the shoe fits. And the shoe rarely ever fits my boats.

Penny grabs both pairs as a wispy-thin saleswoman floats over to us.

"I'm Jane. May I help you?"

Penny smiles and hands her the shoes. "Size ten, please."

What can I say? I have huge feet, and I have no clue how it happened. I don't have the excuse of being very tall. I'm simply a five-seven gal with size-ten flippers.

"Let me see what I can find," Jane says, flashing a perfect grin that shows off straight white teeth. She heads to that magical land in the back of shoe boutiques. Seriously, how is it possible for any shoe store to house as many pairs as they need unless there's an enchanted lair in the back or a portal to another dimension full of boxes of shoes?

Penny grabs my arm and tugs me into a corner beside a display of fuck-me ankle boots. "Ooh, touch these," she says, her hand darting out to stroke a dove gray pair.

I join her and moan softly. "Like velvet."

"See my point? You couldn't resist touching the shoes."

I laugh. "You set a shoe trap."

"So explain to me how it worked this morning. I want to understand how it went down."

"I've already told you. He showed up in my spa this morning, then stripped down to nothing but a smile and asked me out."

"Totally clear on that part." She narrows her brown eyes. "Now, tell me the part about how you somehow developed Superwoman-esque resistance and refrained from either, one, dropping down to your knees and taking him in your mouth, or two, at the very least, stroking his free-range dick."

I laugh as I check out a pair of black leather boots with a sleek zipper up the back. "I don't think giving a blow job at my place of work is in the best practices handbook for small business owners in Manhattan."

She huffs. "Fine. But what about my second point? You didn't want to wrap a hand around it? Just to test it? I'm not saying you should have done any handiwork. But, dear Lord, it was pointing at you."

"Amazing how I was able to control all my baser instincts."

"How? I'm completely serious. Not because I think you're some crazy perv"—her voice softens—"but because I know how much you liked him. How attracted you were to him. And for him to just get into his birthday suit for you . . ." Penny's voice trails off, and she blows out a long stream of air like she's mystified.

"I was wildly attracted to him, and look, I'm not going to lie—I still am." It feels good to admit the truth. "But I needed time to process his nudity."

"Have you processed it now?"

I smile. "Shoe shopping helps me process *everything*."

Because . . . shoes.

"Fair enough." Penny grabs the black zippered boots. "I saw you staring at these. Let's try them on your flipper-feet."

"I love that you have no problem mocking my clodhoppers."

She tucks a strand of hair behind her ear, making sure I see her little bitty ears. "You've seen my ears right?"

I laugh. "They're cute."

She shakes her head. "They're tiny. They're like mouse ears. One of the many reasons I grew my hair out years ago. Anyway, I want you to know that once we finish this emergency shopping session, I'm going to order you a gold medal trophy for resistance."

"I look forward to displaying it proudly on my shelf." I wag my finger at her. "But don't forget—I did touch his chest and his abs."

"Oh, that's true. I'll make it a silver medal."

We wander to a plush, blue suede couch, as the saleswoman returns from the enchanted storage room, her arms laden with boxes of shoes.

"Here you go," she says brightly, handing me the red shoes and the black Mary Janes. "I brought you the red peep toes in a ten, and the Mary Janes in a nine and a half because we don't have them in a ten."

"Thanks," I say, even though her effort is futile. Sales women always think a nine and a half is the same as a ten. But I have never jammed my hooves into anything less than a full and proper ten. It's a myth that women with petite feet cling to—the mistaken notion that one half size smaller will fit just fine. But we big-footed ladies know that single digit sizes will never fit our German-shepherd-puppy paws.

Penny hands Jane the black boots. "And we saw these beauties and couldn't resist. Can we try these in a ten, please?"

Jane's expression turns crestfallen, placing a hand on her heart. "Oh, I'm so sorry. They only go to nine."

I sigh. The curse of banana boats.

Penny's eyes light up. In a stage whisper, she says to Jane, "Then just bring them back in a seven."

I fix her with a searing stare. "You are the luckiest bitch in the world."

She blows on her fingernails as the saleswoman takes off once more. "I'd still trade you my ears for your feet."

I run my finger over the shell of her ear. "Stop it. Your ears are perfect."

She taps her toe to mine. "So are your feet."

"Fine. We're both awesome."

"We absolutely are," Penny adds.

I open the box of red shoes and tug the silica gel packs and the stuffing from the left one. "But seriously, though. What do you *think*? And I don't mean about the physical stuff. Obviously we've established the connection is still there. What do you make of the whole effort he's gone to?"

Penny inhales and downshifts to a more serious tone. "It's kind of like a grand gesture. Only he had to do it at the start, not at the end." She sets her hand on my arm. "And I do love that he's not just making lip service about wanting to see you again. He sent you a salad. Your favorite salad at that. He sent you lilacs. And he sent you himself, in all his naked glory."

I scrunch my forehead. "So the lilacs and salad and nudity are all on the same level?"

Penny scoffs. "No. The flowers and the salad—let's be honest, those are a total swoon. But him risking being naked in public for you." She fans herself. "That's the big gesture." She drops her voice. "I mean, it was big, right?"

I pretend to zip my lips. Then I nod the answer. *Yes.*

"That's what I'm talking about. It's not only a big gesture. It's a you-can't-ignore-me gesture. The man clearly wanted you to take him seriously, as in pay-attention-to-me-because-I'm-not-going-away."

"He was kind of *hard* to ignore," I say with a waggle of my eyebrows.

Penny holds up a hand, and we smack palms.

She clears her throat. "But seriously, I do think he's making a big play for you. And I'm impressed. But don't tell Nicole I've become head cheerleader or she'll have my neck." She scans the shop like Nicole might be listening, picking up a pair of brown leather pumps and searching underneath them. "Just making sure she didn't bug this shop."

I crack up. "Nicole knows what happened. I did invite both of you here today. She's on deadline, though, writing a column about how to deal with bizarre sexual proposals, so she's occupied thinking up tips for turning down pegging, toe-sucking, or hot sauce fetishes."

An eyebrow rises. "Hot sauce fetish? Is that a thing?"

I nod. "There's a fetish for everything. However, Nicole still managed to berate me for a full minute." I shudder as I recall the full weight of Nicole's vexation. I'd texted her, and moments later she called and shouted *"You can't be serious?"* over the line. Even when I gave her the CliffNotes, she warned me to be careful. Then she made me tell her all about my date with Trevor and proceeded to remind me why he's a great catch.

"He *is* a great catch. I've no doubt about that," I'd told her.

"And he said he had a wonderful time with you, so please keep him on the front burner."

"I will," I promised before she jumped off to bang out more words.

But now the question on the front burner in my mind is how to do drinks with Tyler. I meet Penny's eyes as I drop the tissue from the right shoe into the box. "Can you give me some advice?"

"Anything."

"How do I know if I can trust him again? It's only drinks, but what should I be on the lookout for? I feel like understanding men has eluded me in the last few years. My dating experience is woeful. But you're back with Gabriel. How were you able to let go of the past?"

Penny sighs. "We didn't have the sort of past you guys did. But even so, the way I put it behind us was to learn who he is today. What made him tick. How he was the same. How he was different. When you see Tyler, don't just get caught up in a swirl of reminiscence. Learn about the man he's become. See if that man is someone you want to spend time with."

That feels way more intense than I'm ready for. I backpedal from the idea, kicking off my work flip-flops. "I'm only going out for drinks."

Penny smirks and reins in a laugh. She holds it in so hard, it's as if her face is about to burst.

"You don't believe me?" I ask defensively as I slide my bare feet into the red sling-backs.

Penny erupts in laughter as the saleswoman returns with boots. "Say. That. Again," Penny says in between gasping breaths.

"I'm only going out for drinks," I mutter.

The rail-thin saleswoman tries to straighten out a smile, and Penny points at her. "Even Blue Suede Jane doesn't believe it's just drinks."

I cock my head, eyeing one then the other. "Seriously, ladies? Both of you?"

Jane laughs sweetly and gestures to my feet as I stand up in the red heels. "Well, you are shopping for shoes. I can't think of a bigger sign that something *isn't* just drinks. A new pair of shoes means you really like a guy."

We all let our eyes drift down to my toes. Jane gasps first, Penny clasps her hand on her mouth, and I beam at the heavenly vision before me.

The shoes are divine.

In fact, these red peep-toes are perfect for a date with a man who went to such lengths just to earn the right to drinks.

* * *

Just drinks.

Just drinks.

Just drinks.

That mantra echoes in my head as I walk to the bar, listening to a podcast on local politics. The poli-sci major in me can't resist, and I like to be informed on the issues facing my city. But I have a harder time focusing on the words of the hosts because my heart beats faster and my skin prickles as memories fight their way to the front of my brain.

Memories I haven't let myself linger on in ages.

At Brown, Tyler and I were a team, a pack of two, fueled by our shared desire to learn everything. We studied together, quizzing each other for our tests on modern United States history or on twentieth-century literature. We hunted for interesting lectures from guest speakers on the hottest issues of the day. We walked to and from classes together, and spent many nights in the library, hunched over our laptops.

When it came to our backgrounds, we were as different as they come. I didn't grow up with much, and my dad took off when I was fourteen and my little brother, Caleb, was twelve. I can't really overstate how much that sucked.

But I dealt with it and moved on, and that's why I'm in a better spot now to be able to track him down.

At the time, though, he left us with nothing. I went to public high school outside of Tampa and busted my butt in my classes so I could go to a good school. Hard work paid off, and I nabbed a scholarship to Brown. Tyler came from money and a happy home in Los Angeles, growing up with his brother and their two parents, who ran a successful business together.

His parents had already finished saving for his full education by the time he was five.

Our drive, though, was parallel, along with our love of learning. We spent many late nights at the college snack bar, debating anything and everything. We'd share an ice cream with sprinkles, and we'd talk, then head back to my dorm, or his. Once the door closed, all the talk would vanish, and we'd find ourselves engaged in the most favorite collegiate activity of all.

Getting horizontal.

The second the clothes came undone the aspiring lawyers disappeared, and we became those people who couldn't keep their hands off each other. Skin to skin, lips to lips, we came together, and I'd never felt so close to anyone in my life. It was a perfect union of respect, desire, and love.

It was everything I'd never felt in my home, but wanted in my life.

Sometimes on weekends, we went on long drives. He had a black BMW, and during the fall, we'd get claustrophobic and take off, driving through the tree-lined neighborhoods in Providence, then beyond. We escaped a few towns over, finding hills, and hidden places, and then we'd pull over.

We got to know our way around the front and back seats of his Beemer quite well. Every time he touched me, I felt cherished. Whether in the car, the shower, the dorm, the library, the bed, or the car, he adored me.

He fought for a chance with me, and then once we were together, I was never second best. I was his equal, and that made me love him even more.

That's what hurt so much when he broke up with me. Not the end to our plans, not his tactless and callous word choices, not even what went down at the debate.

What hurt the most was that I'd lost him.

When I reach the bar, I remember Penny's words and focus on the here and now.

Today.

Tonight.

Not the past.

CHAPTER NINE

Tyler

She looks like a sexy angel as she walks toward me. Blond hair, flowing and silky over her bare shoulders. A slash of pink gloss on those fantastic lips.

And those hot-as-fuck red shoes.

I'm not sure I ever saw her in heels before. College wasn't exactly the place for four-inch fuck-me pumps. So I'm not sure she knows that I have a thing for shoes. Not wearing them. *Please.* But I do have it bad for how fucking sexy a woman looks in a gorgeous pair of heels.

And no one, no woman in the history of the world, has ever looked this good in red shoes.

"Hey you," I say.

She greets me with a smile. "Hi."

We walk through the bar.

"Ladies first." I gesture to the small, circular booth at the back of the Lucky Spot bar. A low white candle in the middle of the table flickers, casting a faint glow across the wood.

Delaney slides in first and I follow her.

Questions ping-pong in my head. How close can I sit to her? Do I launch right into the catch-up banter? Or dive into those-were-the-days chitchat that reminds her of how good we were together? Do I tell her when I saw her last weekend it stirred up something inside me? And I don't just mean the physical. Seeing her was a knockout blow I didn't see coming.

Clay might say it ignited regret. But I see it more as a storm of possibilities and "what ifs." Perhaps the biggest one is this—what if I hadn't followed Professor Blair's advice at the end of college?

I shake off the thoughts that have been plaguing me all day.

Delaney's here. I'm here. Time to treat this night like a first date, not a stroll down memory lane.

I'm dressed for a first date—jeans, a button-down shirt, the cuffs rolled up to my forearms. Delaney wears a pair of jeans that do nothing but stoke my desire to stare at her ass all night, but that's not possible since we're sitting. A black sleeveless top affords a lovely hint of cleavage, and that same turtle charm I spotted earlier glints in the soft blue lighting.

"So," I begin, clearing my throat as I rub my palms against my thighs. I'm fucking nervous. This is not acceptable. Yesterday, I stood naked in front of her, and tonight I'm dressed, yet at a loss for meaningful words. "How are you?"

"Good," she says, taking her time. "How are you?"

Stupid. Nervous. Ready to kick myself.

"Great. Totally great. How was your day?" I ask, and yep, I'm going to bitch-slap my own face in front of the mirror.

This is so not me. I need to get my shit together right now.

"I had a great day. Work was crazy busy."

That's a perfect opening to make a joke about yesterday, and what kept her crazy busy in the morning, emphasis on crazy.

But for some dumbass reason, I say, "Your shoes are nice."

Can I just smack myself now? Because what in the fuckity fuck was that?

She smiles, and seeing her lips curve up makes my heart beat faster. "Thank you. I got them after work yesterday."

"Oh yeah?" I sit up straighter. Her shopping habits are a most excellent sign.

She nods. "And I only had to go to one store. Amazingly, they had these shoes in my size." She casts her gaze downward. "Me and my big feet."

"Hey, I always liked your big feet," I say, and inside I wipe my hand across my forehead because just maybe I can pull out of this conversational nosedive.

She lifts her face. "Thanks."

C'mon, man. Pull up on the stick before this plane crashes and burns.

Okay, she likes shoes. Shoes are sexy. I'll stick with footwear. But for some reason, the words out of my mouth are about the least sexy part of them. "Did they have those little packets in the shoebox?"

Nice one, dickhead.

She furrows her brow. "Silica gel, you mean? Those packets?"

I've got to sell this to the jury like I *meant* to bring up fucking silica gel. Like it's the most fascinating subject in the universe. "The ones that say 'Do not eat.'"

She shoots me a look that says *why on earth are you asking me this question.* "Yes. There was one in the box for these red shoes, in fact," she says slowly, like she's talking to someone who needs extra time to understand speech.

But I don't try to stop the slide into awkward. Instead, I embrace the weirdness. I dive into it, roll around in it, embrace it. "Were you tempted to nibble on it?"

She laughs lightly, and that sound tells me my bizarre topic has leveled out the plane in spite of myself. "Well, if they didn't have that warning, surely I would have."

I breathe a sigh of relief. We're getting into the swing of things. "How do you think the silica gel makers started those warnings? Let's be frank here." I stab my finger on the table like I'm making a serious point in court. "Somebody must have tried to eat one in order to get that warning."

She narrows her eyes. "Probably the same person who started ripping tags off mattresses."

I slam a palm on the table. "It's horrible to think some scofflaw is going around tearing off tags on mattresses."

"Hey there!"

I turn toward the upbeat voice. The waitress has materialized at our table like she's arrived magically in a cloud of smoke. I didn't even see her coming. She's young, maybe twenty-two, and she bounces on her toes, making her black ponytail swing back and forth.

"Hello there," Delaney says with a smile.

"How is everyone doing tonight?"

"Grand," I answer, then wink at Delaney. "Just grand."

"Grander," Delaney says, weighing in, too.

Whatever nerves or worries I had before are officially squashed. They've gone sayonara, and I couldn't be happier to see them skedaddle.

"Excellent," the chipper waitress says as she slides an orange ceramic bowl to the middle of the table. "These are mustard-dusted pretzels and honey-roasted nuts to get you started."

I arch an eyebrow as my mouth waters.

Delaney points her thumb at me. "You just named his two favorite snack foods in the universe."

The waitress beams. "I'm so glad to hear that. You will love these pretzels. We use a special house recipe for the mustard coating."

"Bring it on then," I say, grabbing a handful. I pop the mini pretzels in my mouth along with a few nuts and crunch down. I roll my eyes in over-the-top delight and mouth "so good."

Delaney laughs then says to the waitress, "Better bring him a beer. He can't manage his nuts without a brew."

As I swallow drily, I say, "I so can."

"Get this man a pale ale, and a Riesling for me, please," Delaney says, meeting my gaze briefly as if to say *That okay?* I say yes with my eyes—I like her drink order.

"Be back soon." The waitress turns on her heel and takes off.

A dry spot lodges in my throat as I chew on the pretzels.

I swallow.

Roughly.

And then a dreaded sensation descends on me. I look around for a glass of water, but we don't have any yet. I draw a breath, but I'm not about to cough. Nor am I about to choke to death. Instead, this rough, Saharan-like feeling spreads in my throat, and it's followed by literally my least favorite thing in the world.

Hiccups.

Delaney's laughter ceases. "Not the dreaded—"

I nod, as an errant "erp" bursts from my lips.

Fuck me.

I hate hiccups because they hurt. I hate them because they're hard to get rid of. And I hate them because they are my weakness. I get hiccups at the mere sight of crackers, or bread, or nuts. I've tried everything from handstands to holding my breath while staring in a mirror to drinking water upside down and half drowning myself.

Delaney grabs my hand. "Hold your breath."

Inhaling deeply, I purse my lips. I count in my head, and she counts under her breath. When she gets to fifteen, a brand new noise rattles free.

It sounds like I'm beeping.

I curse.

"I'll go get you some water," she says, scooting out of the booth and rushing away to find a beverage. I hold my breath once more, to no avail.

Hiccups and I have a love-hate relationship. I hate them, but they love me. A few seconds later, the click-clack of heels grows louder, and I look up to see Delaney sliding back into the booth. She thrusts a big glass of water at me. "Thank you," I mutter, before I down half of it. Hoping. Praying.

Begging for this to be the end of tonight's hiccup episode brought to you by mustard-dusted pretzels.

I set down the glass and take a quick stock of my insides. My chest feels quiet. Throat, too. All's well in America, it seems, and I flash a smile.

Delaney wipes her forehead. "Whew. I thought you were going to hiccup forever like that time—"

And another evil gremlin shoots up my chest and springs free.

That time is the night we had dinner with Professor Blair, my senior advisor, who also mentored me in my pre-law endeavors. He invited us to his home, one of those stately Victorian affairs in Providence, less than one mile from campus. His wife was in academia, too, the headmistress of a local girls' school. He invited some of his top students for dinner, and it was an honor. We actually dressed like the Ivy League students we were. The fire roared in their fireplace, and his wife sat perched on the edge of a cranberry red couch with ornately carved oak arms, a glass of red wine in her hand. One entire wall in their living room was lined with floor-to-ceiling shelves, filled with the kind of books that if cracked open gave off the opium scent of old, rich, timeworn pages.

The whole crew of pre-law suck-ups like myself gathered around the mahogany coffee table. Professor Blair brought a tray of cheese, crackers, and bread to the table.

I swear that fucking bread was drier than the Gobi. It contained less water than a pitcher of sand. And instantly, I hiccuped.

Hiccups are a natural phenomenon, but it's everyone's reaction to them that's unbearably awkward. The "can I get you something, dear?" from Mrs. Blair. The way everyone tries to pretend you're fine, even though you kept firing off every twenty seconds.

But that's what I try to do with Delaney right now. Pretend it's not happening.

"So, you were saying something about shoes?" I say, trying my best to rewind the night.

Delaney points behind me. "Holy shit. Did you see that guy? He's coming straight at us."

I snap my gaze in that direction, but don't see anyone. "Who?" I furrow my brow.

She waves wildly. "There. He's huge. The one with the ring in his nose."

My shoulders sag, and I turn back to her. "Nice try. But you weren't scary enough."

I hiccup again.

Once more, she scoots out of the booth, and this time she grabs my hand. She tugs me away from the table and grabs the water glass in one hand. "Follow me. Eyes on this the whole time." She points to her ass.

"I can do that," I say, a surge of confidence coursing through me, and I watch her butt as she walks through the bar. My eyes don't stray from the sight of that firm, tight ass that I used to love to squeeze as she rode me.

And my dick stands up and pays attention.

Well, what have we here? Yep, the shameless bastard in my pants is on alert now, its one eye watching the lovely woman strutting in front of me. And I do believe we may have uncovered a cure for what ails me. As an antidote, this is the best distraction in the universe. Delaney rounds the corner to the restroom, and I sigh happily. This is the cure, and I want it over and over.

She turns around and stops me in the hallway. "Did it work?" She parks her hand on her hips.

I stare at my gorgeous ex-girlfriend, my whole body buzzing as I take in her warm brown eyes, her high cheekbones, her lovely, kissable lips.

I give her a long, lingering nod, and stare at her fantastic body with nothing but red-hot desire in my eyes. "By 'work,' do you mean am I ridiculously aroused in—"

Erp.

My chest hurts, and I mutter a string of curse words.

She snaps her fingers. "I thought distraction would do the trick."

I gesture to my dick. "You could distract me in other ways. I'm willing to try."

She rolls her eyes. "Do this." She bends at the waist, still holding the water glass, and takes a sip from the opposite side. She stands up. "It works for me every time."

I arch a brow, giving her a dubious glare.

"I swear it does." Her dark eyes brook no argument.

I've got nothing to lose. I grab the glass, bend, and drink up. Or down. Or upside down. Whatever. It flows weirdly and slowly, and I have to focus to keep the water from sliding into my nose. I guess that's the point.

Delaney places her hand on my lower back, rubbing. She's a toucher. Always has been. Part of me feels like an ass, like a helpless fucking pathetic male who can't hold his pretzels.

The other part wants to get back to the table and hit the nuclear option so we can restart this date.

As I finish draining the glass, a sense of calm descends on my body. Like maybe I've been freed from the vile hiccups. I stand, smile, and meet her eyes. Mine are twinkling, I'm sure, saying "we did it, babe."

"All better?" she asks, hopeful.

"I think so—"

And then I'm not.

She grabs the water glass, sets it on the floor, and then backs me up to the wall. In a blur, she cups my cheeks, and then the breath whooshes from my lungs.

My world turns black and hot and hazy as she crushes her lips to mine.

Delaney kisses me hard and rough, an ambush of lips and mouth and soft breath. Her lips seal to mine, her hands grasp my face, and her tongue finds its way inside my mouth. Exploring, seeking, and setting me to flames.

My head goes haywire, my brain is full of static, and I can barely process this night.

I'm kissing Delaney Stewart on our first date, and it's astonishing.

My body takes over, and my hands make their way to her hair. I thread my fingers through that silky blond waterfall, groaning into her mouth as I savor the feel of those strands.

As if she's handing off the next leg of this relay race of a kiss, she lets her hands fall from my face, roping them around my neck. "I can't believe I did that," she murmurs.

"Kissed me senseless?"

She nods, almost in disbelief. "I think I've gone crazy," she whispers.

"I like your style of crazy, then."

"You have to know I didn't plan to just kiss you out of the blue tonight." It sounds more like she's trying to convince herself than me. Or maybe exonerate herself.

I hate the thought that she might regret this, though, so I curl a strand of her hair around my finger, and she murmurs. Yeah, she likes when I touch her hair as much as I do. "Don't second guess yourself. And let's not stop kissing each other senseless."

Breath rushes over her lips, and her tiny nod is my cue to take the wheel.

I sweep my lips across hers. Her sweet, delicious mouth. She tastes so sinful, so sexy, so fucking warm. Her kiss is like fire and chocolate. It's hot and it's sweet and I can't fucking resist. I spin her around and back her to the wall, her spine hitting the brick of the hallway. I press my body to hers, and we fit like long-lost puzzle pieces. My chest is against her breasts, my hard-on wedged against her hip. I suck on her bottom lip, tugging it between my teeth, and she makes a throaty moan. Then an anguished *oh*.

What I love most about this kiss?

It's all brand new.

It's not the way we kissed in college. It's not a prelude to a screw. It's not an I-know-how-you-like-it kiss. It's a little rougher, a bit harder, and a lot needier.

It's a first kiss that rocks my world and blows my mind. It's like lightning, and when it crashes through the sky, I'm lit up, hot and electric. She moans and murmurs and rubs against me, and her passion turns me on ten thousand times more. Her eagerness is an endorphin, and pleasure from it crackles across my whole body. My skin sizzles, my blood heats, and I want to drown in this hot, wild, passionate kiss.

I can't stop.

Teeth click, and tongues tangle, and lips tug and pull. We don't stop. We devour. The more I have of her mouth, the more I want all of her.

My hands drop from her hair, traveling down her sides then around to that absolutely fantastic ass. "It worked. Your distraction ploy," I mutter as I squeeze. A surprised but sexy moan lands in my ears as I knead that delicious flesh, soft, but firm. "The only trouble is, your sweet ass is far too covered in clothes."

She rubs her pelvis against me. "And you're ridiculously aroused," she says, giggling softly.

I growl a yes as I dive in for another kiss. Her laughter is swallowed whole as I crush my lips to hers. It's replaced by a needy whimper, and the way she grinds against me becomes more frantic. I can't get enough of this woman. Especially when she rocks her hips against me, like her body's taking over, like she's saying how much she wants this kiss to become down and dirty, hot and heavy.

Hell yeah. I tug her closer, squeeze her ass tighter.

If we were anyplace else, I have no doubt we could fall into a fast and frenzied kind of hallway screw where you can't even be bothered to undress all the way. The kind of fuck where you need the other person so badly all you manage is to hike up her skirt, unzip your pants, and that's it.

I want that more than air right now.

And maybe, just maybe, she does, too. As she digs her nails into my neck, I break the kiss for one brief second, raise a hand, and drag my finger along her cheek. She turns into my touch. Softly, with longing in her eyes. An electric charge runs through me. "I want to take you home, strip these clothes off your beautiful body, and have my way with you," I say. Then, because some things change but some things stay the same, I brush my lips against the column of her throat and kiss a hot trail to her ear, like she used to crave. She moans and her knees start to give. My hand darts out to her waist, holding her as I kiss her neck. I reach her ear. "You look like a sexy angel in those shoes."

That's what I should have said earlier. That's how I should have begun the date, instead of with my awkward small talk that led to dumb pretzel-eating bravado that led to stupid hiccups.

But then, the hiccups led to this.

A kiss.

The real reboot of this first date. "And you should leave on the shoes." I wiggle my eyebrows. "Just wanted to put that out there. You in nothing but these red heels . . ." My voice trails off as my eyes rake over her lovely frame, taking in the luscious sight of her once more.

She smiles, seeming to enjoy my stare, then she presses a hand to my chest. "I want that. You know I want that."

"Me, too." My voice is rough with need.

"But I was really enjoying our awkward first date banter, too," she says with a twitch of her lips, that makes me grin as well.

"We were rocking the I-have-no-clue-what-to-say chitchat, weren't we?"

"Like nobody's business." She raises her hand, so we can smack palms.

We high-five like old friends rather than old lovers. It isn't so weird. We were friends once upon a time, as well as lovers.

"Let's do it. Let's have more awkward conversation."

"Or," she says, taking her time, like she's going to present a revolutionary idea. "Now, hear me out. But we *could* try for *un*-awkward."

I laugh again. "Our new challenge. Let's go for it."

"I'm game. Also, I'm glad your hiccups are gone." She runs her hands over the collar of my shirt, adjusting it.

"Can you use that trick on me every time?"

She taps my shoulder. "I can. And, by the way, if I were president, I'd abolish litter, hiccups, and bad hair days."

I drape an arm over her shoulder. "I can honestly say I've never had a bad hair day, but you've got my vote for the two other points of your platform."

She ruffles my hair. "Glad I can count on your support."

I flash a smile. "Though, to offer a counter argument—if I can get your hiccup remedy every time, I don't know that I want them abolished."

"I guess we'll see about that, then."

I guess we will indeed.

We leave the hall and make our way back to the table.

CHAPTER TEN

Tyler

It's funny how some things change on a dime.

When Delaney and I were together in college, I was certain I'd be a trial lawyer. King of the courtroom, arguing points and persuading juries. *Twelve Angry Men*, *Presumed Innocent, A Few Good Men,* anything by John Grisham . . . those were just some of my inspirations. Not to mention *To Kill a Mockingbird*, but I wasn't so high-minded that I thought I'd be the next Atticus Finch. I didn't think I could save the world through my oratory. Even I'm not that cocky.

Still, I felt the *call* of the courtroom, the thrill of the debate, the opportunity to make an impassioned plea before twelve men and women.

Besides, I'd decided when I was six and fell in love with *L.A. Law* reruns that I had to be an attorney.

Perhaps that's why following Professor Blair's advice my senior year of college was, all things considered, relatively easy to do.

He called me into his office the Monday morning after the dinner at his home. With his glasses perched on the bridge of his nose, he peered at me with wise green eyes. Cleared his throat. Took off his glasses. Grabbed a cloth. Began cleaning them.

Like he was in a goddamn movie. The Wise Old Mentor. "Tyler, I'm going to give you a piece of advice. Call this unsolicited," he said, his voice gravelly with the years.

"Unsolicited works for me, sir."

Leaning back in his chair, he started wiping the other lens. "You want to be the best attorney you can be?"

"Absolutely."

He tossed the orange cloth on his desk, put his glasses back on, and steepled his fingers. "Do you know what a good lawyer needs more than anything?"

"A good lawyer?" I joked.

The corner of his lips lifted in a small smile, but then it disappeared. "He needs an ironclad focus."

I nodded again. "That's me. I'm one hundred percent focused."

He cocked his head and narrowed his eyes. "Are you, though?"

How could he think I was anything but focused? In addition to serving as my advisor, he was also prepping me for an upcoming debate tournament. The Elite was one of the most prestigious debate competitions for pre-law students. Delaney and I had been working together as debate partners. "Absolutely, sir. I'm already practicing for the Elite with Delaney. My LSATs are done, and I should hear from law schools any day. And I've mapped out my plans post-law school, too."

"With Ms. Stewart?"

Ever formal, he never called Delaney by her first name only. At the time I thought it was politeness. Looking back, I see he was putting distance already between her and me.

"Yes," I said, feeling oddly defensive, like I needed to justify our plans. "We definitely want to be together." Delaney and I had planned to go to schools near each other then find work in the same city. But to his ears, I'm sure I sounded weak.

"Hmm."

"Hmm, what?" I pressed.

He leaned forward, set his hands on his thighs, and leveled me with his stare. "You want to be successful in law, yes?"

"Of course I do, sir."

"And you know I only have your best interests at heart?"

"Absolutely," I said, as my stomach churned with nerves.

"Then, you need to remember that, at your young age, the key to success lies in the elimination of distractions. If you want to be the best, you can't let anything or anyone slow you down." He paused, taking a beat to let that sink in. "You get my meaning?"

Ms. Stewart.

Distraction.

Elimination.

He didn't have to make a closing argument. His meaning was crystal clear—being in love was ill-advised. Making plans together was a no-go. Commitment at my age was a mistake.

Slowly, I nodded. "I do, sir," I said, my tone heavy. "I do understand your meaning."

He handed me the paper I'd worked on for his graduate-level seminar, and across the top he'd scrawled a *D* in bright red ink. I flinched. I'd never received that kind of grade before.

He tapped the paper. "I don't like to see this sort of score from my top student. See what you can do to improve it."

I'd been dismissed. A wave of embarrassment flooded me, followed by self-loathing. How the hell could I have slipped like that? As I left his office, I scratched my head, trying to figure out where I'd gone wrong with the assignment.

I didn't break up with Delaney that day, or the next, or the next.

But over the days that followed, an insidious doubt crept through me, making me question whether I could have the career I'd always wanted and the girl, too.

Could I balance a serious relationship and law school? Was it possible to have that kind of love and that kind of devotion to the law?

I didn't have the answer, and I was cold and distant with her. Her father had even phoned her, something he rarely did, but I was so focused on myself that I barely pressed her to find out about the call. Instead, I asked myself a whole slew of questions. What if I couldn't manage both? What kind of lawyer would I be? Would I even become an attorney?

I wanted my career more than anything in the world.

I'd wanted it my whole life.

I couldn't take the risk, so I jettisoned the girl.

Now, she's here with me enjoying a glass of wine, and I'm struck with the realization that Clay was right. I didn't just want to see her again because I was curious what she was up to.

There's something else driving me, too.

Chapter Eleven

Delaney

I can't stop thinking about our kiss.

Yes, I kissed him to get rid of his hiccups because I know how much he hates them and how much they embarrass him.

Funny, in a way, that this fearless, cocky, confident man is brought to his knees by something so . . . pedestrian and annoying. But we all have our Achilles' heel. I didn't want him to feel uncomfortable. I care about him, and I had to do everything I could to help.

But let's be honest here, too.

I wasn't merely a do-gooder. I didn't exactly throw myself in front of the bus. I wanted to kiss him. Hell, I've been dying to touch him since he juggled his way back into my life. Desire for this man has camped out in me for far too long.

And now I know there's a damn good reason he's been the starring act in countless late night fantasies.

Because he kisses me like it's the only thing on earth he wants to do. Like I'm the best thing he's ever touched. He makes me believe that no man has ever kissed a woman with such intensity, such passion, such desire.

It makes me woozy.

It makes me heady.

It makes me giddy.

Maybe all these floaty, blissful feelings are simply the illusion of chemistry.

Or maybe it's the *power* of chemistry. But how can chemistry grow even more intense over time when it was already mind-blowing back then?

If I were a scientist, I'd apply for a grant and study the subject. For now, my only conclusion is that with some people, chemistry never fades. Perhaps for some, it intensifies.

The real question, though, is whether it extends beyond the physical.

That's why I had to stop the kiss.

And that's why I've soaked up every detail of our conversation since we returned to the booth post-hallway kiss.

We've been talking for the last two hours, getting to know each other again.

I've learned he spends as much time with his niece as he can, taking her on excursions around the city to zoos and parks, pottery-making studios, and M&M stores, indulging nearly every whim simply because he can. Naturally, I find this part of him ridiculously adorable. I learn, too, that in addition to his work in entertainment law, he takes on a few civil rights cases pro bono every year. This doesn't just warm my heart. It makes me feel a tiny bit better about the state of the world.

He asks me about Nirvana and whether I named it for the band. I laugh, then explain the name represents the state of mind. I tell him I opened my spa three years ago, and that while I practice all kinds of massage, I've become known for helping those suffering from a range of ailments—from headaches to nerve pain to arthritis, and even fatigue from cancer treatments.

We move on from the subject of work when he gestures to my necklace, inquiring about the turtle charm.

"It comes from the Cayman Islands," I say, running my finger over the smooth silver. "I picked it up during a scuba and rock climbing trip last year with my two closest friends —Nicole and Penny. They're the ones I was running with the other day."

"Your pack," he says with a smile and a note of appreciation in his voice. "You're close with them, I take it?"

I cross my index finger with the middle one. "Like family. I'm going out with them tomorrow night."

"Speaking of family, how's your mom?"

We chat about my mom and brother, but only briefly, and I don't mention I hired a private detective to find out what my dad has been up to after all these years. Tyler knows better than anyone that family is a tough topic for me, and he doesn't push. Nor do I want to get into the *why* of my pursuit. It's too much, too personal. I haven't even told Penny or Nicole. Besides, when your parents spend the better part of your childhood making up and breaking up, fighting and cursing until the day your dad walks out the door and never looks back, it's hard for the subject of family to be anything but sandpaper in the mouth.

We keep the rest of the conversation simpler, lubricated by talk of music and books, TV and film. He wants to know if I'm still a fan of "skinny boy rockers with eye makeup."

Oh yeah.

I show him my latest playlist, so he knows some loves never die. "And don't try to pretend you don't like Poison. You were just as hooked on the band as I was when we played Guitar Hero's 'Talk Dirty to Me.'" I give him my best I'm-cross-examining-you stare. "I heard you sing that one under your breath when we played the video game."

"I was *hooked* on the directive of that one song title, and I believe you, as well, enjoyed the dirty talk."

A hint of heat floods my cheeks. He's right. I sure did love his naughty mouth.

While we catch up, I drink another glass of wine, and he finishes his beer. This Riesling tastes delicious, and maybe it's the alcohol warming me up and breaking me down at once, but this buzzy feeling inside makes me want to flirt.

We were so damn good at flirting, and I just can't resist.

I twirl a strand of hair and bite the corner of my lip. My go-to move and it always worked on Tyler. If I wanted him to grab a book from my shelf, pick up some snacks, turn up the thermostat, I'd do the move.

He joked that he was silly putty, and that one touch, one look, one press of my teeth into a little nibble, and he'd groan sexily, then give me the moon with some sprinkles on top.

I brush my fingers along his forearm then drag one over the top of his hand. His eyes darken with heat, and I like knowing I still affect him. "Don't think I've forgotten you were going to tell me about the cat with superpowers. Spill the beans, Nichols."

"Ah, yes," he says with a wiggle of his eyebrows. "Seems I have something you want." He moves in closer, and the temperature in me rises. "You really want to know about the pussycat on the TV show?"

"I do want to know," I say, breathily.

He brushes the hair from my neck, and I shiver from his touch. "You won't tell a soul?"

"I promise." My voice is feathery soft, and maybe I'm the one who's putty. Because he melts me. He just fucking melts me with every little touch.

"Swear?"

I make an X over my chest, and he follows the path of my fingers, lingering on the tops of my breasts. The weight of his stare makes my nipples hard. My God, this man. I want him to touch me. It's so damn difficult to last more than a few minutes with him without longing for contact, for the intensity of the physical. He bends his neck, brings his mouth near my ear. I draw a quick breath as he whispers, "Mind control."

I swat his chest. "Get out of here."

"Scout's honor," he says with a believe-me grin. "Cat Crazypants, the Great Illusionist, has sick powers of mind control. His paws also are like suction cups so that he can climb the sides of tall buildings. He uses them to vanquish the forces of evil."

"Be still my heart—a do-gooder. Don't tell me he can fly, too."

He scoffs. "He's an animated cat with kickass superpowers, Delaney. Of course he can fly."

I grin, loving these details. Maybe it's the little girl in me, who gobbled up fairy tales once upon a time. Perhaps as an adult I've graduated to late-night cartoons and naughtier shows. But the common thread remains—a little bit of magic to grease the way out of a bad situation. Magical stories have always been my escape. "I can't believe I have all the classified intel on Cat Crazypants." I shift gears slightly. "I've been thinking about adopting a cat. Maybe I should name him Cat Crazypants."

"Let me ask a question. If you're already picking out names, why don't you have the cat yet?"

I shrug then toss out a possibility. "I have commitment issues?"

Yeah, the wine is definitely working. I don't usually blurt stuff out. I don't serve up my emotional baggage on a platter while out on dates. Or maybe it's not just the wine. Perhaps I can speak freely with Tyler because he knows this already. He's well aware that I've struggled with closeness thanks to mom and dear old dad.

"I know all about your commitment issues," he says with a laugh, and I'm relieved he can joke. "You'll just have to take it slow, then, with your someday feline companion."

"I don't know if taking it slow works when you adopt a cat. You can't really try it out. You need to be ready to take the plunge."

"That is true. You definitely can't date a cat," he says.

"Also, I want a cuddly cat, and that's hard to find."

"Fuck, woman. You've got quite a long list of requirements in a pussycat." His brown eyes sparkle like he knows we're talking about more than domestic animals right now. I suppose I do have a list, but what modern woman doesn't? I want what I want—the very best man.

I mean cat.

I want a good cat.

That's all I want. Four legs, a tail, and one that won't pee on the floor or scratch the furniture. Is that so much to ask? Sure, the extra toes would be fun and all, but that's like asking for eight inches in a man. Ideal, but hard to find. I raise my wine glass. "To the quest for a perfect six-toed cat," I say, offering my glass for clinking. He tips his beer glass to mine.

After I swallow the rest of the Reisling, another wave of warmth sweeps over me and threatens to tear down my defenses.

But these defenses exist for a reason.

Cats have claws.

And cat analogies seem fitting right now. Felines seduce you. They ask to be petted. Then they unleash those claws.

Cats can hurt you.

This is the man who hurt me. This is the guy who coldly left me with barely an explanation. I know someone else who did that too—my dad did that to my mom, and I haven't seen or talked to the person who's responsible for half my DNA in nearly a decade. I eye my nearly empty glass. "I better slow down."

"Still a lightweight?"

"Yes. One more of these, and I'll be toast." I force a smile, as if that's the real issue. Truth be told, drinking makes me frisky. And that's a chance I can't take right now. I can't just flirt my way back into friendship with him. Or into whatever-ship this is.

No matter how good he kisses, no matter how well we can shoot the breeze, I need to remember the pain.

I stop the flirting and ask the real question. "Tyler," I say, clearing my throat. "I'm curious if this is why you wanted to have drinks."

He tilts his head like the RCA dog. "What do you mean?"

"Did you really want to talk about cats and life and friends and work? Is that what you wanted?"

I wait for his answer.

Chapter Twelve

Tyler

What I *want* is rooted in why I *needed* to see her.

I thought it was curiosity. That's what I told my cousin last weekend. And while I did want to learn all these things about her present life, I now know tonight's not just about my curiosity.

This date is about everything I've denied for the last week.

My need to reconnect with her has stemmed straight from regret.

Like an alarm blaring in my ear at five a.m., blasting me from bed, it's an unavoidable truth—I regret breaking up with her.

Oh hell, do I ever.

Maybe it doesn't make sense, but I thought I was driven by a *new* need to see her again, not by an old need. Now, after the talking and the joking, the teasing about bad hair days, and the hot, searing kiss that nearly turned into fucking, I'm sure that regret has barreled past curiosity. It's fueling me. I *miss* this woman. I fucking miss what we could have had if I hadn't been so pigheaded about ending us years ago.

That's why I have to talk to her about what went down.

I'd hinted at the subject in my striptease. The *why*.

And now I need to tell her.

"Yes. To talk to you and hear about what you're up to now. But that's not the only reason I wanted to see you." I drum my fingers on the table. "Remember the other day when I stopped by your office?"

She laughs. "Is that how you refer to it? *Stopping by my office?*"

I flash her a crooked grin. "Why, yes. Seems an apropos way to describe my visit." Then my smile fades. The moment turns more serious. "While I was there, I said breaking up with you was something I thought I had to do."

A dark cloud passes over her eyes. She sits up straighter, shifting away from me. "I remember."

I hold up my hands like I have nothing to hide. "I'm not being a revisionist historian here. Please know I'm not trying to justify how I ended it. I simply want to clear up the past. When I said I thought I had to split up with you, that was because I didn't believe I could have both you and the career I wanted."

"I know that, Tyler," she says, her tone exasperated. "That was very clear then. You don't have to remind me."

Shit. I'm making it worse. I lay my hand on her forearm. Her skin is soft and warm, and this close, I catch a faint scent of her again. She smells fresh, like flowers and springtime. "I'm not trying to pour salt into a wound. And I'm not trying to shift the blame. I'm saying I was an idiot because I believed Professor Blair."

She frowns in confusion.

Then I tell her the whole story. From the *D* on the paper, to the way he cleaned his glasses, to his cutthroat advice.

She sneers when I finish. "Honestly, I'm not surprised he was against me."

"Why do you say that?"

"I always thought he was a pompous windbag."

I laugh. "He kind of was. But he was my advisor and seemed to be looking out for my best interests. I was obsessed with my career at the time, or its potential. It seemed an all or nothing choice to me, and you were the casualty. I'm not saying that was a wise choice. It was just *the* choice I made. That's why I ended things the way I did. I didn't explain it well at the time, and I'm not saying an explanation would have made it better, but I owe you the reason why I was so cold, and I want to give it to you."

She reaches for her glass, but she doesn't drink. She runs the pad of her finger along the rim and shoots me a pointed look. "Okay." Her tone is cool. "You've given it."

"Ouch."

She shrugs.

But even if she's giving up on me, I'm not done. "Look," I say, making my case, keeping my gaze locked with hers, "wrong or right, I did believe any distractions would get in the way of law school." I tap my chest. "That's on me. I made that choice. And it was a bad fucking choice. But I did it, and once I decided—stupidly—that I couldn't have both, I knew I had to go cold turkey on you."

"Cold turkey is putting it mildly," she scoffs. "One minute, we meant everything to each other. The next minute, you were gone from my life. Clean break."

For a moment, I let my head hang. Then I raise my face, meet her eyes once more, and take the wine glass from her hand. I set it on the table, and hold both her hands in mine. The fact that she allows it emboldens me. It's crazy that I've already backed her up to the wall and kissed her like the world was on fire, and yet I still get excited to hold her hand. "I know," I say, imploring her. "I loved you so fucking much it was the only way I could do it."

She blinks, then her lips part. "What?" she speaks softly, gently.

I squeeze her hands. "It's true. It killed me ending things, and I knew I would've caved if I saw you at all or kept in touch. That's why I didn't call, or email, or anything." I grip her hands harder. "I wanted to. I fought the urge every day. But if I had talked to you, I would've caved."

She sighs heavily. "I get why you felt you had to do it. I don't like it, but I do understand. But you need to know how much it hurt. And it's all fine and good to sit here with you and laugh and have a drink, because I'm a big girl and I'm over it. But that doesn't change how it felt at the time—like a huge hole in my heart. And not just because of my parents. It hurt when you left me because I loved you, and because we had planned a future together."

I won't give her any platitudes about how it hurt me, too. Nor will I try to Psych 101 away her family history. I have to man up and own my choices. The breakup is all on me. "I regret what I did, Delaney. That's what I want to say. I can't go back in time and rewrite things, but I want you to know that sitting here with you, talking to you, kissing you—every second is like drinking a big bottle of regret."

"How does it taste, counselor?" she asks, a small curve in her lips.

"Bitter. It tastes bitter."

"I know that taste well," she says, then she sighs deeply. Neither one of us says anything more. I'm not usually good with silence, but perhaps it's necessary to process what went down.

Well, for a few seconds at least. I'm glad she breaks it when she speaks again. "But I'm curious about something. If you wanted to be Mr. Courtroom Trial Lawyer so badly that you walked away from me, how the heck did you wind up in entertainment law? That's not really a courtroom-centric field of law."

I laugh and lean back, glad that the tough part is over for now. "You're right. Entertainment law is mostly deal and contract focused. And as for the change, it's a funny story, and a short one."

She stares at me expectantly. "Waiting."

I scratch my chin. "I learned pretty quickly what excited me about law. It turns out what I really liked wasn't the drama of the courtroom. It was the entertainment part."

She cracks up, tossing her head back. "Oh my God, are you kidding me?"

I shrug sheepishly. "Don't get me wrong. I do think that part of the business is ridiculously cool. But once I was in law school, I realized, thanks to my cousin, that what I loved was entertainment itself. Movies, TV shows, books. That's what inspired me in the first place. And I love helping clients in those areas to realize their dreams."

"I always knew you'd be great at your job. I'm not surprised you're a superstar now in your field and you're barely thirty."

I arch one eyebrow. "How do you know I'm a superstar?"

Her lips curve up. "I looked you up after we talked. Read up on your client list. Saw what you were up to. It's impressive. I'm proud of you."

And fuck, if I don't still have it bad for her, those words reel me in. Yeah, I'm feeling regret big-time, but that feeling is mixed with some hope now, and it's chased with potential. Maybe I have a second chance with her.

A burst of excitement flares inside me. To get there, I want to understand more of who she is today, this woman with the red shoes, and the magic hands, and the turtle charm, who loves her posse madly.

"What about you? You always did give me amazing shoulder rubs, but your career change is a lot bigger than simply practicing a different area of law. What's that all about? How did you make the change?"

Before she can answer, though, the waitress appears, asking if we want refills.

Delaney shakes her head. She turns to me as the waitress leaves, and taps her empty glass. "If I have another one of these, I might do something I regret."

My chest falls.

There's that word again. I'm not the only one dealing with regret, or the prospect of it.

Then, she meets my eyes, and says softly, "I had a change of heart. That's all. And now I really need to go."

Change of heart.

That's exactly what I don't want her to have with me right now. I need to plead my case for another shot. And since she's seeing her friends tomorrow, they're the real judge and jury I'll have to impress. I've got a small window to make sure Delaney knows I'm not the same guy who walked away eight years ago. I can be different.

After I pay, we head outside. Standing on the sidewalk in front of the bar, I raise my hand and finger the strands of her hair. I play to my strengths again. The physical. She leans into my hand. There. Yeah. That.

And another strength? Memory for details, especially about the things that are important to me. "Are you going for a run tomorrow morning?"

She gives me a "how'd you know my schedule" look.

"I figured you go for a run nearly every morning."

A small smile is my answer. "I do."

"With your friends?"

She shakes her head. "Tomorrow I'm solo. I like to run early on Saturday, since I have appointments in the morning. And getting Nicole out of bed at that hour is like asking a dog to eat broccoli."

"Early wake-up calls don't bother me, nor does broccoli. Tell me where to meet you."

"Tyler," she says, resisting.

I drop my hand to her shoulder. "Just a run. That's all. We can run and talk. Or we can run and not talk."

"Why?"

I cup her cheek and run my thumb over her top lip. "Because seeing you reminds me that I was wrong to listen to Professor Blair. And since I don't have Cat Crazypants's power to turn back time, all I can do is ask to be your running companion tomorrow morning."

Her brown eyes sparkle. "Cat Crazypants can turn back time?"

"He sure as hell can."

And maybe I can, too, in my own way, since she says yes.

I've been granted a continuance.

Chapter Thirteen

Tyler

In the half light of the early dawn, I jog lightly from my apartment and through the tree-lined streets on the Upper East Side, my phone pressed to my ear.

It's a Saturday morning and early as hell, but I have a nervous client to talk down again. "Jay, I spoke with Craig yesterday and told him we weren't going to budge on the last point for *After Dark*. It's a deal-breaker."

Jay hums, and he hems, and he haws. I'm sure he's pacing like a caged animal at his pad. "Are you sure we should be so firm?" His voice squeaks.

"Jay, my man," I say with calm and confidence as I slow at the crosswalk, "trust me on this. I've dealt with Craig before. I know his issues. But more than that, this is a point we need to hold out for."

"A hill worth dying on?"

As I cross Fifth Avenue when the light changes, I assure him that yes, this is our hill. "We can do this, man. Sometimes you have to take a chance to get what you want. You believe that, don't you?"

He doesn't answer at first, and part of me is ready to answer my own damn question. Life is all about chances. If you want something, you simply have to go for it.

He exhales nervously. "Okay. If you say so, boss."

"I do say so," I tell him, keeping up the energy, especially since he's stewing in a worrisome funk. "Listen, it's six in the morning. Get back to sleep, and trust that we're taking this leap together and I won't let you down."

I swear I can see him nodding and smiling from his apartment in Brooklyn. "Okay, Tyler. I'm getting back in bed right now. Orders of my attorney."

"Excellent," I say, then I hang up and coast into the park, cruising past tall trees and fat bushes until I spot a sexy angel stretching near the reservoir.

Holy good morning view.

As the sun rises, I thank the Lord for my eyesight. Hot pink shorts hug her rear today, and I enjoy every second of the view as she practices hamstring lunges with her back to me. My dick likes the view, too, so I adjust myself in my shorts, lest I show up sporting a maypole.

But then again, who the fuck cares if she knows I'm hot for her? Pretty sure she got that memo.

I head over to Delaney.

She turns her head.

And waves.

And smiles.

That smile makes me feel like I can do this. Like I can win her heart again. Mine pounds faster as I near her, and it's not just because I happen to think she's the most stunning woman I've ever seen, but because of who she is.

I arrive at her side, and she straightens. "Hey."

"Hey."

There's that awkwardness again, and I want no part of it today. Like the bungee jumper I am, I lean in and dust a quick kiss on her lips. At first, she freezes. That won't fucking do at all. My tongue darts out, flicking her top lip. A soft breath escapes her, and she gives in. Her sweet lips linger on mine, sending a charge down my spine. My brain leapfrogs ahead, and I picture scooping her up in my arms, carrying her to a quiet little patch of trees, and kissing her till she begs me to take her home.

I want that badly—I want her to beg for it because she's at her happiest when she's overcome—but I suspect it's too soon for her.

Not to mention, screwing in Central Park usually results in a public citation. Public fornicators are never as clandestine as they think they are.

I nibble lightly on her bottom lip for a few seconds, drawing out a throaty murmur from her. Then I somehow find the will to separate.

She blinks. Several times. She sways the slightest bit, like her feet barely touch the ground. Good. I want her to be affected.

She furrows her brow. "I'm sorry, but do we kiss now when we see each other in the park?"

"Evidently we do."

"Weird. Because I didn't get that memo."

I rock on my heels. "Want me to take it back?"

"The kiss or the memo?"

"The memo," I say matter-of-factly, like this is all so obvious. "You can't take a kiss back."

"You sure on that, Nichols?"

"I can *try* to take back the kiss. Want me to, sweet girl?" I use the term of endearment I once called her. She doesn't blanch, and that's a damn good sign.

She smirks. "Be my guest."

I kiss her once more, like I'm reversing the lip lock, doing it all in rewind, pulling away ever so slowly, ever so softly, leaving her dazed once more.

Perfect.

If she can drive me this crazy, make me this hard, send the temperature in my blood to beyond incendiary, the least I can do is return the favor.

Judging from her reaction, I'm doing it right.

I gesture from her to me. "Like that. I think that's how you take back a kiss."

Chuckling, she nods to the running path. "Ready for me to kick your ass?"

Every competitive bone in my body snaps to attention. "We'll see about that," I say, then I smack her pink nylon covered behind.

Her eyes widen, saying *oh-no-you-didn't.*

But there's a twinkle in those baby browns that says the lady might like spanking.

That's new, and it's most interesting.

I pencil in a new item on my mental to-do list. Find out how much she likes spanking. I never spanked her in college—just wasn't part of the repertoire. But judging from her response now, I'm more determined than ever to find out everything she likes in and out of bed.

For the first minute of our run, we're quiet as we find our pace.

A fast one, to be sure. She wasn't kidding when she said she wanted to beat me. The woman possesses some serious speed. I like it. Keeping up with her is yet another way she challenges me. As that thought takes shape, I realize that's a key part of why I'm so into her. She always kept me on my toes.

We round the first bend, curving past a cluster of tall maple trees that canopy the path. "So, Delaney. It's your turn to spill the beans."

She glances at me out of the corner of her eye. "What beans?"

I hold up my hands like I'm kneading dough. "How the hell did you become the woman with magic hands? I had a seriously sore neck from reading contracts, and you worked some wonders on me the other morning," I say, rubbing the back of my neck.

She shoots me a warm smile. "I'm glad you felt better. Do you get tightness there a lot?"

"Yes," I say, but before I go into more detail, I realize she's deflecting. She's dancing around my question. I don't follow her lead. "How did it happen?"

She waggles her hands as we jog. "The magic in my hands? Simple. I wished upon a star when I was a little girl. And voilà."

I roll my eyes, and swat her backside lightly once more. She pretends to yelp.

"Permission to treat opposing counsel as hostile," I say playfully.

"Objection. I'm not hostile. Just making you work hard."

"You definitely make me . . ." I let my eyes drift downward, and Delaney follows my gaze as we keep a steady pace, and I finish the thought, ". . . *hard*."

"I noticed when you showed up." She winks.

And I'm about to just slide right into the repartee when I remind myself that I can't let the naughty banter distract me from my mission—to get to know her again. Delaney's the type of person who keeps her feelings close to the vest. She takes her time to open up. Once she does, it's a glorious thing, but sometimes the process is like questioning a reluctant witness, and you've got to stay on it. Good thing I'm a tenacious bastard. "Let's get back to the question, sexy angel." I pause a moment, realizing I like *sexy angel* better than *sweet girl*. It suits her now. "How'd you ditch law school and become a masseuse?"

She sighs then fixes her eyes ahead of her, narrowly sidestepping a twig in the middle of the path. "My story is quite simple. Remember the debate competition?"

How could I forget? The Elite was the last time I saw her. Professor Blair found a way for me to pair up with someone else in the competition, and when I did, we went full throttle. I prepped my ass off, treating the competition like a goddamn national debate. We took no prisoners while winning, and winning soundly.

Which also meant I beat Delaney, even though she was sharp that day.

"I remember it," I say as we run past a group of gray-haired men likely training together for a marathon or race. "We were supposed to partner together."

"But you wound up with some other partner, and we faced off against each other. There was some prize money that was to be used for law school," she says, and I nearly stumble on the hard dirt path.

I feel like I've been clobbered, like her words smacked my chest with a bag of bricks. Why didn't I see it before? That money must have been her path to law school. I didn't know going in that there was a prize—it was announced at the end. Did I take her chance at law school away from her when I won?

"Right," I say, swallowing roughly. "Were you counting on that money?"

She looks at me as I regain my steady footing. "It would have helped defray some of the costs. But truth be told, the competition itself—the debate itself—was the eye-opener. Especially the way I felt arguing with you."

A darkness seems to cross her eyes. Maybe sadness. I'm not sure, but I cringe as I recall the way I devoured the competition that day. I kicked unholy ass, and won a three-thousand-dollar award at the end. Three thousand dollars hardly makes a dent in law school. But for Delaney, maybe it would have paved the way.

"Was it the money?" I ask, holding my breath in hope that she says no, because I will fucking kick myself in the jaw with a steel-toed boot if she says yes.

"Honestly, no," she says, and reflexively I run a hand over my jaw, glad I won't be bashing in that part of my facial structure. "Sure, the money would have been nice if I still had wanted to go. But the debate itself was my . . ." She slows and looks up at the peach streaks of the sun showing above the horizon. "My tipping point. It made me realize once and for all that law was not for me."

That *should* make me feel better, but it doesn't. Not only did I break up with her, but what if I broke her fucking spirit in the debate? What if my approach, guns blazing, did her in? *Jesus Christ.* Could I have been a bigger dick?

"That debate made you reconsider all your graduate school plans?" I ask, because for some strange reason, I feel like she's not telling me something. I don't mean some dreaded big secret like a baby or a sickness. I mean something *emotional* about her decision. Something personal—Delaney was like that—she didn't always share right away, and I can't help but wonder if there's more to the story.

A strand of hair slips from her ponytail as we run, and she tucks it over her ear. "Yes. The debate was a tough one."

"It sure was. You were tough, Delaney," I say, remembering how focused she was at the podium, making her points. "A ferocious competitor."

She nods a quick thank-you. "There was a lot riding on it for me. It forced me to look long and hard at what I wanted to do in life. Like you, I once felt that justice was my calling. That I could fight for it and deliver on it."

I wince as I ask the next question. "And one debate turned all that around for you?"

"Well," she says, laughing, "not entirely. But it was pretty illuminating."

"What did it illuminate?" A stone lodges in my chest.

She darts away from me, and I turn quickly to follow her. She stops, bends to pick up a discarded soda cup, and resumes running. "Litter. One of my pet peeves."

I grab the cup from her and toss it in the nearest recycling bin, shooting it like a basketball.

"Two points," she says, as we keep running. "And to answer your question, the debate made it easy for me to turn down all my law school acceptances."

"Whoa. You turned down everything?" I can't even imagine doing that.

"I did indeed. I was accepted into all but my first choice, and I declined them all."

I'm rarely speechless, but this new intel just surprises the hell out of me, and I take a minute to gather my thoughts. "Why did you turn them all down? Because you only wanted your first choice?"

She shrugs. "I didn't want to go, Tyler," she says, but her tone is so light, so even, that I can't figure out if her answer is good or bad. The problem is this is how she used to segue out of tough conversations before, too. I'm not sure if I should push her. Or just accept that my crime was worse than I thought. That my winner-take-all attitude played some part in derailing her dreams.

I chew on that pill for a half mile or so as we run in relative silence. Then, her hand darts out, and she smacks my ass. "Payback, slowpoke."

She takes off, racing ahead of me.

It's clear the school conversation is over, and maybe I've made too much of it. Maybe she's not pissed anymore. Either way, the woman is sprinting, and I'm chasing, and at least that means I'm still in the ballgame. She's a blur, just like last Sunday. But this time I won't let her get away. I pick up my pace, my long stride eating up the dirt path, and seconds later I'm by her side once more. "Are you running away from me, sexy angel?"

A mischievous glint twinkles in her eyes as we reach the top of the hill. She stops, grabs my shirt, and tugs me close. For a second, I think she's going to kiss me, but instead she says, "I was, but you caught me."

"I'll catch you again if I have to."

"Will you now?"

Double talk. Tap dancing around the topic. Sometimes, that's how she rolls. How she *needs* to roll. I get it; I respect it. The woman had a shitty hand of cards dealt her in life, and then again by me. She protects herself with flirting, with banter, with playful words.

It's all armor to protect her heart.

"I will absolutely catch you," I say, my voice confident, and my meaning clear.

She arches an eyebrow then flashes a quick smile. "Good," she whispers, and hell if that doesn't sound like an invitation.

We start running again. "Why'd you choose massage instead?"

"That is a very good question," she says, arms swinging back and forth as her breath comes faster.

"Then give me a very good answer."

A shrieking lands on my ears as a slim woman with a short, sleek, black haircut runs at us, arms wide open. "Delaney!" the thin woman shouts, practically barreling into her.

"Gigi! How are you?" Delaney beams, too, as the women clasp each other in a massive hug.

When they separate, Gigi runs a hand over her cropped hair. "Worlds better."

"Really?"

Gigi nods. "I swear." She gestures to her midsection. "I put on weight. I look better when I'm not a skinny chicken."

"You were adorable as a skinny chicken, and you're adorable as a fluffy chicken, too," Delaney says, then turns to me. "Tyler, this is one of my clients. Gigi. She's a cancer ass-kicker."

"Nice!" I hold up a fist for Gigi, and we knock.

Gigi juts out her hip and punches the air, understandably proud of herself.

"This miracle worker helped me through," Gigi says, planting her hands on Delaney's shoulders. Gigi lowers her voice to a stage whisper. "She was like my marijuana."

I crack up. "Delaney's a natural high. She makes everything feel better."

Delaney waves a hand as if to say she had nothing to do with it. "I'm glad you're doing well."

"So well," she says, then drags a hand through her spiky hair. "Especially since my locks are coming back nicely. Speaking of, I'm having a wig party this week. Did you get my invite? I dropped it off the other day at Nirvana."

Delaney snaps her fingers. "Yes! I meant to RSVP. I should be able to make it. But . . . confession. I don't have a wig."

Gigi points at Delaney and gives her a stern stare. "No, my dear. What you have is an excellent reason to go shopping."

They both laugh, then Gigi meets my eyes and gestures to Delaney. "Make sure she goes shopping, you hear me now?"

I salute her. "Your wish is my command."

Gigi bumps shoulders with Delaney then pats my arm. "By the way, he's super cute." Gigi doesn't whisper the compliment. She says it while looking at me.

Delaney snaps her gaze to her client. "No, he's not super cute, Gigi. Super cute is for kittens, hedgehogs, and dogs that wear bow ties."

Dogs with bow ties? I mouth.

"Work with us," Delaney whispers, and all I can figure is this is some inside joke between them. Fine by me.

Delaney returns her focus to Gigi. "If he's not cute, then what is he? Hint. He's the very definition of this word . . ."

Gigi claps once in excitement. "Can I say it?"

"You better."

"He's fuckhot," Gigi says, and they laugh, while I, meanwhile, feel like a million bucks. I square my shoulders and smile a little wider.

"Why thank you very much. Especially coming from such lovely women," I say, complimenting them too. Because they both deserve it. I'm struck with the realization of how easily Delaney connects with her friends—not just Nicole and Penny, but now Gigi in this unexpected and unguarded moment. Delaney's gorgeous on the outside, but a woman who has friends like this is beautiful inside too.

Gigi explains. "We had many conversations on the massage table about anything and everything, from life, liberty, and the pursuit of happiness, to levels of attractiveness, ranging from bow tie-wearing dogs to ridiculously good-looking men."

"I.e., fuckhot men," Delaney adds.

"Glad I received that ruling rather than the bow tie one," I say, because I am 100 percent clear on this point and 100 percent A-OK to be talked about like a piece of meat.

Gigi holds out her hand. "Nice to meet you, Tyler."

I shake hands with her. "You too, Gigi."

She jogs in place for a few seconds before she takes off along the path. She calls back, "See you with your wig on."

After she disappears, Delaney points her thumb in the direction of the flamboyant woman. "Does that answer your question about my change of heart in careers?"

I nod, instantly getting it. "Yep. I can see. You really can touch people's lives."

"Not all my clients have battled medical issues. But for those that do, I'm glad I'm able to give them a little relief, a little peace from what hurts. I'm not a doctor or a nurse, but in my own small way I like to think I can make a difference for some. That's why I switched to massage."

"I'd say you're making a big difference. She called you a miracle worker."

Delaney beams, and I love that the simplest of compliments lights her up, so I keep going. "You can make someone feel truly better. That's not just a gift. It's a skill and a talent. I always thought you'd be a fantastic attorney because you're damn good at reasoning, making a point, and arguing a position, but judging from your clients' reactions, and from the wonders you worked on my neck, you chose the right field."

I'm not just saying that because a kernel of guilt has lodged inside my brain, making me think I'm responsible for destroying her dreams. I'm saying it because it's so apparent she's happy in her work today.

"Thank you. And hey, can't beat the attire at the spa. Yoga pants all the way. I was never particularly fond of suits, and I don't think I look good in them."

"Wrong on that one. I bet you look fuckhot in them."

"I bet you'd like to see me in one."

"Or out of one."

And there goes my focus again.

My eyes roam over her, and though she is sexy as sin in her little running shorts and T-shirt, the woman would also look extraordinary in a tight skirt, form-fitting blouse, and fuck-me pumps. Wait. Let's add sexy glasses that rest on the bridge of her nose, and a shelf full of books behind her. She can perch on the edge of her desk, and I can rip off the blouse, buttons spilling all over the floor, then hike up that skirt, and wrap her legs around my waist.

"You okay?"

I blink, realizing she's staring at me, and I wonder how long I've been in dirty dreamland.

"What?"

"You drifted off."

"Go figure. I was picturing you wearing four-inch heels, and my thoughts went haywire."

"You've turned into quite a shoe man, haven't you?"

I groan. "There's something I have to tell you."

"What is it?"

I rake my gaze over her tight, trim frame, then linger on her . . . white sneakers. "Your sneakers are turning me on," I say in a salacious tone.

She raises her right leg then strokes her calf down to her foot. "Does this get you going?"

This time, I growl, and huff like a bull. "Oh yeah, baby."

She rubs the side of her sneakered foot against my leg, and yep, it gets me revved up. Maybe I'm that easy when it comes to her. Or it could be that I fucking love when she's like this—this playful, this fun, this fucking cool enough to go with the moment.

"Do it again," I command her, and she grabs hold of my arm for balance, sliding her foot higher up my leg.

"More? You want more?" she asks, egging me on.

"So much more."

She cracks up and sets her foot back on the ground. "Glad to know my big feet turn you on."

"Your big feet and the person they're attached to," I say, correcting her.

"Thanks for the clarification," she says, and puts one big foot in front of the other, starting us running again.

"So," I begin. "A wig party."

"Should be fun."

"Need help shopping for one?" I ask, because I'm really hoping she'll invite me.

"I'll probably go shopping with the girls. But thanks for the offer."

I'm not going down without a fight. And I'm not going to dance around what I want. *Her.*

Even if I screwed her over years ago, I have a new chance. Back then I was so singularly focused on my own selfish goals that it didn't occur to me I could seriously derail hers with my all-or-nothing approach to that *illuminating* last debate.

Although she had a change of heart, I played a part in it.

But that's the past. I can't change it. I can, however, let her know that I'm a different man in the present.

This lovely, sassy, strong, sexy woman. I've got to make her mine again.

Time to let her know it is on.

Chapter Fourteen

Delaney

"Delaney," he says my name without any trace of nerves. "I would love to take you to the party. Would that work for you?"

No *can I.* No *I wanna go.* He just lays it out. A small voice in my head, a long-held part of me that fights to protect my heart, wants to say no.

But another part of me is surprised he wants to go so badly. Another part is intrigued. Tyler wasn't the type of guy who'd go to a wig party back in the day. Yes, he went all out to get me to go on a first date. But even though he wanted me, we didn't do every single thing together. Case in point—he was never into Halloween. When the rest of us dressed up and trick-or-treated in the dorms—for candy and small bottles of liquor because . . . college, obviously—he declined. Not his thing, he'd said. "May I never own a costume," he told me, holding up his hand like he was taking an oath on a Bible. I didn't really get the aversion, but I figured some guys don't like pretending to be someone else. I could live with that. I was never going to insist he slip on a Superman suit for my entertainment.

Though, he did enjoy stripping me out of my black cat costume that year.

Yes, of course I went as a cat. Cats are sexy.

That's why I'm surprised he's inviting himself.

A hint of a smile tugs at my lips. "You'd want to go?"

"I would absolutely love to go."

My eyes narrow as we crunch along a grassy section of the path. "Do you have a wig?"

He shakes his head.

"But you'd wear one? You'd really wear a wig?" I ask, skeptical. Because this Tyler doesn't quite align with the man I knew. I haven't seen this side of him. This willingness.

It is, admittedly, alluring.

"Of course I'd wear a wig. It's a goddamn wig party," he says, his voice booming like he's making a speech. "I will wear a wig, and I will wear it with pride."

Color me impressed. I tilt my head and stare at him, as I concoct a plan. "Any kind of wig?"

He shakes his finger at me as we round a bend in the path. "I know what you're doing, and I won't back down. Yes, I will wear a wig, and yes, you can pick it out. You know why I say that?"

"Why do you say that?"

"Because if wearing a long black wig, or a combover pink wig, or a kinky, curly Richard Simmons wig means I get to spend more time with you, I will do it." He taps his chest with both hands. "Let me introduce you to me. I'm the guy who wants you back. Badly."

My heart races, and I don't think it's from exercise. He's always been a daring man. He's always gone after what he wanted. But I've never seen him bend like this to get it. Fine, we're only talking about a wig. But it's also a step. A sign. An olive branch. "I'm tempted."

"Good. I can work with tempted. I like you tempted."

He is tempting. So incredibly tempting. "Then I guess I need to shop for two wigs."

Happiness dances across his chestnut brown eyes, and the look stirs butterflies in my chest. I should probably question my own decision to agree to another date. Clearly, I'm not ready to just crack open my heart again and share all my thoughts and feelings—I couldn't find it in me to tell him about the call with my dad that set in motion the change in career.

But at least I said enough about my choice.

I'm not ready to dig up all my emotions yet for a man who broke me.

Truthfully, I should probably put on my anti-heartbreak armor. Nicole would surely tell me to run the other way.

Wait. That's not true. She'd say I should march right up to him and say "see you later, I'm outta here," then strut off into the sunset, having protected my heart, but *also* had the last word.

But that's not what I want to do.

What I want is something else entirely.

More of these butterflies.

We run in silence the rest of the way, and I let my mind go blank. I stop telling myself to keep Tyler at arm's length. I don't entirely want an arm's length between us.

I want less length between us.

That's why after our run, when my muscles are the good kind of sore, and he offers to walk me home, I say yes.

And that's why I do the next thing, too. When we near my apartment, and he looks at me with the most vulnerable expression on his handsome face, and the most genuine look in his beautiful eyes, and says, "I want a second chance with you," I invite him in.

* * *

I want him.

It's just that simple.

There are no two ways about it.

I know what will happen, though, if I take him upstairs to my apartment on the fifth floor. The door will creak shut, since it's one of those doors that cries out for WD-40 as it closes molasses-slow, and before it clicks shut, my clothes will be in a puddle.

I'll grab his neck, rope my hands in his hair, and beg him.

I will absolutely beg him.

But we're not at that point yet, so I tug him into the mail alcove at the end of the first-floor hallway.

My building consists of five floors and twenty apartments. We're a quiet bunch in this building on the Upper West Side. It's early on a Saturday, and even on weekday evenings, I rarely run into other residents, not even in the mail alcove. Since this isn't a doorman building, we're all alone.

"Remember what you said about the time in the library?"

He nods. He knows what I want.

"And the English lecture hall," I add.

Another nod. He steps closer, like he's stalking me. I back up to the mailboxes. His eyes darken with desire. I feel it, too. It swoops down my chest, flies through my belly, settles between my legs like a pulse beating.

"We were good together," I whisper, a new boldness taking over. Because I want to touch him. I want to know if all those things I've imagined at night are still true. If he can take me away. Lord knows, we could barely keep our hands to ourselves in the park. We were like kittens, paws all over each other, swatting, playing, nipping.

But it's not just physical.

I like this man.

The parts of him that I loved before and still see in him, I still like. But more than that, I like the man I'm getting to know today. How he laughs, how he needles me, how we tease and scratch and bite in the way we talk. I like, too, that he's a fighter. That he can't seem to back down from me.

Now I want to know if contact with him is still as good.

The metal on the bottom row of mailboxes digs into my spine. Tyler plants his hands on either side of my head. Those tingles? They fly now, like a roller-coaster car soaring downhill. I tug on the neck of his T-shirt, slightly sweaty from the run.

"So good together," he rasps, echoing my words.

I twist more on the fabric. "Kiss me good-bye."

He leans in, closing his eyes. But I stop him with a hand on his chest before he hits my lips.

He frowns in confusion.

"Remember the time in the laundry room?"

He growls, and it's the sexiest sound, deep, masculine, and rough. "I remember everything," he says, then he sets his hands on my shoulders and spins me around.

One time when we were doing laundry late at night, he pushed me up against the two-stack of dryers and did unspeakably erotic things to my neck.

Kisses that made my knees weak.

That soaked my panties.

That made me so primed to come.

He grabs my wrists, slides my hands up the metal rows, and pushes them flat to the mailboxes.

I shiver.

Releasing his hold on me, he says, "Don't move your hands." He drags his thumb over my wrist. Then up my arm to my shoulder. He cups my jaw, brushing his thumb along my face.

I nearly melt.

I always liked it best when he took over.

Sure, our kiss last night was outrageously passionate, and I started it. But I like to give him the keys. Tyler is a pursuer. He likes to chase, he likes to catch, and I like to be caught.

That's what he does now, pinning me with his body. His chest is sealed to my back, and with one hand he gathers my ponytail and moves it off my neck. With his other hand holding my jaw, he gently, but firmly, stretches my neck to the side, exposing the flesh for him.

He dusts a kiss on my collarbone.

My stomach flips.

Then another. His lips travel across my neck, along my hairline, down to the top of my spine. He kisses me everywhere, imprinting his lips all over my shoulders, my collarbone, the back of my neck.

I moan, and he presses his cock harder against me. That only makes me moan louder.

"You missed this?" he asks, his voice smoky and ridiculously sexy.

"So much," I admit, and it's the whole damn truth.

"I bet no one else has kissed you like this."

"You'd be right."

"And did you miss this?" he asks, then sucks on my neck, hard. "Or this?" He nips me with his teeth.

"I did," I say, my breath coming fast.

"But maybe you missed it more like this . . ." He bites down harder, and I shudder.

The fireworks show begins. He kisses harder, his lips crushing against my skin, his bruising kisses turning my world hazy.

He kisses the shell of my ear, and the fireworks explode. When he bites down on my earlobe, I am nothing but tingles. Everywhere. Just everywhere.

A door creaks somewhere. Maybe above us. He freezes, and I want to care that someone is around, but I want him more. "Don't stop."

"Never," he tells me, as the door closes and silence once

more surrounds us. There's just the squeak of pipes and the far-off pads of footsteps on floors above.

I just don't care who's coming or going, because if anyone decides to get mail at this early hour on a Saturday, they'll surely turn the other way when they see us—his mouth all over my neck, his hands traveling down my sides, me pushing against him, seeking as much closeness as I can get.

His hand slinks to my belly, splays over my shirt. He yanks it up and presses his palm against me, flesh to flesh, and it feels so damn good.

"The things I want to do to you," he murmurs in my ear as he plays with the waistband of my running shorts . . . "Strip off your clothes." Tugs at the material . . . "Bring you to the bed." Dips a finger inside my shorts . . . "Spread those gorgeous legs wide open for me."

I groan. I am nothing but flames and sparks and heat.

"Would you like that?" he growls, low and dirty in my ear.

I answer with a nod, as wetness gathers between my legs. I'm dying for him to touch me, I'm praying for him to taste me, I'm wishing for him to fuck me.

Even though the rational part of my brain knows I'll only allow one of those three right now, I want them all. I want all of him.

"I'd put you on your belly, and kiss you everywhere. I'd drive you wild," he says, then slides his fingers lower into my shorts, tangoing with my panties.

I want to fuck him. I want him to fuck me. I want him to slide his fingers inside me and know what he does to me. I rock against him, seeking more with my body. "Please," I murmur.

He shoves his hand inside my panties all the way. "Jesus Christ," he groans as he touches me.

I can't speak. I can't say anything. My mouth falls open, and my entire body crackles.

"Look at my sexy angel. So fucking wet for me." He slides his fingers through my wetness, and groans with each glide and stroke. "My sexy angel still gets turned on by me. Is that right?"

I pant out a yes.

Another stroke, and I shudder. A whole body shudder.

"You've never been this wet," he rasps out. "I'm thinking you might still want me."

I moan my agreement.

"And I bet you still think about me."

All the time, I want to say, but he knows from my body that I do.

"Do I fuck you when you're alone? Do I put you on your knees and take you?"

I nod as his fingers part me, and my whole body vibrates. Dear God, this man gets to me.

His chin brushes my ear. His breath is hot against my skin. "What else do I do to you when you're all alone?"

"Everything."

"Your favorite thing?" Tyler's mouth scrapes against my shoulder, the bristles of his chin rough and hard.

I shake. White-hot tension grips me, tight in my belly, and it courses through me, flooding me as he sends me closer to the edge with his words, and his hands, and the reminders of how he owns my body.

"Yes," I whisper, and I've never known the word *desperate* so completely till this moment. I am *desperate* everywhere.

He rubs his chin over my shoulder, like he's stirring up my memory. "My face buried between those pretty legs of yours."

Groans and curses fall uncontrollably from my mouth. Because . . . *that.* I want *that* so much.

Nothing, nothing, nothing in the world compares to the way he went down on me. I can't even describe it, but the first time he did it he promised I'd love it, and I didn't just love it, I'd have died for it. He kissed me down there like I was heaven, and he made me feel I'd gone there, too, but even better. I was in heaven, but I was still alive.

"And do I make love to you, too?" he asks.

My voice breaks as I give a yes while he strokes me, his fingers moving faster, sliding between my legs, then over my clit, then back again. A noise comes from my lips. It sounds like a cry.

My God, it's so good I swear I might cry.

"God," I breathe out. "Kiss me and fuck me with your fingers."

His only response is a growl.

He doesn't turn me around. He doesn't change positions. He simply presses his cock harder, rubs me faster, then turns my face.

And like this, his front to my back, my face turned to the side, his hand in my shorts, he kisses me hard and fucks me relentlessly with his fingers.

Tightness builds in my belly in seconds. The tension escalates. It grips me as the need to come radiates in my whole body. I grind against his hand, dipping down, riding his fingers as he kisses me like a madman.

I groan into his mouth, then it turns into the start of a scream.

"Oh God," I say, breaking the kiss. "I'm going to—"

"Quiet," he instructs, then he slams his mouth to mine again. He steals my kiss, his greedy mouth swallowing the sound of my orgasm. A climax detonates in my body and rattles through me, spreading to every corner.

I shake everywhere. My knees, my chest, my hips.

My feet barely touch the ground as I come on his hand. Kissing and coming, coming and kissing.

And it's mind blowing.

When I start to float down, he pulls out his fingers, brings them to his mouth, and sucks me off.

I'm dizzy and drugged and so turned on.

He gently spins me around, and shoots me a cocky, lopsided grin. "Have I mentioned how good it is to see you again, angel?"

I sigh happily. "It is good to see you, Tyler."

He presses his forehead to mine, and that small gesture melts me for him. Butterflies rule my body as he gently kisses my face. "And it's equally good to make you come again. Don't forget there's a whole lot more of that in store for you." He takes a few steps back and says, "Let me know where to pick you up for the party."

He turns on his heel and leaves.

My legs are jelly as I walk upstairs to get ready for work.

But I wouldn't change a thing.

Except my panties. I change those.

Chapter Fifteen

Delaney

Later that day, I set a hand on my belly, to quiet the burst of nerves. Little morsels of guilt slip and slide over my skin.

But it's just an email. It's not even the email from the private detective. But even so—why do I feel like I've done something wrong?

I squeeze my eyes shut, as I grip the bureau in my bedroom, white-knuckling the wood.

Shake it off.

I open my eyes, flop down on my bed, and grab my phone. I re-read Trevor's note that he sent while I was working today.

Hey Delaney,

Hope this doesn't sound weird, but I saw a six-pack of plastic rings on the ground and thought of you. And, truth be told, the straw I found on my sidewalk the other day reminded me of you, too. Come to think of it, so did the crumpled-up newspaper skittering around outside my office building.

But, I'll have you know, I cleaned them up and disposed of them properly.

In any case, I had a great time with you the other night, and I swear I'm not just saying that because we share a pet peeve. I'll be taking off tomorrow for my trip, and I'll do my best to make sure the contestants don't shed a tear from my critiques. By the way, do you have a favorite cuisine? Let me know, and I can book a reservation for dinner when I return.

Hope you have a great Girls' Night Out tonight. No doubt it'll be a blast.

Talk soon,
Trevor

I toss the phone to the middle of the bed, grab a pillow, slam it on top of my face, and curse into the downy feathers.

But my pillow tirade solves nothing.

So I sit up, drag my hands through my hair, and try to figure out what the hell to do.

Trevor is such a catch.

He's so normal.

And fun.

And witty.

And similar enough to me.

And thoughtful.

He's exactly the type of guy I wanted to date during my last spin of the dating merry-go-round more than a year ago. Why the hell didn't I meet a guy like Trevor then? Instead, my wanna-get-a-coffee adventures with the opposite sex consisted of a guy who texted me obsessively pre- and post-date, never once using a complete word in his texts, another who confessed to being a big fan of tickling (the date didn't last long enough for me to learn if he was a tickler or ticklee), and finally a buff, muscular banker who spent our date sharing the details of his workout routine and the bond market. I'm not sure which was more dull, the amount of weight he bench pressed or the amount of money he'd invested.

But no Trevors.

Not a single one.

And now here's this perfectly normal guy walking into my life without a dick pic, a fetish, or a narcissistic bone to be seen.

I *should* be writing back to him with a goofy smile on my face. I should be parked cross-legged on my bed, grinning happily as I tap out an equally witty and sweet reply. I should share his email with Penny and Nicole, oohing and ahhing over each word.

Instead, my stomach churns.

I don't want to feel this way.

I try to center myself with a few deep breaths. I imagine my massage room, and I pretend I hear the gentle patter of falling rain. I let it wash away the strange sense that I've done something wrong.

I haven't. Have I?

That thing this morning in the mailroom has nothing to do with this email, and vice versa.

I head to the mirror on the back of my closet door and check out my outfit for tonight's Girls' Night Out—jeans, a slouchy emerald green top that slopes off one shoulder, and a pair of silvery pumps that Penny picked up for me when she and Gabriel traveled to Paris last month. "*Quarante-et-un*," Penny declared with excitement, using the French word for my shoe size as she presented them to me. "They have gobs of size 41 shoes in Paris, and I couldn't resist these."

As I appraise the shiny shoes in the mirror, I imagine Tyler's reaction to them. The way his eyes would linger on the heels, the throaty growl that would rumble up his chest, how he'd push me against the wall, cage me in, and whisper hot, dirty words in my ear about what he wanted to do to me while I wear nothing but these shoes.

My hand drifts over my belly, then down, down. My eyes float closed as a blast of heat floods my body. A pulse beats between my legs as I imagine what happens next. All my late-night fantasies suddenly feel thrillingly real.

Like they can happen. Like they *will* happen. My fingers travel lower over my clothes. A gasp rushes across my lips, and shockingly, I find I'm aroused just from that fleeting vision.

I'm so ridiculously aroused I'm about to touch myself again.

Get it together.

I open my eyes and pinch the bridge of my nose, as if I can ward off the fantasies. This thing with my ex is just physical, right? It's butterflies and tingles. It's sizzle and spark. It's a man who has my number. My interest in him is like my lust for a pair of shoes.

That's all.

Nothing more.

There can't be anything more to it.

My phone buzzes, vibrating on my bed.

I stride over, grab it and slide open a group message from my girls. Nicole says she's on her way to the wig shop. Penny chimes in that she's running a few minutes late. I hastily reply that I'm on my way.

Grabbing my wristlet, I stuff my phone inside and ignore Trevor's message as I catch a subway downtown.

I'll write back later.

On the train, I stare at my shoes the whole time, day-dreaming.

CHAPTER SIXTEEN

Tyler

The yo-yo soars in a wide circle, around and back down. I punch the air as Carly lands her second trick.

She jumps in the park, squealing.

"Around the world! You did it." I hold up my palm and she slams hers against it. "Who rocks?"

She giggles and points to herself. "I do."

"You absolutely do."

Earlier in the week, she mastered walk-the-dog. Yep, I'm going to teach her a whole slew of yo-yo tricks. Shocking in a world of Candy Crush and Pokémon Go, but we do all kinds of shit that doesn't involve a phone or a battery. I'm an old-school uncle. She'll have plenty of time to stare at screens all throughout her life, but it doesn't have to be on my watch.

"You are the yo-yo master," I tell her.

"Can you teach me some more?"

"Absolutely."

We tackle the elevator trick, as I show her how to make the yo-yo look like it's rising up along the string. It's a tough one, and after a few tries, she decides she wants to scale the rock climbing wall, so I head over there with her and stand behind her as she climbs.

"How's second grade treating you, little lady? You learning about complex algebra and writing essays on Shakespeare yet?"

She narrows her eyes as she looks back at me from a purple handhold. "Who's Shakespeare?"

I set my hands on my hips. "Only the most famous poet and playwright of all time. But you'll get to him soon enough."

"Did you know I'm learning how to do big multiplication?" she asks as she grabs a red climbing divot on the wall.

"Tell me more."

As she moves up and down and across the wall, she updates me on second-grade math, and how she's moved *way past easy stuff* like eight times eight and onto bigger numbers like twelve times sixteen, which sounds damn impressive for a second grader to me.

"I'm advanced at math," she says as she hops down, wiping her hands on her jeans. "Beyond second grade level."

I arch an eyebrow. "That so?"

"Is so."

"Well, what's fourteen times thirteen, then?"

She closes her eyes, and draws on an imaginary chalkboard with her finger, mouthing the multiplication. "One hundred eighty-two," she says as she opens her eyes.

I nod approvingly.

"My teacher says the key is to follow the steps. Don't cut corners, and take your time."

"Smart teacher. That's not bad advice at all. Matter of fact, that's great advice on just about everything."

We leave the park and head through the streets to meet up with her parents, chatting about the type of poetry she'd write if she were a famous poet someday.

"And I'd make sure to take my time," she adds.

I linger on the notion of time, wondering how much I have with Delaney. What will it take to win her over? How many days or nights will she give me? But I also wonder what I'm trying to accomplish. Sometimes, I focus so much on the doing that I don't always think about the why. Do I want to go back to the way it was with us or start something new entirely?

And the most important question of all is this—how do I get any of that without hurting her again?

When we meet Clay and Julia at a café for lunch, Carly climbs into her dad's lap and throws her arms around him. He nuzzles her face, then Carly gives her mom a kiss on the cheek.

Later, when the meal ends and Julia and Carly head off to the ladies' room, it's just Clay and me at the table.

I meet his eyes. "You were right."

"I usually am. But about what this time?"

"It was regret fueling me with Delaney. Not just curiosity. Not just the possibilities."

He nods knowingly. "Thought it might be."

"I was an ass when I ended it with her. I fucking regret it. And I want her back."

He holds up a hand. "One question first. Is it still regret that's driving you?"

I flash back to this morning in her mailroom, to earlier in the park, to last night at the bar. Yes, I acknowledged my regret, but that's a damn good thing. Regret can make you change. "It's that, but it's also something more. Something deeper." I tap my breastbone. "Something in here."

I don't name it. Not yet. Instead, I give him a quick overview of what's transpired in the last week. "Tell me what to do next," I say, wanting, needing his insight. The man is older, wiser, smarter.

Clay chuckles deeply and leans back in his chair. "How much time do you have to win her back?"

"That's the question. I don't actually know."

He sets his elbows on the table and looks me square in the eyes. "Look, there's no roadmap. There's no set of instructions to follow. You hurt the woman before, but she seems to be giving you another chance. Let's start with this —don't be an asshole. The world is full of pricks and selfish fuckers and far too many man-children. Then, you've got the guys who are so goddamn self-absorbed you wonder if they were raised by coddlers, and then you've got men who have so little fucking backbone they can't wipe their own ass."

I shudder, and he points at me, that intense look in his dark eyes. "You're not any of those, Tyler. You're a man, and you behave like a man. The number one rule that most men today forget is this —don't be an asshole. The world is full of assholes. Be a man."

Chapter Seventeen

Delaney

Nicole marches along the cobblestones, stops in front of me, and shoots me a dagger stare outside Jen and Dena's Wig Emporium in Greenwich Village. A mannequin head sporting a leprechaun green bob cut peers at us with unblinking eyes.

Nicole parks her hands on her hips. "What do you have to say for yourself, missy?"

"I'm in the market for a fun new wig?" I offer tentatively, hoping to deflect a lashing from one of my closest friends even as I brace for it.

The only saving grace will be strength in numbers, since Penny's on my team. But she's not here yet, and these bodiless heads in the display window aren't going to save me from Nicole's ire. I gird myself for the verbal whipping.

Her green eyes narrow. "Let's talk about why we're getting *two* wigs." She taps her toe on the sidewalk, the leather boot beating a rhythm of frustration. "Well?"

"Well, what?"

She opens her mouth wide, but words seem to fail her. I smirk. Nicole is rarely speechless. But the dialogue desertion doesn't last long. "You have some serious explaining to do." She pokes my shoulder. "How did one drink turn into a morning jog, and then another date? A date we need to go wig shopping for, of all things?"

I break down her question into the easily manageable parts. "I try to run every morning, and you're allergic to six a.m. starts. So Tyler went with me, and then we ran into a client in the park, and she invited us to her party."

Yes, there. Blame it on Gigi.

Nicole huffs and wags a scolding finger at me. "Now you're trying to talk circles around me, when all I'm trying to do is protect you from getting hurt."

"*Nicole*," I say plaintively. I know she means well. I know she's only pissed because she's looking out for me in a super protective, mama bear, slash-anyone-who-comes-near-her-cubs way.

She heaves a sigh and then softens. "'Laney-girl, exes are bad news. Do I need to remind you of the top five reasons you should never get back together with an ex even if he blows your mind in bed?"

That was the title of one of her recent columns. I read it, but I didn't memorize it. Seems I didn't need to, though, because she holds up her index finger, and I've got a feeling she knows this quintet cold.

"Number one. You broke up for a reason." She stares me down.

I hold out my hands, admitting that much.

"Number two." She counts off with two fingers. "He hurt you like a son of a bitch."

I screw up the corner of my lips. "I don't think you said *son of a bitch* in your column."

Like I can catch this woman on a technicality. But hey, I have to try.

"I write online. You bet I used 'son of a bitch,' and if I have to use 'motherfucker,' too, I will."

I raise my hands in surrender. "Wouldn't want to run into you in a dark alley."

"Damn straight. I know Krav Maga. On to number three. They often have new bad habits, and the new ones can be even more disgusting than the old ones."

I scrunch my brow. "Seriously? That's a reason?"

She nods. "What if he hogs the bed now? What if he cuts his toenails in front of you? What if he expects you to pick up his dirty socks?" She cringes to emphasize the horror of this parade of possible gross behaviors. "Burps? Picks his teeth? Doesn't text back in a timely manner? Leaves cabinet doors open? Sucks annoyingly on a water bottle?"

I give her a look like she's insane. Because, seriously? "Leaves cabinet doors open? That's a thing?"

Her eyes blaze with anger. "Has that ever happened to you? Because it is a living hell. Shoulder bruises. Smacked eyes. Scratched temples. It's like evil elves booby-trapped your home."

I lean my hip against the store window, where a rainbow-colored head stares at me. I point at Nicole. "I'm feeling like that might be something someone did to you."

"And it drove me insane," she says, gripping her head.

"Nicole, anyone can do those things. Why is that uniquely annoying with an ex?"

"My point exactly. Everything, literally everything"—she slashes an emphatic hand through the air—"is more annoying with an ex. It's all amplified, especially bad habits. That's the nature of a second chance. You already gave him a first chance. Everything is in stereo the second time around."

"Tyler never did those things before, though. No cupboard doors swinging madly and no slurping of bottles. So I'm not biting on the habit issue."

She huffs. "Number four. The sex might be different."

I laugh and shake my head. "That one is not an issue. Whatsoever."

She stalks me, backs me up to the window, and sets a hand against the display, breathing fire. "You did *not* sleep with him."

"There was no . . . *penetration* involved," I say, then I clasp my hand over my mouth. "Oops. Wait. There was." I waggle my fingers.

"You dirty girl," she says, but her lips twitch, and it's clear she's reining in a smile.

I wiggle my eyebrows. "Also, the penetration was even better than before, and that's saying something."

She inhales through her nose again and stares through slits of eyes. "Fine, you lucky bitch. Then, how's this? Number five. The two of you want different things."

I have no rebuttal. I can't protest because I don't know the answer. He might want different things. I might, too. I don't know yet what he wants, besides me. Tyler has shown he wants me intensely, but what does that mean? Does he want the same type of future we mapped out once upon a time, or just someone to spend the night with now and then? Does he want a girlfriend, a playmate, or a partner? More than that, what do I want from him? Sure, I agreed to go to a party in a week. But what am I opening myself up to by buying wigs and wearing them? What comes after the party, and am I even ready for that?

Bells clink lightly against glass. A pair of thirty-something women stumble out of the store. But it's the fun kind of stumble, the one girlfriends do as they laugh and wrap arms around each other. One of the women sports a strawberry-blond bob and the other wears a lemon-yellow shoulder-length do. I vaguely wonder why they have wigs. For fun? For necessity? For a party? But the answer's not apparent as they walk on by.

Just like the answer to Tyler and me.

I turn back to Nicole. "We might want different things, but I don't know what he wants. And more important, I don't yet know what *I* want. That's actually *why* I said yes to the party. To try to figure that out," I say, speaking plainly now. No teasing or hard times, just the truth.

Nicole reaches for my arm and circles a hand softly around it. "It's hard, to know what you want." She squeezes. "It's the hardest thing, isn't it?"

"And to know if going for it is worth the risk."

"It's insanity out there," she says and sweeps her arm in an arc encompassing everything but us, I suppose. "It's all a big complicated sea of garbage and madness and magic all at once, and sometimes you can't separate one from the other."

"Garbage and madness and magic?" I arch a brow and laugh. "Is that your next column on dating and mating in the online, Snapchat, Plenty of Fish, sexting, dick pic, no-one-knows-what's-true-anymore world?"

"Maybe it should be. But then, that's the basic premise of what I do—navigate the sea of shit and dating." She shades her eyes with her palm like she's checking out the rolling waves from the deck of her ship.

"Captain Nicole, aye aye."

Her eyes shift to the end of the block, landing on the couple strolling in our direction. Penny waves. Her beau, Gabriel, is by her side. He's tall and lean, with longish hair and tattooed arms. The two of them are a perfect pair. He's crazy for her, and she's mad about him.

Nicole nudges my shoulder. "But I'm not done. Here's the final point—people don't change."

I gesture to Penny and her man as my evidence. "Penny's with Gabriel. He's changed."

"Their story is different. Fate intervened and prevented them from seeing each other."

Before I can answer, the pair in question arrives at our side. Ever the sophisticated European, Gabriel drops cheek kisses on Nicole then me.

I can't deny that I adore his classy side. And him too, because he's made Penny incandescently happy. Ergo, he gets gold stars from me. "Gabriel, tell me something. Do people change?"

He chuckles, then squares his shoulders. "Of course they do."

Nicole casts a doubtful look his way, and Gabriel places his hand on his chest as if to say *who me?* "I've changed. I'm not the idiot I was when I was twenty-four."

Nicole rolls her eyes then waggles her fingers, dismissing him. "You're disqualified. Be on your way."

"As a matter of fact, I will. I'm heading to my restaurant. Where I will create a delicious dessert for my lovely fiancée." He roams his eyes over Penny possessively. "Something I would have done for her years ago, and I do now. Perhaps some things don't change." He winks and kisses Penny goodbye.

Penny turns to us. "He wants me to have something when I get home tonight from our night out."

I sigh happily. "He's so sweet."

"And sexy," she adds, with a naughty glint in her eyes. She gestures to the store. "Are we going in, girls? Or are we going to stare at the leprechaun wig in the window all night? Incidentally, if you can get Tyler to wear that wig I will buy drinks forever and ever and then some."

I yank open the door. "Don't leprechauns have red hair, though? Isn't it more a Jolly Green Giant wig or an Emerald City wig?"

Nicole pipes in. "Or a Wicked Witch wig." Nicole taps her finger on her chin. "Hmm. Now that I realize we can truly torture your ex by making him wear any wig we choose, I might actually approve of this date with him." Nicole spins and points to Penny. "I know I've already lost your support."

Penny laughs as she fiddles with a cherry-red hairstyle. "I just don't happen to agree with your more—how shall we say—strident position?"

Nicole spots a long blond wig. "I've always wanted to see if you blondes have more fun," she says to me, then asks the shopworker if she can try it on. The woman brings us thin nylon caps to cover our hair under the wigs. As Nicole adjusts the blond locks, she says, "Look, I don't know if people can change. I just worry. I know you all think I'm a hard-ass—"

"Gee," Penny interjects, placing her index finger on her temple. "Why would anyone think that?"

Nicole sighs. "And I don't deny being a practitioner of tough love. But the reality is this—I'm a witness to the hazards, pitfalls, and potholes of dating in this decade, and I've seen much more of the bad and the ugly than the good. I don't want to see Delaney get hurt, and I'm not convinced men can change."

She peers into the mirror, tugs the bangs down lower, and spins around, showing us her new look.

"But hairstyles *can* definitely change," I say. "And you look good as a blonde."

Penny fiddles with her new fire-engine 'do and meets our gazes in the mirror. "But see, I do think people can change. Maybe it's because I work with animals, but just hear me out. I've seen what adopting a pet can do for a person. How it can soften hearts and change priorities and turn you into someone who loves another creature nearly as unconditionally as that creature loves you."

I wrap an arm around her shoulders and squeeze. I adore the dog-loving heart of my bestie. "You're right."

Nicole tilts her head back and forth, like she's weighing Penny's observation. Then she utters a quiet, "That's true."

"Why don't we let Delaney find out for herself?" Penny asks us through the reflection. "Go out with him and see how much he has changed."

As I adjust a sapphire blue wig, I don't just marinate on Penny's questions about Tyler. I turn them back on myself. Sure, I want to know how he's different, but I already see signs of that. What I also want to know is this—how have *I* changed?

I'd like to think I've changed for the better. I want to believe that my career shift from the sharp edges of law to the more peaceful waves of massage made me a better person. But, did it? A pebble wedges into the corner of my heart. Irritating and completely unpleasant, it's a reminder that I didn't tell Tyler the whole truth about my change of heart regarding my career. I didn't open up fully to him about the phone call with my dad, even though Tyler seemed patently honest with me.

Do I need to share that detail with him? It's not like I hid something terrible from him.

But even so, I didn't tell him the full truth at the time, and I haven't told him now either. I know why I hold back —if I don't share everything I might not be fully hurt. By keeping parts of myself just for me, I like to think I can guard them from hurt.

I know that's not true though.

We can't ever protect ourselves from hurt, from broken hearts, from damaged love.

But we can try to live our lives differently.

If people *do* change, I sure as hell ought to be looking at myself first. It should start with me.

As I run my fingers through the blue hair, I vow to tell him the full story about why I didn't go to law school, even if I feel like I'm taking off all my armor with the mere mention of my father's words—words that had sent my future into a whole new direction.

This chance with Tyler isn't only a romantic one. It's an opportunity to face the past and deal with the future.

I raise my chin and stare at my friends. "One week. I'm going to give it a week."

Penny shrieks and claps. Nicole nods solemnly then drapes her arm around me.

"Group hug," Nicole says, and we all join in, setting aside our differences and coming together.

They might come at my love life from opposite sides, but in the end I have what any girl wants from her friends—solidarity. Maybe it's odd, maybe a tad controlling, that my friends have so much say in my love life. But they're my family, we're as close as sisters, and I need them in the same bone-deep, always-there-for-me manner. We stick our noses into each other's lives more than most, but we do it out of love.

Theirs is a love I never worry might leave. That's why they are my inner circle. That's why they have my unconditional trust.

"One week," Nicole echoes. "You have my full support.

But you need to decide at the end of the week. If you keep giving him more and more time, then you're giving him the keys to breaking your heart, and trust me on this—a broken heart the second time around doesn't just hurt twice as much. The pain is exponentially greater."

Human beings always have the keys to breaking each other's hearts. One week, one year, a lifetime—doesn't matter. We can always hurt the ones we love. Even so, I do understand why she wants me to be wise, and on this time limit, I have to agree with her. "I'll give it a week." Then my tone lightens, and I shrug like this is no big deal. "What's the harm in a week?"

Neither replies, and I hope I don't answer my own question the hard way.

"We'll be here no matter what." Nicole grips my shoulder, then whispers, "Especially if you decide at the end of the week you really want Trevor instead."

I laugh. "Yeah, about Trevor . . ."

Nicole arches a brow. "What about him?"

I update my friends on the latest as we find a perfect wig for my ex-boyfriend, who's now jostled his way to the front of the dating pack. I buy the wigs and drop them in a canvas bag, then we head to our Girls' Night Out, enjoying dancing, drinks, and friendship, as I reflect on whether people can change.

I think about my mom and how strong she was after my father left. She was always a tough woman, but she had to shore up that foundation when she became a single parent, remaining sturdy for us. That's change, too—it's the kind that intensifies your core. I think of my brother and how easy it would have been for him to turn into a fuck-up, a messed-up teenage boy who skipped school after his daddy left. Instead, he doubled down on his studying and, like me, he won a scholarship to college.

We were forced to change.

But do we only change when we have no choice? A fault line had split our lives into *before* and *after*, and we had to shed our old selves. Can men and women, wanting to win back an old flame, choose to change in a deep and true way?

I don't have the answers to that, but as I rewind to the morning, and the night before, and the massage table earlier in the week, and the phone calls, I know Tyler and I are more than two elements in a beaker that combust on contact.

We are more than the physical.

We combust for so many reasons. Because of history, of emotion, of connection, of respect, of need, of understanding.

Because of a once-great love.

And because of who he is now, the man I'm spending time with these days.

That's why at the end of the night, after I find my way home and settle into bed, I write back to Trevor.

Dear Trevor,

Your trip sounds amazing, and I know you're going to have a great time. I want you to know that while I'm confident we would have a fantastic date, I need to cancel before we even start. In the last few days, after we went out, someone has come back into my life, and I'm going to explore what's there. It wouldn't be fair to keep you both in play.

That's why I need to send this email now, before I give it a go with him. Rather than hedge my bets, even though I know you'd be a great guy to bet on and you'll make someone ridiculously happy, I should say thank you and good-bye.

My best,
Delaney

After I hit send, the stone in my heart shrinks, claiming less of my real estate. There's more to say, and more to do, but I've taken one important step.

I was patently open with Trevor. I need to do the same with my ex.

The next morning, my phone dings with a jackpot full of notes. A sweet reply from Trevor, thanking me for my honesty. A Facebook message from Tyler, asking me if I'm free for lunch. And an email from Joe Thomas telling me my father now lives in Vancouver, Canada, that he's still married, and he'll have an email and a phone number for me shortly.

Do I want the address, he asks?

Nerves skate over my skin. I do, and I don't. I don't, and I do. But I also know if I have his address, I'll just google it over and over.

I tell Joe I'll wait. I've been waiting for years.

I make plans with Tyler, and I do the one thing that makes the most sense.

Since I want him desperately, I decide not to sleep with him yet.

To prove to myself that I can change.

Chapter Eighteen

Tyler

She says yes.

Hell fucking yeah.

She adds *just lunch*, and I send her a GIF of a cartwheeling eggplant, because I understand what she needs —*just lunch*. She needs to know that the heat of the mailroom encounter isn't all we still have in common. The passion between us is incontrovertible, but she wants to know we're more than that.

Over a pesto artichoke sandwich and fries at a sidewalk café in the Eighties, she gives me the details of her night out dancing with her friends.

"We could have entered a dance marathon, it seemed."

"Did you do the Macarena?"

"All night long."

"How about a conga line?" I ask, demonstrating the moves in my chair.

She nods. "And then we did a square dance."

"Hope you wore your cowgirl boots."

She shakes her head. "I wore silver heels," she says, with a strangely shy little smile. Then she's not so shy when she meets my eyes and says, "And I thought of you."

Images flash before me that make my throat dry. I groan, then lean across the plate that holds my chicken sandwich and tell her in a rough voice, "I like hearing that. I thought of you last night, too, and then I did a lot more than think. And I'm also sure you'd look hot in cowgirl boots."

The next day I get my reward.

She texts me a location for breakfast, and when I meet her there, she's got on a short jean skirt, a red checked short-sleeve blouse, and cowgirl boots.

"Fuck me now," I mumble as I give her a kiss on the cheek.

She laughs. "Maybe not *right* now . . ."

"But later?"

She shrugs, but the gesture comes complete with a wink that says *we'll see.*

We sit down and I order eggs, but no bacon.

After the waiter leaves, Delaney tips her forehead in my direction. "No bacon?" She stretches across the table and places the back of her hand on my forehead. "You're not feeling so hot today?"

I laugh. "Nope. I feel great. Just wanted to prove I can abstain."

"Prove to whom?"

I point at the gorgeous woman sitting across from me. Her blond hair is swept up in a high ponytail, and her cheeks are morning-fresh and rosy. "You."

Her brown eyes seem to sparkle. "Your abstinence is impressive, but you do know you won't offend me if you eat bacon?"

I nod. "I know you're not offended, and I appreciate that." Delaney's eating choices have always been for her, not something she tries to impose on others. "But let's call a pig a pig. Bacon isn't that good for you. And, truth be told, maybe some of your vegetarianism is rubbing off on me." I hold up both hands. "Not saying I'm going the full nothing-with-a-face route. I just mean I've cut back. I'll survive without it."

An eyebrow rises. "You sure?"

I pretend to choke, then to cough, then I slump in the chair as if the last breath is fading from me.

A few seconds later I sit up, and she asks me if I'm going to live.

"It'll be rough."

She pretends to toss her napkin at me. "You'll learn to love fake bacon. With avocado and lettuce," she says, then as if an idea has just taken root, her eyes light up. "Actually, I'll make one for you someday. My veggie BLTs are six shades of awesome."

"Six shades? Not five and not seven, but six?"

"Yes. Six shades just like six toes. And maybe you'll get to experience all six shades of my world-renowned BLT."

"You mean FLT. Fake-on."

She laughs as she folds the napkin across her lap once more, "What do you most like to do outside of work?" Her eyes drift northward. "Besides . . . *that*."

"Besides *that*, I'd have to say rock climbing," I answer. "Also, rafting and kayaking. And going to watch the Dodgers kick the asses of any New York baseball team."

"Some things never change," she says with a smile.

"And some things never should."

She holds up her water glass in a toast, and I clink mine with hers.

The next day, we go for another run in the park in the early dawn. At the end of our five miles, we bump into Oliver. He's stretching at the edge of the reservoir.

"Nichols, how's it hanging?" he says in his best imitation of an American accent.

I clap him on the shoulder. "A little to the left, thank you very much." Delaney snickers, and I turn to my running partner and make intros. "Delaney, this is Oliver. He works at my firm and pretends to talk American sometimes. Oliver, this is the lovely Delaney. We went to college together."

Oliver pushes his mess of dark hair off his forehead and smiles at Delaney. With a slight bow of the head, he reaches for her hand and kisses the top. "Charmed," he says, this time in his proper accent.

"I see you're from Italy," she jokes.

Oliver laughs and points at me. "She's a keeper."

I take her hand. "That's the goal."

Oliver turns his attention back to Delaney. "I trust you demolished him on the running path?"

"I did my absolute best to make sure he ate my dust."

I adopt an abject frown. "It was terrible to have to watch her backside the entire time."

On Wednesday, we plan a mid-afternoon coffee date. I wait for her outside a café on Columbus, shades on, head bent, answering emails on my phone.

As I tap out a reply to a client, soft lips flutter across my cheek. Sweet and delicious, they light sparks down my spine. I stop writing, stuff the phone in my pocket, and cup her cheek in my hand.

Turning her face to me, I kiss her on the street, and we spend our whole coffee date like that. Sans coffee and with kissing.

We walk and talk and kiss, like we're practicing all the kinds of kissing in the world.

There's the street corner kiss, the nibble on the lips kiss, then the so soft it's barely there lip-lock. Somehow, even that last one sets my bones on fire.

But none more than the one I give her on Seventy-Eighth Street, as I push her up against the stoop outside a brownstone. Grabbing her jaw, I hold her face as I bestow a harsh, hungry kiss on those lips I fucking love.

She moans so helplessly that I have no choice but to crowd her against the banister and kiss her more cruelly, using teeth, sucking lips, devouring her taste. Her body melts into mine, and her arms rope round my neck. Her every sound and sigh tells me she likes it like this.

But I stop soon because the clock is ticking and I have a conference call at four. "I need to get back to work soon. I only have ten more minutes."

"Me, too. I need to return to work, too." She drops her gaze to the sidewalk, then looks up. Gone is the dark desire.

In its place is something I haven't seen in a while. She looks like a deer. She looks scared.

She swallows. Shit. Fuck. No. She's going to end things, and they've barely started. My brain goes into hyperdrive, cycling back through the last few days to figure out where I've gone wrong. Did I say something thoughtless? Do something careless?

She runs her finger over the collar of my shirt. "I made a mistake."

My throat clogs now. "What do you mean?"

"I wasn't completely honest with you."

I furrow my brow. "About what?"

She draws a sharp breath. "I'm sorry it took me so long to say this, but you know the other day when I said why I didn't go to law school?"

She takes a beat, and I'm finally able to take a breath. "Sure. When we went for a run last Saturday?"

"Yes. I didn't share the full story. I wasn't sure how to say it all then, or if I was even ready to. But I want to be open with you even if it's hard for me."

I brush some hair off her face, tucking a strand behind her ear. "What is it, angel?"

Because whatever it is, I can handle it.

I mean, I think I can.

"When I said the debate competition was an eye-opener, it was. But, I'd already started thinking I didn't want to go to law school."

"Yeah? For how long?"

"For a few weeks. My father called me, and said something that made me rethink everything. I didn't tell you all the details at the time."

"I remember you mentioned the call. Why wouldn't you tell me the details?" I ask, because I thought we'd worked through this issue before—her struggle to open up and share her hopes and fears.

"You were checking out, honestly. You were distant. But I can't blame you entirely. I didn't want to open up about the things he said. I didn't want to give him all the credit for changing my mind." She sighs. "Even though he was right."

"What did he say?"

She inhales and raises her chin. "He said I'd make a good lawyer because I was like him. Because I'd always liked to fight. Just like he had with my mom."

I cringe. "That must have hurt."

She nods. "It hurt, and it was completely true. I liked to argue, but it ultimately wasn't who I wanted to be. I didn't want to be like him." Her voice wobbles. "That's why I didn't tell you."

I frown. "Why wouldn't you tell me?"

"I didn't want to give anyone any more power to hurt me. I didn't want to keep serving up all these raw and exposed parts of myself to the men in my life, and let them just walk out."

My heart aches for her—that she felt that way. But it aches too since she was right. I *did* walk out on her. "I wish you'd have said something then. But I guess I understand why you didn't want to open up to me."

She fixes me with a thoughtful stare. "It probably wouldn't even have made a difference." Her tone is wistful, not angry.

"Delaney," I say, wishing she wasn't right.

"Would it have though?"

I sigh heavily, then shake my head. "No. But let's do things differently this time around. I want you to be open with me now. I want you to tell me about your doubts and fears." I grip her shoulders, holding her tight, so she gets it. So she knows I want to be there for her. And the least I can do is try to understand her heart and mind, even about something that happened eight years ago. "Tell me what you were thinking at the time. Tell me how the conversation made you feel."

She fiddles with the collar on my shirt. Her nervous habit. "I started realizing he was right, and I didn't want to fight. I didn't want to argue. I saw too much of it growing up. Maybe that's what drew me to law in the first place, but then I realized I want to heal, not to tear apart. That's all the law felt like to me then. It was one long argument, and that's what my home was like." She takes a deep breath. It seems to fuel her. "I wanted a new path. One I chose for me. And when I went into the last debate, that's why I said it was illuminating. I told myself it would be my last chance to decide what I truly wanted for my own future. When you won and I didn't care that I'd lost, I knew I was done with law. I should have told you that when you asked me the other day in the park . . . but I didn't."

She's shivering, even though it's not cold. I wish this wasn't always so hard for her to open up. But I understand why it is. I run my thumb along her jawline. "It's okay. Thank you for telling me now."

"I wasn't sure what was happening between us that morning when we ran. And I wasn't sure I wanted to say anything if I wasn't going to see you again."

My heart speeds up. "Are you sure now that you're going to see me again? Because you better keep seeing me."

She swats me playfully. "You better be sure too. Because I want to keep seeing you, Tyler Nichols."

"And you will see me. And I want you to talk to me. To trust me. To open up. Do you want that?"

She draws a sharp breath. "I do."

And I smile once more. Because there it is. She isn't going to keep everything hidden. She isn't going to spend her days wrapping herself in armor. She'll take it off, so long as she knows I'll be here. I drop a kiss to her forehead and linger there. "I want you to know your heart is safe with me."

"I want it to be safe with you," she whispers. She pulls back and shoots me a coy little look. Her voice turns flirty. "But are you sure you aren't mad at me for not telling you the full truth when we went running?"

I scoff. "Not even a little."

She snaps her fingers in an aw-shucks gesture.

"Shame. Because I was ready to come to your office and grovel."

I arch an eyebrow. "Did you say *grovel*?"

CHAPTER NINETEEN

Delaney

The next morning, I ransack my closet, slip on some shoes, and make my way to Tyler's office.

When the elevator dings on his floor, I smooth a hand over my hastily assembled outfit. Tight black skirt. Short-sleeve white blouse. Heels. They're black and make me four inches taller.

Enough said.

He doesn't know I'm coming. But the lift of his brow yesterday afternoon, and the glint in his eye, told me he'd be fine with an unexpected visitor who's come to grovel.

The receptionist greets me with a cheery hello.

"I'm looking for Oliver Edgecombe."

"Of course. Who shall I say is here?"

I set my hands on her desk, dart my eyes around, and whisper, "It's Delaney, but can you keep it a secret? I'm surprising Tyler, and I need Oliver's help. I don't want Tyler to know I'm here to give him a neck massage."

That's my cover. Well, I suspect Oliver knows what a neck massage will probably turn into. But when I called him this morning to ask for his help, he went along with the premise. Bless him.

Holly smiles. "Of course."

She dials Tyler's coworker, and a few seconds later, the handsome man strides to the front of the office to greet me. We review the plan, and he gives me a thumbs-up.

"You're a doll," he says, rubbing the back of his neck as he winks. "I hope someday some hot, strapping thing surprises me at my office with a neck massage. Someday soon, come to think of it."

I smile. "I'll hope that for you, too."

The receptionist waves her hand, cutting in. "Yoo-hoo. Can I get in on this, too?"

"Of course, Holly." Oliver whispers to her, and her blue eyes light up. She guides me to the copy room, ushers me in, and shuts the door.

"I love surprises," Holly says, her tone giddy. "Tyler's going to be so psyched to see you."

I wonder how she knows that. "He is?"

Holly nods and keeps her voice hushed. "He's crazy about you."

"He mentions me?"

"Yes. Several times. All good. Plus, he's always stretching his neck back and forth."

I want to ask more, but I've already procured enough good news to float away on a cloud of bliss. I cock my head when I hear Oliver ask Tyler to come into his office. That's the cue. Holly opens the copy room door, scans the hall, then beckons to me. She points across the hallway to Tyler's office, sets a hand on my back, and guides me inside with a gentle shove.

"Should I shut the door?" she whispers.

I nod and mouth *yes, please*.

As soon as it clicks shut, I unbutton the top two buttons of my shirt and wait.

My heart jackhammers, and my skin heats up. With excitement. With hope. With desire.

"You got this, man. You're the IP king," Tyler's voice booms from the hall, and a stupid grin spreads on my face. Is it crazy that I love that he's praising his colleague? But I do. I love that he's good to them. I love, too, that they want to help surprise him.

Most of all, I'm thrilled he's about to open the door.

The doorknob creaks and then turns.

It's now or never.

With a quickness, my fingers open more buttons.

"Weird. Don't remember closing this," he says to himself, as he opens the door all the way, and I pray he's alone.

"You didn't close it."

He blinks and roams his eyes over me. It takes all of one second to register what's happening, and in that wink of time, he slams the door shut. "Please say you're not an illusion."

"I'm not an illusion or a figment of your dirty imagination. But I am sorry." I work open another button.

He shakes his head and gestures to me. "Never apologize for this."

"I'm sorry I wasn't more forthright when we went for a run," I clarify, as I finish the final button.

"Feel free to keep everything inside again if it gets me this type of groveling," he says, his voice husky.

My white blouse is undone now, so I strip it off, tossing it on his office couch. I'm wearing a black demi-cup bra, and his eyes linger on my breasts as I say, "I want you to know that I'm trying to share what's on my mind."

"What's on it right now?"

I nod to the door. "Right now, I'm thinking you ought to lock the door."

His hand darts out and flicks the lock.

I close the distance between us, park my palms on his strong chest, then walk him backward.

All the way to his desk chair. I push him down into the black leather. He looks like a king of the boardroom in his charcoal pants, white shirt, and maroon tie. He loosens the silk tie as he stares up at me with hooded eyes.

"Now what?" he asks, challenging me.

"Now, I'm going to show you that I remember everything you taught me."

He groans, carnal and masculine and so damn sexy. Raising his chin confidently, he reaches for my face and runs the pad of his thumb across my top lip. In a dirty growl, he says, "Then get down on your knees like a good girl so I can fuck your mouth like a bad one."

Heat flares through me, and I fall to my knees, quickly working open the zipper to his pants. His thick erection strains against the fabric, and that only makes me want him more. He helps me along, untucking his shirt as I release him from the confines of his boxer briefs.

His cock springs free, and I'm hungry and eager. I curl a fist around his hard length, and he hisses. "Fuck," he grunts.

I haven't even wrapped my lips around him, and he's so turned on. So am I. I ache between my legs just thinking about what I'm about to do to him.

"First step," I whisper, my lips hovering near the head of his dick. "Open wide."

He smiles as he clamps his hands to the side of my head. "You remember."

"I remember it all." This man taught me how to give a blow job. Step by step, he showed me the basics. He instructed me on what he liked, and how to blow his mind. And I did it the way he liked it, over and over, because I loved making him feel good.

Chapter Twenty

Tyler

She drops her lips to the head of my dick and licks. "Just a little flick at first," she whispers, and I moan my gratitude.

Lust charges through me as she proceeds to show off all the skills I taught her. "Tease me, angel. Fucking tease me. Drive me crazy with that wicked tongue of yours."

She flicks her tongue up and down my cock. That's step two. Tongue action. Like she's licking a candy cane. Like she's savoring it top to bottom, stem to stern. She settles in closer, and I make room for her, opening my knees wider. Like I've got a good buzz going, my skin sizzles as she licks all over. Then she grabs the base of my shaft and squeezes.

I shudder.

Yeah, I love that move, too. But I especially love *this.* She wraps her lips around me and draws me into the warm, wet tunnel of her mouth. Sparks tear through me, and it's like two wires connecting as she sucks and squeezes, sucks and squeezes.

"Yes, baby. Nice and wide. Like that," I say, my hands clutching her skull as I guide her head up and down.

There is no better view on earth than this. Delaney's hair is spread across my lap. Her red lips are stretched wide and filled with my cock. Her head bobs.

I'm not going to last long, and I don't care. She's working my dick over something fierce.

But I want more. Because more is how I like it. More is step three. "Can you take me all the way?" I ask as she swirls her tongue around the head, distracting me and making me grunt and groan.

She nods against my lap, and I curl my hands around her throat. Not tight, just massaging, running my thumbs across her neck. "Open for me, baby. Deep."

Her eyes twinkle as she glances up, like she's full of naughtiness, full of surprises. I gently rub my hands over her delicate and fucking delicious throat. The next thing I know, she's going down, down, down on my dick, and holy fuck. White-hot flames torch my body.

I'm. All. The. Way. In.

I want to close my eyes and fuck her mouth, but I want to watch every goddamn second. This woman is on her knees, and I'm balls-deep in her throat, and she's sucking me like a champion. Like *my* champion. Like she wants my cock as much as I want her to be the one sucking it. And fuck, I do. I really fucking do, so much that tremors roll through my body. Shockwaves of pleasure rumble over my flesh as she goes to town.

My bones vibrate and desire builds inside me, flooding every corner of my body.

My fingers curl around her skull. My chest heats, and the back of my neck is in flames. I want to be consumed by this fire, feel it spread everywhere.

As she swirls her tongue around my dick, I utter a guttural *yes*.

Can barely speak.

Can hardly think.

I feel like I'm falling under, like I'm sliding into some alternate world of bliss and desire and pleasure. Her eyes are glossy, almost watering, but she doesn't stop. She won't stop, and maybe this sounds nuts, but God, I think I'm fucking in love with her for that alone.

Because she *can't* be doing this just because she likes it. She can't possibly crave my cock, no matter how magic she says it is, so much she'd nearly gag. She's taking me all the way because she wants to blow my mind.

She wants this to be good for me, and, fuck, that's what does it for me.

My dick is hitting the back of her throat, getting acquainted with the far corners of her mouth, and my sexy angel sucks like she's never letting go.

I'm nearly there, but I still want one more thing. Somehow I manage words. They come out harsh and stuttered. "Baby, you know what I want."

She nods against my cock, and then I feel her hand on my thigh, and she cups my balls. Then she squeezes them. *Yes, fucking yes.* She tugs on them—not too hard, but just enough, and my brain goes haywire. My balls tighten, and my dick thickens even more. I unravel as a climax barrels through my body, knocking out lights, frying wires. It's an obliteration of the senses as I unleash my orgasm in her mouth.

"*Coming.* Coming so fucking hard," I say, gripping tighter, and I'm done. I'm toast. I'm in blow job heaven. This orgasm finishes me off, my legs shaking, my heart racing, and pleasure partying in every cell.

I shudder as an aftershock wracks my body.

With a loud, wet pop, she lets go of my dick. I sigh happily. So fucking happily. There's nothing inside me but the lovely, druggy aftereffects of the best blow job ever.

She lifts her chin and clasps my thighs. "Told you I had a good teacher."

"Get up here, student," I say, and offer her my hand. I tug her into my lap, and she sits on my half-mast dick. I wrap an arm around her and graze my lips against her forehead. But that's all the time I've got for basking. Time to take care of my woman. I grab her hips, lift her up, and set her on the edge of my desk.

She arches a brow in question. I push up her skirt and spread her legs, catching a peek of black lacy panties. I drag a finger across them, murmuring as the pad of my finger slips over her wetness through the fabric. "Let me do that to you. Right here. With you sitting on my desk. Let me eat you out."

She gasps like I've said the most shocking, scandalous thing. Maybe I have. We were always daring, always playing with fire in public. Even though this is private, it still feels dirty. The good kind of dirty.

But she shakes her head and slips off the desk, sinking back to my lap. "Not now."

I frown. "Why not?" I dart my hand between her legs, rubbing her once more. I love how much of her slick heat has soaked through. She's silky even with this tiny layer of lace between her flesh and my fingers. "Sure seems like you want it."

"I do," she says, but she pushes my hand away and looks me in the eyes. "I want it so much. But it makes me feel really vulnerable, and I want to be one hundred percent ready for that. I want to be able to let go completely and give in to it. You know how I love it when you do that to me."

"I do know that."

"And I want to be able to be in the moment completely."

I pull her closer, my nose nearly touching hers. "You will be, angel. You won't be anyplace else when I undress you, spread your legs, and bury my face between these beautiful thighs that I've been dreaming about. I don't want anything but your complete abandon."

She murmurs. "That's what I want, too."

I press a closed-mouth kiss to her lips. "Hey."

She pulls back and meets my eyes. "Yeah?"

"Thanks for being open with me. For telling me that. That you're not ready yet."

"An old dog can learn new tricks."

I sit up and beg. "Same here."

Her lips twitch in a smile. "And thanks for letting me blow you in your office like the world is ending."

Laughing deeply, I lean back in my chair. I drop a hand to her ass and squeeze her cheek. "There's something I need to tell you."

"Ruh roh," she says, like Scooby Doo, and I'm glad she's not worried. She shouldn't be.

Tucking a finger under her chin, I raise her face, keeping her gaze locked on me. "I like you. A lot."

"I like you, too. A lot," she says, as she snuggles in closer. "It's the sex, right?"

I crack up. "Yeah, it's all the sex. I'm overdosing on all the sex."

Her smile grows wider. "We are pretty good in that department."

I knead those lovely cheeks again. "We were always good together. In every way. We can be good again, too."

She raises an eyebrow. "You think so?"

"I know so."

Her smile disappears. "But it's not just this part you like, right?" She gestures from my chest to her breasts.

"Your boobs like my pecs?"

She swats me. "You know what I'm saying."

"Angel. It's not just sex." I rub my hands over her arms, reassuring her. "We haven't even had sex, and I'll wait months if you want to." Then I lower my voice. "Though, I really hope we don't wait months."

She screws up the corner of her lips. "I was thinking more like ninety days?"

"You think I can't last, but let me tell you something." I slide my hand under her skirt and up her inner thigh, grazing the soft skin. "I know it would drive you crazy to wait that long, too."

She whimpers, but then it turns to a little chuckle. "Pot. Kettle." She moves my hand away. "Seriously, though. Tell me, Tyler. Is it just sex?"

I shake my head. "Woman, the way I feel is not just coming from how much I want to fuck you."

"Or how much I want you to fuck me," she tosses back, with a naughty little lilt to her voice that tells me all her worries have been assuaged.

"Exactly. There's way more to this, and you know it."

* * *

Later that day, I toss a crumpled up sheet of paper into the wastebasket and swivel my chair so I face Oliver. He's slumped back on the couch with his navy tie loosened as we review contracts. "Let me ask you a question," I say.

"Hit me."

"You ever fallen in love when getting a blow job?"

Oliver cracks up, his hand on his belly. "Oh dear Lord. You have come to the right man with that inquiry."

"That so?"

"Oh, yes," he says confidently. "I've fallen in love when getting them, and when giving them. But that's not all. I've also seen God, witnessed angels, traveled to the stars, and seen the light of distant planets." I roll my eyes, but Oliver's not done. He sits up straighter. "I'll have you know I've also walked through the pearly gates and back."

"You've died and gone to heaven and back all from giving and getting head?"

He laughs deeply. "No, no, no. During the heavenly experience, I was absolutely the recipient. Bloke had the most astonishing—"

I hold up a hand. "Don't tell me. I don't want to know what was so astonishing about—"

Oliver jumps back in, a quizzical look on his features. "About his tongue?" he asks, 100 percent deadpan.

"You're the worst."

He wiggles his eyebrows and sticks out his tongue, flicking it around.

Dragging my hands through my hair, I mutter, "Why do I even ask you this shit?"

Oliver taps his chin as if in deep thought. "Hmm. Let me guess. Might it be because you fell in love during a blow job today?"

I sigh heavily, then I smile stupidly.

I did fall in love during a blow job. Only it wasn't because of the *astonishing* friction or the magnificent deep throating. But trust me, her ability to go deep is, indeed, astonishing. What did it for me was her passion. Her zest, if you will. She wanted it to be amazing for me, and after what I put her through eight years ago, that's saying something.

It says something about *her*. About her heart. About her willingness to try again. She's all in when it comes to starting over. She surprised me at my fucking office with a striptease and some oral loving to say she was sorry for something she didn't even need to apologize for. But she did it anyway, and I loved the gesture.

Am I falling in love through my dick?

That's not how I see it. A man puts himself at a woman's mercy with a blow job. On the surface, I have the power. She's on her knees, my hands are in her hair, and I've got her where I want her.

But no.

During a blow job, a woman holds all the cards. She's got a man's most valuable possession in her mouth, and next to her *teeth.*

To top it off, Delaney had me by the goddamn balls. Literally.

And like that, I surrendered to her, and she gave me the best time ever, even though I'm the asshole who broke her heart.

Now, I hope to hell I'm the man she lets back in.

And make no mistake, I want her heart badly.

How to win it is the big question.

CHAPTER TWENTY-ONE

Tyler

When I leave Craig Buckley's office that afternoon, you'd have to wipe the grin off my face with a street sweeper.

My go-big-or-go-home strategy worked. It performed like a Bugatti hugging the curves on the Autobahn. We won nearly every point, making this one beautiful deal for Jay Benator. I punch the air when I exit the revolving glass doors of the Midtown office building then call Jay on my cell phone.

As soon as he answers, I dive in. "Congratulations! You are now the lead prime-time show on LGO, and you'll be getting a fifteen percent raise."

"Holy shit." His voice is rich with elation and relief all at once. "I can't believe it." He repeats those words over and over as I tell him the details.

"You did it, man," I say with a grin as wide as the traffic jam near Times Square.

"No, you did it, Tyler. I'm amazed," he says, awestruck.

I like having a client who's amazed. We took a risk and it paid off. Proof that sometimes you have to swing for the fences.

We chat for a little longer, and then I call Clay. I give him the good news as I walk up Broadway through the late afternoon crowds, feeling like I own this city. I might even be strutting, and that's fine with me. I'm in one helluva New York groove. My cousin has been a fantastic mentor, guiding me through the ins and outs of entertainment law and giving me the opportunity to pursue riskier opportunities.

When we're through, my workday is officially over, so I head to Speakeasy, a bar in Midtown where I'm slated to meet Simon. We toast to the good news as we grab some stools at the counter.

Then he clears his throat. "I've got some good news, too."

"You do?"

The man nods with a grin. "I asked Abby to move in with me, and she said yes."

"Excellent," I say, and I knock fists with him. "You've got the whole happy Brady Bunch thing going on, don't you?"

"Life with my ladies truly couldn't be any more perfect." Simon has a five-year-old daughter, and I can already tell that Simon, Abby, and Hayden will be the happiest blended family around.

"Wait. Don't tell me you need moving help."

Simon laughs and shakes his head. "Pretty sure my phone still works."

I wipe a hand across my brow. "Isn't that one of the nice things about being an adult and having a J-O-B? You can call up a moving company and have them do the heavy lifting."

"You know it. I'll drink to no longer needing to ask my buddies to move futons and milk crates." He lifts his glass and takes a sip. "How's your insane campaign to win back Delaney going?"

"Better than expected," I say, then I get him up to speed on that front, letting him know the dates are going outrageously well.

"I'm impressed, Nichols. I knew this was going to be a tough one, but you're defying the odds."

I grin like a son of a bitch. "And I need to keep doing that. Tomorrow night we're going to a party that one of her clients is throwing, and she seems pretty psyched for it." I scrub a hand over my jaw. "Should I get her a gift before we go? What do you think?"

Simon nods. "Women like gifts."

"Wisdom from on high," I say, knocking my glass to his. "The question is what to get her. Flowers? Or chocolate? Or something quirkier, like a necklace made from recycled bike chains?"

Simon furrows his brow. "They make that?"

"Yeah, they're actually kind of cool looking. Stark and sort of industrial, but sexy. And Delaney's all about being green, so I think she'd dig it."

"Seems you have your answer."

"But is that enough? Is it defying the odds? The thing is, I think I'm already in love with her again. I want to prove myself. Show her how seriously I care about her. Remember when you said I needed a grand gesture?"

Simon laughs. “You’re going to show up naked at her doorstep this time? Run down the street in your birthday suit? Wait. Wait.” He holds up his hand. “I know. Take her to a Yankees game and do the full monty on the Jumbotron.”

I give him a look. “If that’s what it takes, I’d do it.”

He whistles. “You’ve got cojones. Oh, and feel free to call me when you need to post bail.”

I spin my coaster. “Don’t worry, Travers. I’ve got you on speed dial.”

But I’ve got something else in mind—something that doesn’t involve my balls on a Jumbotron.

CHAPTER TWENTY-TWO

Delaney

Tyler stands in my sliver of a hallway, his eyes closed.

I run my fingers lightly through his lush brown locks, savoring the soft feel of his thick hair. I could do this for a while. But we have a party to go to.

"Ready?"

"Absolutely."

His eyes are closed. The hairstyle I picked for him is a surprise. I slide the banana-blond wig over his skull, tucking his brown hair into the wig cap. He smirks and smiles the whole time. He's wearing jeans and a T-shirt, per my instructions.

I adjust the wig, then I tell him to stand still as I grab a red-checked bandana from the coffee table. I tie that around his forehead, tucking it under the bright bangs. He wiggles his eyebrows as I do that.

Next, I grab some leather wristbands and snap them on his right arm.

"I'm going to look so hot," he says.

I drop a kiss on the tip of his nose. "Even like this, yes, you are." I step back, appraising my handiwork. Technically, Gigi's fete isn't a costume party so I didn't plan to go full-on dress-up, but I couldn't help myself once I saw the wig. I had no choice but to accessorize it.

I put my hands on his shoulders and walk him to the mirror. "Open your eyes."

He does as told, and his laughter starts with a trickle, then small little burst. Then, like a dam unleashed, it becomes a waterfall of belly laughs.

He shakes his head at his reflection and turns to me. "I'm your Axl Rose, angel. You got me a mullet."

A grin spreads. Technically, Axl didn't have a true mullet but a lot of hair band rockers did, and this wig simply called out to me. "And no one has ever rocked a mullet like you have."

"You do have a big thing for hair bands." He runs a palm over the too-bright blond hair that's spiky on the top and sides and long in the back.

I hope he knows it's a compliment that I picked this look for him. Sure, it's ironic, but it's also a nod to one of my guilty pleasures. "You do know I had a huge crush on Axl Rose back in the day?"

He runs the back of his fingers over my cheek. "I am one hundred percent aware of that crush, and I couldn't be more honored to rock the look. And will you be wearing a Joan Jett rocker-chick 'do?" He presses his hands together in prayer. "Please say yes, please say yes, please say yes."

I laugh and drag a hand down his chest, enjoying the feel of his hard muscles through the fabric of his T-shirt. "Just you wait."

I head to my bedroom and shut the door. I won't be playing Joan Jett or Belinda Carlisle tonight. But I think he'll like my look anyway, even though I didn't pick it for him. I picked it for me. It's fun, playful, and bold. It's the opposite of the more muted looks I wear to work.

But more than anything, the wig I picked makes me happy. I twist my hair up, tuck it into a nylon cap, and then pull on a sapphire blue wig. The fake hair hits me just below the chin in a cute bob. I kick off my jeans and slip on a white dress.

For the pièce de résistance, I grab a pair of boots from my closet. Nicole tracked them down for me. She hoofed it all over the city in hot pursuit of the sexiest pair of size-ten flipper-feet ankle boots she could find. When she presented these gray beauties to me last night over happy hour drinks, she said, "A peace offering."

I arched a brow. "There's no need for an olive branch when you've done nothing wrong."

Nicole shook her head. "I do need to make peace. Because I want you to know, without a shadow of a doubt, that I'm here for you. I support you. When you go on your date tomorrow night, I want you to know I'm behind you." She squeezed my hand, and her green eyes teared up. "I mean it, hon. All I want is for you to be happy. If this man makes you happy, then you should go for it, and you should have the hottest pair of boots in existence to match your little go-go outfit." She smiled and threw her arms around me. "You're going to look like Katy Perry."

But after I slip on the boots, which jack me up by three inches, it's not the pop star I look like. It's a kids' TV star. When I return to the hallway where Tyler's leaning against the wall, his eyes roam my figure from head to toe. His jaw falls in slow motion like a crank is winding it wide open, as he takes me in. "You . . ."

He doesn't say anything more. I think he might be speechless. He licks his lips and tries again. "You look . . ."

I smile and jut out a hip, giving him a sexy little pose.

He detaches himself from the wall, strides over to me, and sets his hands on my hips, clasping me tight. "I can't believe you have just given me Smurf fantasies. But you have. You are the sexiest fucking woman I've ever seen, my Smurfette."

I'll take that over a pop star anyway, considering what he does next.

He slams his mouth to mine. He sweeps his tongue over my lips, then insistently pushes inside my mouth. He kisses me roughly, with hunger. His stubble scratches my chin, and the whiskery burn sends a rush of heat down my chest and straight between my legs.

Already I'm hot for him, needy for him. He bends me back, demanding more from my lips, wanting all of my mouth, kissing me like it's the only thing on earth left to do.

Kiss and crush and devour.

I moan into his mouth, and he swallows all my sounds then kisses me impossibly harder. My head goes fuzzy, my brain turning into a haze of heat.

And I know as he marks my lips, and takes what he needs from my mouth, that my quip about ninety days is going to be pretty goddamn funny later. The joke will be on me. Like 89.5 days sooner.

When he kisses me like this, and he touches me like that, I fall harder for him.

That's what I've been doing all week, with the dates, and the coffee, and the breakfast, and the office visit, and the walking and talking and kissing, and the running. Through it all, I've been falling for this man again.

My heart hammers with the realization. It crashes against my sternum, demanding attention. And I absolutely notice it. I feel everything—the pounding against my ribcage, the flush over my skin as it turns hot, the blood speeding through the freeways in my body. Most of all, I pay attention to how every molecule in me wants to get closer to him.

These feelings scared me in the past.

They scare me again now.

But not as much, and not as deeply, and not enough to stop me. I didn't expect to fall again so quickly, but here it is. I'm in his arms, and I know this is where I belong.

At some point, we come up for air. His eyes are fiery. Blazing with need.

He licks his lips then shakes his head like he's clearing his thoughts. He pulls me up and cups my cheeks in his big hands. "I'm crazy for you, my Smurf."

"Oh Tyler," I say with a happy murmur. "I'm so crazy for you." Then I add, with a little wink, "Axl."

That earns me yet another kiss.

As we leave, with his hand in mind, my heart stutters. For a moment, it feels like a skipped beat. Like fear. How have I let myself fall under his spell again so easily? But then, as I loop an arm around his shoulder and absently rub, kneading the knots as he moans his approval, the answer is clear.

I believe in healing. It's my job, but it's also my mantra.

I try to repair ailments for a living. I like to think I've healed the wounds inside me.

Through forgiveness. Through moving on. Through letting go.

Now, I'm letting go in a whole new way as I fall again and more wildly for this daring, cocky, funny, caring man with a mullet, a big mouth, and a heart of gold.

I'm not sure I ever forgave my father for leaving us. But he's my dad. He was supposed to stay.

With Tyler, I have a chance to forgive in a way I never could with my dad. To move beyond the past. Looking back, I can see I made mistakes, too. I didn't always open my heart when I should have. Sometimes, I kept my fears too close to the vest. I put up walls from time to time.

And just as he has a new chance with me, I have a new chance to be the person I want to be. As we walk through the New York evening, hand in hand on our way to a wig party, I thread my fingers more tightly through his.

I take a breath.

Shore up my heart.

Prepare to say something I haven't told a soul. Not Penny, not Nicole, and certainly not my mom. "I'm trying to find my dad."

My chest pinches and my throat squeezes.

Tyler slows his pace and meets my gaze. "Yeah? How's that going?"

His tone is so normal, so measured, so wonderfully calm, that it eases the pain of some of the shards and splinters inside me. "I hired a private detective. I wanted to see where he is. If he's still married. If he has more kids."

"What did you find out?"

"He's in Canada." With each sentence I utter out loud, I feel lighter and freer. As the sounds of the New York evening clatter around us, from cabs screeching by, to buses slogging fumes, to the click-clack of harried New Yorkers, I enter my happy zone.

It's a little bubble with this man who adored me once upon a time and seems to yet again. He makes me feel like all my heart is safe with him—the happy parts, and the scarred parts, and the ones that are still healing, too.

"He's still married." I add, "But I'm waiting for more info."

"What will you do when you get it?"

We stop at the crosswalk as the light turns red. I turn to him and shrug. "I honestly don't know. Contact him, I suppose? See how he's doing? What he's up to?"

Tyler nods and bends to dust a soft kiss on my forehead. "Let me help you when you get the info."

I pull back to meet his gaze. "Help me?"

"Anything you need," he says, the look in his eyes so earnest and caring. "There's nothing I want more than to be there for you if you need me. If you need a shoulder to lean on before, during, or after that call, you know where to find me."

And I float.

My sexy ankle boots are hoverboards, and I rise up and up and up on a cloud of sweetness and bliss. I don't know what's going to happen with my dad, but this man wants to be by my side. And that means something to me—something real and true.

Soon we make it to Gigi's home, and she throws open the door, inviting us into a swirl of music and laughter and appetizers and delicious culinary scents. Her home is awash in brightly colored heads, too. She's donned a rainbow-striped wig herself, which she affectionately calls her Rainbow Dash hair, after one of the My Little Ponies. She introduces us to several of the friends and family stuffed inside her brownstone off Amsterdam Avenue.

There are women with Afros, some with 80s perms, and one with a green wig that looks as bright as the Emerald City. A man wears a woman's strawberry-blond TV anchor cut, and another man has a 1970s *Anchorman*-style mop top. This party is a festival of color and style and lots and lots of locks. It's an homage to survival and to life.

We nibble on appetizers, and we drink champagne, and we toast with Gigi to kicking cancer's ass. Soon, Tyler and I find ourselves in a little nook of the kitchen.

"I won an awesome new deal at work," he says, then tells me about one of his clients and how he pulled off a big contract.

I raise my glass. "You're amazing. You take these chances and they pay off."

He nods. "My cousin calls me Bungee Jump Tyler. I'm owning the nickname. Carving out my niche as one helluva daring attorney."

Something occurs to me. Something I haven't thought much about before, but now I've got to know. "If we'd stayed together before, do you think you'd be one helluva daring attorney?"

He tilts his head. "Why do you ask?"

I lean in closer to him as an idea takes hold. "I just wonder—if we'd stayed together would we be doing what we're doing right now? Maybe we wouldn't be."

He raises an eyebrow and nods, as if considering it. "You think so?"

I hold my hands out wide. "Who knows? Maybe you wouldn't have gone into entertainment law. You love what you do, but maybe if we'd stuck to the path we mapped out, maybe we'd be on those same paths still. Maybe we wouldn't have taken the chance to diverge and try new things?"

"Like a new branch of law for me and a whole new career for you?"

I bounce on my toes, energy coursing through me. "Look, I didn't like our breakup, but maybe we were *supposed* to break up so we could become the people we are. I'm so damn happy to *not* be a lawyer and instead do massage for a living and run my own business. And you—you're practicing a type of law you didn't even plan to go into."

"And our split let us come back together as the people we are today. Like, this is how we're supposed to be with each other?"

"And with ourselves, too. Maybe we *needed* to be pulled apart to become our better selves."

He sets down his champagne glass, loops his arm around my waist, and tugs me close. "Delaney," he says, his voice raspy, "what you just said is another reason why I'm not just crazy for you."

He takes a beat, and I study his face, trying to understand what he meant. "Not just crazy for me?"

"I'm not," he says, shaking his head. "It's way more than that, angel. It's so much deeper. I'm in love with you all over again."

I melt into his touch and breathe out words I haven't said since him. "I'm so in love with you, too."

Chapter Twenty-Three

Tyler

Ask me a few weeks ago if I'd be riding in my elevator, molded to Delaney, kissing the hell out of her.

The answer would have been a blank stare.

A few weeks ago I couldn't have conceived she'd be back in my life.

But the second I saw her in the park the other week, my future turned one, two, three clicks in a new direction. And she was that direction. The future I once wanted desperately to have then stupidly torpedoed has boomeranged back to me. I've been granted a chance to do everything right this time around.

As I kiss her while the elevator chugs upward in my building, I'm struck by the awareness of how absolutely fucking lucky I am.

I'm here because of random luck.

If I hadn't gone to the park with my niece . . . if I hadn't walked past that dude with the Rubik's Cube . . . if I hadn't opened my eyes at just that moment . . .

The elevator dings and the door opens on my floor.

A quick trip down the hall and I unlock my apartment. A strange flurry of tension settles over me. But as I watch Delaney's eyes roam around my living room, taking in the crisp white walls, the blond hardwood floors, the light airy feel of my home, I realize I'm not tense at all.

I'm nervous.

I want her to like my home.

I want her to *feel* at home here.

I want her to be a part of my life.

She turns in a circle then meets my gaze. "I approve. Now show me the bedroom."

I grin, my heart thumping happily. "As you wish," I say, taking her hand, and walking down the short hallway to the bedroom. We stop just outside the door, and I adopt a serious expression as I set my hands on her shoulders. "I must warn you, though. I have something in here that's quite rare in Manhattan homes."

"A sex swing?"

"I hardly think that's rare. I have"—I lower my voice to a stage whisper—"a king-size bed."

Her brown eyes twinkle. "Don't get me excited."

I slide a hand under her dress, up her thigh. "I'm pretty sure you're already excited."

"I meant about the bed."

I sweep out my arm toward the furniture in question. "Then, by all means, let's get you in my bed."

She swats my shoulder then steps through the doorway and looks around. The room is sparse by design. A bed with a white comforter, a bureau, and a lamp. Some books, some frames, a signed Los Angeles Dodgers baseball, and a few odds and ends.

She turns to me, her eyebrows arched in praise. "Let's put that king-size bed to use."

And those are the hottest words I've heard in a long time because it involves my favorite thing—making her come. That's my first, second, and third priority as I yank off my wig and the bandana in one fast tug.

"No more Axl or Poison lookalike wig, but I'm still going to talk dirty to you," I say and grasp her hips.

"You better."

I strip her. Roping my arms around her, I slide the zipper down the back of her dress. She shivers as I let the material slip off her shoulders, over her arms, and the rest of the way down. I hold her hand as she steps out of the dress.

Before she can bend to pick it up—since I know she will —I grab the dress and fold it gently on top of the bureau.

"Thank you," she whispers.

"No. Thank *you* for wearing this lovely ensemble under the dress."

That would be a white lace bra that lifts her breasts beautifully. My dick thumps hard against the zipper of my jeans as my eyes drink in her sheer white lace panties. I want them off so badly.

She lifts her hand to her hair, fingering the sapphire ends. "Wig on or off?"

"Don't care," I say, as I grab the tail of my T-shirt and yank it over my head. I've got a one-track mind. "All I need is for you to get those panties off and let me finally go down on you."

"You say that like I've been depriving you for ages."

I reach between her legs, dragging my fingers against the wet panel of her panties. She gasps, her gorgeous mouth falling open in an O.

"Considering I want little more than to bury my face between your legs, then yes, I'd say deprivation is what you've been cruelly practicing."

"Then we should end your cruel punishment."

I stroke her slippery wetness as I back her up to the bed. She loops her arms around my neck and tilts her chin up. She says my name like she's going to tell me the secret to her world. "*Tyler.* I have a confession."

I pull down her panties. "I'm all ears."

"I've been getting off to you for the last few years," she says as I help her step out of them.

A groan rumbles up my chest. "You have?"

She nods. "You've had some kind of voodoo hold on me. I tried to fight it, but I swear, every time, it was you. Your face, your voice, your hands." Her tone goes gravelly, and I've never heard her more turned on. It makes me harder. Makes me hotter, until my skin burns with desire for her. "And your tongue. I'm obsessed with your tongue and your mouth and your lips."

I groan, rough and husky, then seize her jaw and stare in her eyes. "I think you're the one talking dirty to me."

"It was always you. I always thought of you. You made me feel . . . so much."

"Angel, you make me feel everything." I dip my face to her neck, bring my teeth to her skin, and nip.

She yelps playfully. "That's why I made you wait."

I wrench back. "Because you thought of me?"

She nods then extracts herself from me, unhooking her bra and sinking down to the mattress. "Because I knew once you did that to me, there would be no going back. It was always my favorite thing. It always made me feel . . . vulnerable. More than sex. More than anything."

"You've got to know it's okay to be vulnerable with me. It's okay to let yourself go." I bend lower and park my palms on the edge of the mattress, pinning her with my eyes. "I love your abandon. I love it so much. Almost as much as I fucking love you. And I love how you respond to me."

She falls back to her elbows. She's naked save for her shoes. I run my hand along the leather of her boots. "I fucking love that you left these on."

She scoots farther onto the bed, inching nearer the headboard. I climb up and prowl after her. She rests her head on some pillows. Then she parts her lovely legs and invites me to heaven.

And my dick sings hallelujah.

I scrub a hand over my jaw, marveling—just fucking marveling at this woman.

"Your pussy is so fucking pretty, Delaney," I say, as I press my hands to her ankles.

She lets her knees fall open. I can't do anything but stare helplessly. She's so wet, so slick, so pink and perfect. I drag a finger over the strip of hair. "Love this little landing strip."

She shivers, then shrugs playfully. "I can't embrace the bare-as-a-bottom look."

"No need to when this is hot as fuck." I graze a finger through her wet folds, and her sexy smile disappears. It's replaced by an exquisite cry.

Already.

Al-fucking-ready.

This woman.

She's mine. She's fucking mine.

I drop my face between her legs and flick my tongue across that slick heat.

She arches her hips instantly. "Oh God."

I moan as I taste her. As I lick her. As I fucking savor the sweetness that I've missed. My God, she's like opium. She's addictive. She's incredible. I nearly forgot how much I love going down on this woman, but I'm never forgetting it again. Because we are perfect like this. I flick my tongue against the delicious rise of her clit, and that winds her up. She bucks up against me.

"Tyler," she groans. "It's so good."

I raise my eyes and watch her every reaction as I kiss her sweetness. Her naked body moves like a dancer's when I do this to her. She's languid and loose and so fucking sensual, meeting every lick, every stroke. Her lithe limbs twist, and she spears her fingers in her hair. It's like a fucking dirty ballet, the way we are when I eat her out. There's never been a doubt in my mind how good we are together in bed, but especially like this, ever since I introduced her to the joys and delights of my mouth. That first time, it was like she didn't know what hit her, but she wanted it. She wanted it badly. In my car one evening on the side of a dark road, I pulled her jeans to her knees and told her I'd make her feel so fucking good.

She was nervous, biting her lip even as she nodded.

Now she's the lovely junkie she became with me, and I want her addicted to my mouth for all time.

I groan as I lick a line up her wetness, my dick hardening even more in my jeans. I've got to free that bastard soon. It's tight and uncomfortable, but I will endure because . . . this.

Her.

She lets go of her hair and slams her hands to the covers by her side, her fists curling around the white comforter. "Go wild, baby," I whisper, as I slide my hands under her ass, cupping her cheeks. "Give me all you've got."

She grabs my hair and sinks her fingers deep into my strands, pulling my face closer to her wondrous pussy. She grows wetter with each lick, each flick. I don't need to use my fingers with Delaney. She loves the tongue. She's always loved just the tongue.

"God, it's incredible," she cries out, then lets go of my head with one hand. She brings her right hand up to her tits and starts kneading one. "You drive me so wild."

Oh, fuck.

There is nothing hotter in all creation than a woman playing with her tits while you go down on her. It's the ultimate sign of her abandon, proof of how exquisitely turned on she is. She's so fucking aroused, she *has* to touch herself.

And she flies off the edge like that. Squeezing her breast, moaning my name, arching up into my motherfucking face. I can barely breathe, and I don't care. I'm where I want to be. I'm a live wire. Everything in me sizzles as her pleasure floods my tongue.

"Oh God, I think I'm coming."

Just like she said the first time.

Just like she says every time I've done this. Even though there's no *thinking* about it. She *is* coming, so fucking hard on my face. She rocks and bucks and arches, and I weather her storm of an orgasm because this is what I want more than anything.

Her words cease to be words. They turn into incoherent cries as she shatters beneath me, coming undone on my bed.

Where she belongs.

When she wriggles under me, that's my cue to give her a break. She's too sensitive right now. I raise my face, wipe a hand over my mouth, and crawl up her body, enjoying the flush of her skin. I swear she fucking glows.

"Like that?" I ask, my voice thick with lust for her.

She smiles dopily as her eyes flutter open.

"Yes."

It's the sweetest sound—her yes. She reaches for me, placing her hands on my face. "You," she murmurs. "What am I going to do with you?"

I shrug one shoulder and wink. "Keep me around?"

"That's the plan."

That plan meshes with mine quite nicely. But my plan also includes another orgasm for her. A few minutes later, I slide down the covers, flat on my back, and tap my lips. "Get on me. I want to do that again."

She shoots me a look like she can't believe it. "Are you serious?"

I nod. "Deadly serious. I fucking love your pussy. Get on my face and fuck me hard, woman."

She shivers, and a wave of excitement visibly moves down her body. "Under one condition."

Chapter Twenty-Four

Delaney

I want him naked, too. Is that so much for a woman to ask? I think not.

So I tell him, and he strips off his jeans and boxer briefs, his thick cock jutting proudly against his hard belly. I'm not ashamed to say my mouth waters when I see it. God, I love his dick. I do. I just fucking do. This man has been my weakness. But he's my strength, too. He makes me feel amazing, and he takes me as I am. He doesn't just want part of me—he wants all of me.

The same way I want him.

But I also want this wig off my head, so I yank it free and toss the sapphire hair to the edge of the bed.

"I probably have bed head or wig head," I joke.

"It looks hot."

I reach down to unzip the boots. "Sorry, handsome. The boots need to go now."

"I can live with that. *This time*," he says as he lies down on the white covers, looking like sin come to life. As I straddle him, I brush my palms along his pecs to his abs, then to his beautiful cock.

"Your magic cock," I murmur.

He grins. "It's casting a spell on you."

I laugh, tossing back my head. "So does that enchanted tongue of yours."

He sticks out his tongue and flicks it around, and I spend more time touching him. His body is so stunning. So strong and toned. I travel back up and run my hands along his muscled arms and his big biceps.

He nods and pats his chest. "C'mon. Give me some more." He sits up, grabs me by the hips, then pulls me higher on him.

"But I was going to admire you."

He shakes his head. "I'm a greedy motherfucker. I need your sweetness again. Now stop stalling, climb up, and fuck my face like there's no tomorrow."

A white-hot charge streaks through me, twisting and curling. I heat up everywhere as I climb over his face and sink down.

My body goes up in flames as I rock against his tongue. As I glide against his lips. As I grind and dip against his face.

He grips my hips tightly.

I moan my pleasure as I let my head fall back, my hair sliding down my spine. This man drives me wild. This man adores me. This man knows how to take me higher and higher.

I moan so loud I'm sure it's criminal. I'm not ashamed, though, to be so vocal. I'm turned on, and I'm in love again. Love and sex and second chances have become the world to me. All those thoughts flood my brain, and then the pleasure takes over and I'm nothing but sheer bliss, riding him to the edge.

"I'm so close."

And that drives him crazy. I feel him go faster, and then I'm aware of movement behind me. I turn my head, open my eyes, and find he's only using one hand to hold me, because the other? Dear God. It's between his legs. He's got his fist curled around his cock, and he's stroking. Rough, hard, needy strokes. The sight of him like that is a detonation.

His need for relief, his need to touch himself while he gives me pleasure—it's the most erotic thing I've ever witnessed.

Another orgasm blasts through me, rocketing through my body, blotting out the world. Everything goes dark and black and wonderful.

* * *

Intimacy was never my strong suit. It's the bedfellow of trust, and that's a tough one for me, too. That's why oral sex was something I didn't rush to try. To me, it's even closer than intercourse. It's the ultimate intimacy. To let go and give in.

All that went against my instincts.

But with Tyler, when we were younger, I was ready to try. Damn good thing, too, because I quickly learned I did not want to miss out on that special item on the menu. I took as much as I could get. I was voracious. Easily, it became a daily practice.

Now, as I float down from the clouds, I'm ready to beg for it every day again.

But I also want something else, right this second. I want another form of closeness. I want as much from this man as I can take. My appetite is endless.

I want him bare.

As I slide down his body, nearing his cock, I meet his eyes. They blaze with desire, heating up even more as I rub myself against the head of his dick. God, he feels so incredibly good that sparks fly across my whole body. "I'm on the pill," I say, my breath coming fast as I move against him, wanting to take him into me right now. "Are you safe?"

He swallows and rasps out a scratchy yes.

I sink down on him.

Trembles. Everywhere. Across my entire body.

"Delaney," he moans, and I can hear the sheer pleasure in every syllable of my name. His hands dart out to clasp around my hips. "You feel . . ."

I nod as I breathe out, a long, lingering breath that shudders through me. "I know . . . It's so good."

He pushes up into me, filling me. The waves crash over me once more. Every stroke, every second—it's all my fantasies and more. Because it's real, achingly real, as I ride this man.

This man I loved madly once before.

This man I've fallen in love with once again.

"Look at you. Fucking me again. Your sweet little body taking me deep, my sexy angel," he says, and I shiver from his dirty words. "This is where I want to be. Buried the fuck inside my woman. You're mine, Delaney. You need to know that."

I nod, my breath coming faster as I rock up and down on him. "I do know that. I swear."

"Not letting you go. Not this time. Need you with me."

"Don't let me go," I say on a whimper.

He pulses inside me, and he slides me up and down on his erection. "Love the way you move on me. Love how you want to fuck me so hard."

My body says *thank you* again and again, because this is the best high, the greatest buzz as I rise up, then slam back down. Tremors roll through me, and I swear I'm vibrating. Tyler's eyes squeeze shut, and he grips me so hard, it nearly hurts. When he opens his eyes, they're blazing. His voice is demanding. "On your back. Now."

In seconds, he's flipped me flat, hiked up my legs, and draped them over his shoulders. I can barely move, so I surrender to him.

"Fuck me," I moan, as he begins to punch his hips. A bead of sweat drips down his hard chest.

He shakes his head. "I'm not fucking you right now," he says, as he slams into me.

Another roll of his hips. Another shuddering thrust that sends my world spinning. His palms press hard against the mattress, and he lowers himself against me. "I'm making love to you like this."

I untangle my hands, rope them around his neck, and tug him even closer. "You are."

And then words no longer matter. Only bodies. Only hearts. Only this connection that faded over the years but burned back brightly as soon as we came into each other's lives again. Stronger, better, more certain the second time around.

Another climax claims me, rushing through my body, lighting me up.

My cries flip the switch in him because he fucks harder, relentlessly, taking me, owning me, then finally finding his release inside me.

When he collapses onto me, sweaty and elated, and asks me to spend the night, I tell him there's no place I'd rather be.

Even though when the sun rises, all I want is to leave.

CHAPTER TWENTY-FIVE

Tyler

I've been good at keeping secrets.

I have a great poker face. If I need to keep something to myself, I damn well keep that shit locked up tight. I don't mean dangerous secrets that eat away at your soul. I simply mean that when I was a kid, I never gave up the goods on what my little brother was getting for Christmas even after I saw a receipt for a new bike sticking out of my mom's purse. Likewise, I don't ever let on in a negotiation that I'm one step away from signing a deal, not until I need to play those cards.

Last night, I was a vault, too.

This morning, the cat's coming out of the bag.

I rise before Delaney, toss a fresh, clean T-shirt on the bed for her to tug on when she wakes up, then head quietly to the bathroom to take a piss. I wash my hands and brush my teeth, then put on a pair of boxer briefs. I walk to the kitchen, pull open a utensil drawer, and take out a few items I'll need. Then, I whip up breakfast for my girl.

Eggs, toast, and fake bacon, as well as a steaming cup of green tea since I know she prefers that to coffee.

Soft feet pad across the floor, and she wanders in, sleepy-eyed with matted hair, but a fantastic morning-after smile on her face. My white T-shirt lands at her upper thighs and looks hot as fuck on her. Especially since I know she's bare under it. She rises on tiptoe and gives me a kiss on the cheek. "Morning," she whispers, as her minty fresh breath floats near my mouth.

I turn away from the pot of tea and give her a full and proper kiss. When I break it, I arch an eyebrow. "If I were president, I'd abolish morning breath."

"You so have my vote."

I gesture to the stool at the counter. "Sit. Eat. I made you breakfast. Your favorite. And I got you free-range, farm-fresh, all-natural, one hundred percent organic eggs. Actually, come to think of it, I even hand-picked the eggs from a sustainable local farm, and I met the hen in advance. Nice gal. Her name was Cluckity-cluck."

She shoots me a look that says *impressed*. "And did you thank Cluckity-Cluck for her services?"

"I told her I was most appreciative," I say as I slide a plate to her then set one down for me.

She peers over the counter at the clock on the microwave. "I have a massage at ten. But that give us time for breakfast, and . . ."

"I'll take both the meal and the *and*." I join her at the counter, and we eat and talk. It all feels so natural and right.

I'm more confident than ever that there's so much more to us getting back together than just the sparks in bed. But I need her to know that, too. I want to give her all the security I can. I want her to know this time is for real. I drum my fingers on the counter. "Remember in my office when you said you were worried this was just sex?"

She nods. "Yeah? Why do you ask?"

"It's not, Delaney. It's so much more than that."

She smiles and swipes a strand of hair off her cheek. "I know that, Tyler. I'm good on that front."

But I want her to know it in a bone-deep way. I reach over the counter, grab the box I removed from the utensil drawer, and take her hand in my free one. "Marry me."

She blinks.

This is the secret I kept last night. "I love you. I'm in love with you. I want to do this right. I want us to be together. I'm not going anywhere this time, and I need you to know that." I say it with certainty, with confidence. And yeah, with bravado. She's going to say yes. She has to. This is what we both want.

Her lips part, but no sound comes out. Her irises go wide. Then she closes her eyes, and when she opens them, she regards me as if she's viewing a disaster scene, taking in rubble, broken homes, shards of glass. "I don't . . ."

A seed of doubt roots around in my chest, but I shove it aside. This is my bailiwick. This is what I do well. I go big. And there's no better reason to do it than to win her heart forever.

Fuck doubt.

I flip open the box, and the glint from the diamond ring shines brightly. So brightly, she looks away, like she needs sunglasses.

But I won't lose this one.

I make my case to the jury. "I'm in love with you, and nothing is going to change that. I need you to know I'll be here for you always. I want to prove that I've changed. Prove that I'm worthy."

She crinkles her brow, and her lips pull down. That looks distinctly like a frown, and my chest pinches.

"Tyler," she says, her voice soft but full of warning.

"Yeah?"

She gets off the stool and stands up. She shakes her head. "This is certifiably insane."

"Why?"

She grabs her head, digging her fingers against her temple like she's trying to process what's happening. "We just had sex. And you're trying to prove this isn't about the sex. We just got back together. And you're trying to tell me you're going to love me forever. That's insane," she says, her words falling out in a mad rush.

"It's not insane. It's right." But my voice is the wobbly one now.

"I'm not your next business deal. I'm not your next risk. I'm not your next chance to prove you can roll the dice and win. I'm a person. A woman. And I'm not ready to marry you. I'm not even ready to be engaged."

"Why not? Sounds brilliant to me."

She parks one hand on her hip then gets going, and I remember what a powerhouse debater she was in college.

"Maybe if you'd suggested we get a cat, that might feel a little more normal. But this is twenty steps ahead of where we are. We need time. We need to keep getting to know each other."

"But I thought you wanted—"

"Wait. Let me guess. You thought I wanted you to fix the past? You thought I wanted you to slap a Band-Aid on 'It's too hard to juggle classes and you'?"

"But you said 'don't let me go' when we were having sex." My voice rises, too, as we're firing back and forth at each other. Because I also have a fucking point to make.

She holds out her hands like she's making an impassioned plea. "I meant 'don't let me go' as in 'keep me around. Be with me.' I didn't mean ask me to marry you after barely one week of dating."

I raise an eyebrow, trying to get to the bottom of where I went so wrong. "Is this because of your intimacy challenges? Because it's hard for you to trust?"

Her eyes brim with fire. "No," she hisses. "It's because you're doing it for the wrong reasons."

I fold my arms over my chest. "What the hell? I thought this was what you wanted."

Her tone softens as she speaks. "What I wanted was a new chance to do this right with you. Not to blindly jump off a cliff to prove getting back together makes sense. It already made sense to me an hour ago." She drags a hand through her hair and sighs heavily.

"And now?" I ask, my stomach plummeting like an airplane that's shot down.

"I don't honestly know what makes sense." She peers at the clock. "I should go."

I suppose what seems to make the most sense to her is leaving. Since that's what she does next.

CHAPTER TWENTY-SIX

Delaney

#$@&%*!
$@&%*! #
@&%*! #$
&%*! #$@
%*! #$@&
*! #$@&%
! #$@&%*

* * *

I curse silently once more, alone in the restroom at Nirvana. I clench my fists, stomp my feet, and shake my head. I've got to get this morning out of my system. I have work to do. Massages to give. Clients to take care of.

I take a deep, calming breath, then I bring my palms together in front of my chest and ask the universe to grant me peace right now.

Or at least for the next sixty minutes, since my client Violet waits for me in the Rainfall Room.

As I exit the bathroom, I tell myself I'm leaving Tyler in a trail of dust behind me. I won't think about his absolutely absurd proposal. I won't devote a moment's thought to the utter insanity of him thinking we should get married *so freaking soon.* And I won't let my mind get caught up in second- and third-guessing our fight.

I shudder.

That word.

Fight.

We fought like two bitter people. Like my parents. The thought sickens me. I hate fighting. I detest it. It's not who I want to be. I should have done better this morning. Should have been calmer.

With my chin up, I head into the massage room. Violet is in position, her raven hair spilling over her left shoulder, freeing her right one for some serious deep tissue work.

"Hey, Vi. How's it going?"

She raises her face from the face rest and smiles. "I was a good girl. No iPad in bed for the last two weeks."

I pat her shoulder. "I'm so proud of you. That's great news."

"I broke the habit," she says, as she resumes her position. "Like you told me to."

I drizzle some lavender massage oil on my palm and begin working on her shoulder. "Vi," I whisper, astonished.

"What is it?"

"I can tell. You aren't as knotted and tight."

"See? I've behaved."

I beam, and this is how I get Tyler out of my head. I focus on work, clients, and healing. This is the antidote to my morning. But even though we fought, my reaction was totally reasonable, wasn't it? A proposal the morning after we sleep together is crazypants.

Oh shit.

I'm lingering on him again.

I shoo him from my brain once more as Violet says, "What about you?"

"What *about* me?" I ask as I dig my thumbs around her shoulder blade.

"Last time I saw you, you said that you'd been trying to break the habit of thinking about your ex-boyfriend," she says, reminding me of my own words. I cringe.

"Right," I say, guilty as charged.

"So . . .?"

I swallow and fess up. "Well, we wound up getting back together, actually."

Violet flips up on her side. "You did?"

I tap the headrest, gently reminding her. "I can't work my magic if you're on your side."

"I know, but tell me stuff. How did that happen?"

"I'll tell you, but let me do it as I rub, okay?"

She returns to her front, wriggling around till she's back in the position.

"Here's how it started . . ."

I rub and talk. Violet asks questions as I go. "So what happened after the wig party?"

"We had earth-shattering, toe-curling sex."

"Yum."

"And I spent the night."

"So what's the problem, then?"

"In the morning, things started to go downhill," I say, and then I tell her about the proposal. "It's crazy, right?" I ask as I knead my hands over her lower back.

"Yes, it's too soon to propose. He jumped the gun. He was pretty impulsive." She breathes out heavily as I dig my thumbs along her spine. "But what if there's a middle ground? Something in between you leaving and him proposing?"

"But I didn't leave," I insist. "I had to come here and work."

"Sure," Violet says, her tone understanding. "But to him, it might have felt like leaving."

Leaving.

My chest hurts, a fresh, sharp pain.

I know how that feels. To be left.

Chapter Twenty-Seven

Tyler

Carly pretends to toss a bone to the skeleton of the Tyrannosaurus Rex.

"Good boy," she says, clapping. "Look, Tyler. He's chasing after it."

I point to the bone-retrieving dinosaur. "He's almost got it. You can do it, boy," I say as we weave through the lobby of the Museum of Natural History, one of her favorite places in the city.

She also happens to be a huge fan of *Night at the Museum*, so this trip is a total win-win.

The only problem is I'm not feeling like such a winner today.

I'm feeling like one helluva loser. As we stroll over to the bison exhibit, I try to pinpoint where I went wrong this morning. Asking her to marry me felt so goddamn smart, so fucking strategic when I walked into Katherine's jewelry store on Fifth Avenue after my drinks with Simon the other night.

With one grand gesture indeed, I was rewriting the past. Repairing all the damage that had been done. A clean sweep.

And I'd be keeping her forever.

Or so I thought.

I heave a harsh sigh as I rub a hand over the back of my neck. So much for my plans. I failed abysmally at assessing Delaney's wants and needs. Proposing to her seemed brilliant. The best way to let her know I've changed. I'm not the man who walked away. I'm the man who'll stay.

Carly tugs on my shirt. "Can we go see the capuchin monkey?"

"Let's track down that banana eater," I say.

Now is not the time to sort out my romantic fuck-ups. It's Carly time, and for the next two hours, we do our best to play our own version of *Night at the Museum* as we wander through the exhibits. Along the way, I ask her how the big multiplication is going at school.

Her hazel eyes light up with excitement as she rattles off the new math facts she's learned, and how much she likes her teacher.

Her words from the day at the park echo into my present dilemma.

"My teacher says the key is to follow the steps. Don't cut corners, and take your time."

Ding, ding, ding.

I grab tight to the brass rail in front of the stuffed buffalos to steady myself. That's where I went wrong. Delaney was right. I treated her like a business transaction, focusing solely on the outcome. I thought I could slam dunk my way back into her heart. I didn't take the time. I didn't follow the steps. I cut all the fucking corners.

But a relationship is built on a foundation that *needs* corners.

As well as bricks, mortar, and plenty of time to shore it all up.

I skipped those steps, figuring I could apply my business strategy to romance.

But the truth is, I went only for the endgame with her. While I might go big in deals, I do so with meticulous strategy and preparation. I am a man with a playbook and a rock solid game plan. That's why I can brave the risky deals for my clients, because I've done the homework.

With Delaney, I didn't study, but I thought I'd win the deal anyway. I flash back to Clay's words when I landed the Jay Benator deal. He told me that the deal wasn't as crazy as I thought. "You knew your stuff," he'd told me. "You took the time to understand what Craig needed, and then you delivered so you could get your client's goals met. That's why you're one helluva daring attorney."

After I drop off Carly with her dad that afternoon, I head uptown and go for a walk in my neighborhood, running through scenarios—how to apologize, how to prepare, how to explain what I really want from Delaney. I cycle through all our conversations in the last few weeks, reviewing every detail, weighing what matters most, and adding up the facts.

I stop at a café, grab a coffee, do a little research on my phone, then make a few calls. Just like I did when I showed up at her work ready to strip, I have all my details together. I won't be Bungee Jump Tyler this time.

I'm just grabbing my phone to dial her number when I see a message from her that makes me sit up straight.

Chapter Twenty-Eight

Delaney

My morning is mercifully short, so I do what any self-respecting woman would do in this situation.

Call for backup.

The soldiers are ready. Nicole and Penny wait outside Nirvana, and the second I leave, Nicole declares it's time for a walk and talk.

We march toward one of our favorite lunch spots while I give them the full download. Nicole's eyes approximate saucers and Penny's morph into moons. Great. I've officially shocked my best friends. That's how crazy my love life is.

We stop at the corner of the street, waiting for a light. "Everything was going so well," I say, half-frustrated, half-sad. "It was perfect. It was bliss. It was everything I imagined a second chance would be." I look at Nicole, my voice wavering with emotion as I recall how lovely the last week had been. "You said give it a week, and I did, and we had a great time, and we communicated, and we talked about things. I was open with him, and he was sweet and caring with me. And then *boom*." I slap my palms together, making a loud clap. "A proposal. Out of the blue."

Penny meets Nicole's eyes, and they nod in unison.

"Uh oh. You two are up to something," I say as the light changes and we cross.

Nicole speaks first. "I can't believe I'm saying this, but . . ." She takes a deep breath then exhales. "But I think he only did it because he loves you." I'm about to respond, but she raises a hand. "Hear me out. I'm not saying you should get engaged after one effing week. But I *am* saying, in his own weird, warped, twisted way, the man is trying to show you he's changed."

"By leapfrogging into an engagement?" I ask, narrowing my eyes.

"Men don't always make sense," Penny offers, and I mutter *true* because there's so much wisdom in those words. "Sometimes, they take two steps forward and one step back. Or they take twenty steps forward when they should take two."

Nicole jumps back in. "The point is, he might have missed on the timing of this one. He might not be showcasing change in the best way possible. But, at the heart of all this, I think he is changing."

I shoot her a pointed look. "I thought people don't change."

Nicole shrugs and smiles. "Maybe they do for someone as amazing as you."

Penny says, "Go see him. Try to find a middle ground."

"Something in between twenty steps and two steps?" I ask.

"Exactly," Nicole says.

I look at my watch. "Mind if I skip lunch? I should try to track him down."

They both shoo me away, but as I walk, I see a message that stops me in my tracks.

* * *

When I was younger, my dad used to take me to the park. Anytime I wanted to go, it seemed. A monkey, he'd called me, because I climbed everything. I swung across the bars like they were my personal jungle. I clambered up the slide faster than anyone. Those crazy high crisscross rope structures? They were my stomping grounds.

And my dad always waited for me at the bottom, ready to encourage me to do it all over again.

Then once I wore myself out, he took my hand in his, and we walked home. Together.

He was, by all accounts, a good dad.

As I find myself wandering through Central Park, staring at the email from Joe Thomas, I flash back to those memories, rather than the ones of my parents arguing. I stop at a playground, watching the kids chasing each other, swinging with nannies, scampering with mothers and fathers. And I remember what this felt like when I was one of those little kids.

Wrapping my hands around the edge of the fence, I wait for the storm to lash me.

For the hurt to swoop down like a bat from a darkened sky.

Surely, this is when the memories will wound me the most—as I regard the tableau of what I lost. But as I run my thumb over the screen of my phone, staring at the number in Canada, and the Gmail address, too, I brace myself for the hurt to crash into me.

For the wave to tug me under.

Only, as I look up from the phone to stare at a little blond girl swinging high, kicking her feet happily, all I do is smile.

And the truth hits me.

Beautifully.

Peacefully.

And without regret.

He left and didn't look back.

Time for me to look forward, and only forward.

There's nothing I need from him anymore.

There's nothing he can give me.

Curiosity is a powerful motivator, and it drove me to track him down. But he's not a former classmate from college who I'm curious about. He's not an old friend I'd catch up with over a cocktail.

He's the man who gave half his DNA to me and then walked out fourteen years later.

I don't need to make small talk with him.

I don't need to talk to him at all.

This is my life, and it's just as good as it's been since he left.

I let go of the fence, turn on my heel, and head to the other side of the park.

CHAPTER TWENTY-NINE

Tyler

I stand in my doorway, waiting for the sound of the elevator. A few seconds later, a soft whoosh tells me it's here. When the brass door slides open, I expect her to be sad. Crying. Distraught. But she's none of those. Instead, she walks down the hallway with purpose. She wears yoga pants, sneakers, and a black V-neck T-shirt—her work attire. Her hair is pulled high in a ponytail.

"Hey," I say softly, when she reaches the doorway. The damn organ in my chest hammers hard against my ribcage, thumping like it's trying to escape. I'm fucking nervous and excited all at once. And I'm hopeful, too. "I'm glad you're here." I hold the door wide open, and she comes in. "Tell me what you found out. I want to help you. Like I told you I would."

She stops, licks her lips, and says, "I know you do. But as I was walking over here, I realized something important."

She gestures from me to her. "That I want to talk about *us* first."

The word reverberates. I have no fucking clue what *us* is. I have no idea if I messed up *us* completely. But she came to me. That's a step, and steps are what I need to take, not leaps. "Talk to me."

The door falls shut, but we don't move. We stand in the entryway, not far from where I proposed this morning.

Her features are soft as she speaks. "I wasn't leaving this morning. I know it might have seemed that way, but I was just going to work. I was thrown for a loop, though. I felt like a prize, like just your next victory."

I jump in. "You're not. I swear you're not. I wanted to show you that you're so much more."

"I get that, but at the time that's all it seemed like. It seemed impulsive and unplanned." She runs her hand lightly down my arm. "But I understand now that it came from the best intentions. And I love the sentiment."

"It was impulsive," I admit, with a you-know-me expression. "I'll probably always be a little impulsive. But I also want you to have faith in me."

"But you see, I already do, Tyler," she says, her eyes fixed on me, her voice steady and sure. "You don't need to prove yourself. You don't need to come to my place of work and strip for me again, or jump through any more hoops."

I wiggle an eyebrow. "But you do want me to strip for you again?"

She nibbles on the corner of her lips. "I absolutely do."

"Good. Because I've got some new moves."

She smiles. "I look forward to the next show. And that's because you've already earned your way back in. Let's just move forward now."

I breathe a sigh of relief. *Us*. There's still an us. But it never hurts to confirm. "So we're doing this? You want me, impulsive side and circumspect one both?"

She flashes a flirty smile and slugs my arm. "Yes. I like all your sides, both the naked and the clothed, too. And even though we might argue, I'm not breaking up because you proposed." She rolls her eyes.

I grab her hand and squeeze hard. "You've got to know why I did it. I fucking love you, and I wanted to give you security," I say, needing to explain my actions, needing her to understand. "I couldn't give that to you before, and I want to do it now."

She places a palm on my chest. "I know now that security isn't something I can find from you." She lets go and taps her breastbone. "It's in me. It's right here. I have my inner strength. I've learned. I've grown. I have great friends, an amazing business, and this sexy, smart, and sweet guy who's back in my life," she says, and I mouth *you do have all that*. She gives me a smile, then her voice goes serious again. "All I want is for us to take it day by day. Let's just keep being in love every day."

I smile because that's the easiest thing in the world. "That's not a problem at all. That's like breathing, Delaney."

She smiles softly. "And someday, maybe someday soon, when it feels right to both of us, ask me again. For now, let's just go to parties, and meet for lunch, and kiss on street corners, and make love all night long."

My heart dances a jig. This is the true second chance. Not the one I leaped too hard at this morning. But a real one —a do-over that's not about fixing the past, or erasing mistakes, but one that's about forgiveness and moving on.

I dust a soft kiss on her forehead. Relief floods me as she sways closer to me. But then I wrench back because there are things *I* still need to say. "I'm sorry I was pushy this morning. I've got an asshole in me, and I'm trying to keep him down, but sometimes he crops up." She chuckles, but I'm not done. "I'm especially sorry for what I said about intimacy and challenges. That was unfair. So fucking unfair."

"I was reactive, too. I got angry, and I don't like that side of myself. So let's put it behind us and just be a couple, and see where we go."

"I like the sound of that. I realized this afternoon that I need to just take things as they come and not try to jump fifty feet ahead too soon. My niece actually helped me realize that."

She smiles. "She did? Carly?"

"I'm not sure it was intentional, but sometimes that kid has the wisest observations. The things she says about life and school and whatnot make me realize I need to slow down and take my time, especially when it's something as important as you."

"I like having time with you," Delaney says softly.

"And I like having this second chance with you."

I kiss her. It's soft, but insistent. A kiss that promises we'll make mistakes, but we'll learn from them. A kiss that says we'll try our best not to hurt each other, but when we do we'll work on forgiveness.

When we separate, I look her in the eyes. "I want you to know I'm not going anywhere. Maybe it was crazy to ask you to marry me after a week. But I know in my heart and soul, whether it's this week or next week or next year, you and I can have an amazing future together."

"Me, too," she whispers, her voice breaking. "I believe that, too."

I cup her cheek. "Just let me love you. Let me take care of you."

She smiles as she ropes her hands around my neck. "That sounds perfect to me. And by the way, the ring was gorgeous. You picked perfectly."

A burst of pride spreads through me. "Glad I did that right. And that ring is safe and sound inside my signed Los Angeles Dodgers baseball plexiglass holder for that sometime when you're ready for me to ask again."

"That ring is keeping good company, then."

"You know it." I take her hand, guide her to the couch, and adopt a more serious tone. "Tell me what you learned about your dad," I say, since her message said she'd heard from the detective and wanted to talk to me.

She draws a deep breath. "I *did* want to talk to you about him."

I furrow my brow. "You don't now?"

She nods, then shakes her head, then laughs. "I do, but I don't."

"Dude, I'm confused now."

More laughter comes from Delaney. "As I was walking over here, thinking about calling him and emailing him, something hit me. I don't need to know what he's doing in order to put that bit of the past behind me. Some pieces of the past just need to stay there. And some pieces can become your future." She runs her fingers along my stubbled jaw. "Like you."

I swallow roughly, absorbing the enormity of her words. "You and me, angel," I scratch out, then I press a kiss to her forehead because words fucking fail me sometimes.

She swipes her finger across her phone screen triumphantly. "It's archived. I don't need to save his info, but it'll be there if I need it."

"It will be there. And I'll be here for you."

"I know that. I believe that."

I raise a hand and run my fingers across her silky hair. "Hey. I'm proud of you for this. What you did—tracking him down, then deciding you didn't need it. You did all that on your own. That takes serious cojones."

She wriggles her eyebrows. "Sort of like showing up naked at your ex-girlfriend's place of work to show how much you want her back."

I laugh deeply. "She's not my ex-girlfriend anymore."

Delaney moves in even closer. "No, she's not your ex at all."

I hold up a finger. "And since she's not my ex, and since I want to prove to her I listened, I got her a gift."

My lovely, sexy once-and-present girlfriend arches an eyebrow. "Oh, you did now?"

I straighten my shoulders. "I sure did. To show you I want us to move together at a normal pace."

I take a beat, making her wait for it. She bounces a bit on the cushion. "What is it?" she asks.

I buff my nails on my shirt then blow on them. "You said you wanted a cat, and that I should start with a cat."

Her jaw crashes to the ground. "You got a cat?"

I shift my palm like a seesaw. "That would be impulsive, and I'm trying to take my time and not cut corners. So rather than *getting* you a cat, I *found* you one. And I put money down to adopt him from a cat rescue." I hold up both hands, a gesture of surrender should I need to. "If you're not ready for him, the money can go to the rescue in your name. But I do think you'll like him."

A grin spreads across her face as I grab my phone, swipe it open, and find a picture. "I believe this pussycat fits your specs." I clear my throat and read his description. "They call me Mr. Cuddles. I will curl up next to you, snuggle on the pillow, and sleep in your arms. I'll also rub against you, purr, and even open the door."

She shoves my chest. "Get out of here."

I pretend she slammed me into the armrest. "Polydactyl, baby. Mr. Cuddles has six toes."

She jumps up from the couch and presses her palms together plaintively. "I want him. I want him now."

The woman is literally buzzing with glee. It's amazing to watch her excitement. "You don't want to see him first before you decide?"

She shakes her head. "I'm committing to him. Just like I'm committing to you." She stands up and heads to the door then glances back at me. "Funny. Even though you don't have six toes, I like you just fine."

I raise my right hand, wiggle my fingers, and then stick out my tongue.

Epilogue

Her Epilogue

The cat we renamed Mr. Crazypants was no liar in his ad.

The fluff ball wedges himself between my boyfriend and me that night.

I stare at the orange feline, then at Tyler, and I shrug. "He likes us."

The cat stretches out his right leg then presses his paw to my chest as he purrs.

"I'd say he likes you," Tyler says as the pussycat stretches all six toes then inches even closer to me. "Damn, Mr. Cuddles was an appropriate name if I ever heard one."

I laugh as my new rescued polydactyl kitty snuggles next to me under the covers. "But I like Mr. Crazypants better."

"He was meant to be yours."

"Same for you," I whisper, and Tyler grins, his brown eyes sparkling.

"Now, I know Mr. Crazypants is a grade-A snuggler, but there's something I've got that he doesn't have," Tyler says, as he slinks his hand under my camisole, feathering his fingers across my belly.

"A magic cock?" I ask.

He rolls his eyes. "I don't want to think about a cat's hardware, please."

"Then, whatever did you mean?" I ask, batting my eyelashes innocently.

"What did you call it?" Tyler asks, staring thoughtfully at the ceiling. "I just can't seem to remember the word. Let me see if this reminds you."

He slides under the covers, tugs down my panties, and reminds me why he alone sets my world on fire. His tongue is an instrument of absolute pleasure, and that's what he brings me in mere minutes.

I cry out in bliss, and the new addition even meows in chorus, too.

We both laugh, then Tyler pops his head out. "I believe it's called an enchanted tongue."

"Well, now that you've reminded me, why don't you remind me what that other part does, too."

He makes love to me, and it is magic.

Later, I tell him I have a gift for him, too, and I'll give it to him the next day.

"I can't wait."

Then Mr. Crazypants drapes his feline body over my head, and the three of us drift off like that, a strange new threesome moving well beyond the past, and into a whole new future.

* * *

"Are we there yet?"

"Almost."

My hands cover his eyes for the final few feet to the store. When we reach the entrance, I remove my makeshift blindfold. "Ta-da."

We're at Blue Suede.

He peers at the door, then back at me. "We're going shoe shopping?" Things don't quite compute at first, but a second later, his face transforms. The expression in his eyes is dirty, and his lips twitch up in a naughty grin. "We're going *shoe shopping*."

"Yes." I tap-dance my fingernails along his chest. "And you get to pick the shoes you want me to wear."

"In bed?"

"Wherever you want. My treat."

"I'll say that's *my* treat."

He opens the door for me, and we head into the boutique.

"I should warn you, though, it can be hard to find my size. There might not be too many options."

He grabs my waist and pulls me in closer, pressing his hard body against mine. "Then we will keep on shopping. We will soldier on. We will find you the perfect shoes for your gorgeous feet." He brings his mouth to my ear. "Because I love the way you look when you're wearing nothing but heels."

Twenty minutes later, he's picked out a pair of purple stilettos, some black fuck-me ankle boots, and a pair of red suede pumps.

I swear the man is aroused the entire time we're shopping. I'm convinced at one point he's going to hump me against some shelves of flats.

Then hump me he does.

Later. Back at his house, when I put on the black stilettos and then don his favorite outfit.

When we're done, sweaty, elated and sated, he whispers in my ear. "This whole take-it-day-by-day sure is turning out to be a whole lot of fun."

Yes. Yes, it is. Even though we don't know what tomorrow holds, I love all our todays.

His Epilogue

A flash of orange hits my line of sight, then a gorgeous face, a smile, and the beautiful blonde the grin belongs to. With her two best friends by her side, Delaney crosses the finish line of the 10K run. The women thrust their arms high.

I shout. I hoot. And I holler.

So does Carly, her little voice not quite so little as she happily cheers. The kid has one hell of a set of lungs on her.

As Delaney, Nicole, and Penny slow to a jog, we meet them at the end of the finish line, handing them waters and high-fives. Today's run was to raise money for some of the local animal rescues in Manhattan.

"You ladies are amazing," I say, giving Delaney a quick kiss then congratulating her friends, too.

"And you're amazing for handing us this most delicious bottled water," Nicole says, chiming in as she takes a long and hearty swig in between breaths.

"We beat our time from last year," Penny points out, and Delaney smacks her friend's palm.

"Next year, you're going to join us, right?" Delaney says to Carly.

My niece laughs and shakes her head. "Only if I can do it on rollerblades."

Delaney shrugs. "You drive a hard bargain."

I point a thumb at my chest. "She learned all her negotiation skills from me. And speaking of negotiation, how about I take you all out for breakfast at The Charming Breakfast Spot?"

Four pairs of eyes light up. "Yes, but where's the negotiation in that?" Delaney teases.

I shrug and smile. "Got me. Turns out there's none. But I figured you all earned it with the way you ran for the dogs today."

"And we are looking forward to eggs and toast," Nicole says, then she narrows her eyes. "But don't think you're going to get any details out of me that I wouldn't give up last time."

In unison, Delaney and Penny zip their lips.

The first time I went out with her and her friends last week, the girls had been chatting about a new guy Nicole's interested in, but they clammed up when I joined them. Delaney had asked me to meet up with them for cocktails at Speakeasy. I'll admit it—I was a tad bit nervous meeting her friends. Knowing how close she is to them, I wasn't sure if they'd welcome me with open arms.

I had nothing to worry about. Penny and Nicole love Delaney like a sister, so they grilled me as any family member would do. I can honestly say I enjoyed every second of their cross-examination, especially since I passed it. Nicole even pretended to tap me with a magic wand at the end, declaring, "We like you. Now, be good to our girl always."

I nodded solemnly. "That's a promise."

And as I head to the café, holding Carly's little hand in mine so we can scout out a table in advance, that's exactly what I intend to do.

Another Epilogue

Someday, maybe someday soon

Tyler

I groan when I wake up.

I wish I were making this sound because Delaney's lips were wrapped around my dick.

That would be my favorite kind of alarm clock.

Though, in her defense, she does, indeed, provide cock-a-doodle-doo services on a fairly regular basis.

I am one lucky bastard.

The only part of me that isn't so lucky is the neck.

This damn cat.

Mr. Crazypants is wrapped around my neck, motherfucking purring in my ear. Don't get me wrong. This cat is cool as hell. But his cuddly tendencies have put a crook in my spine.

I've never been so sore in my life.

Fortunately, I'm involved with the best damn masseuse in all of New York City. She insisted on scheduling a massage for me today. Sure, she rubs my neck at home, too, and last night, she gave me one fantastic massage. But she told me I needed to get my behind into Nirvana at nine a.m. sharp so she could work on me properly. It's Saturday, and she's already at work. I gently remove the cat from his scarf pose, swing my legs over the bed, and stretch, trying to work out the kinks.

I hit the shower, get dressed in jeans and a T-shirt, grab my wallet, phone, and shades, and head for the door. The orange fluff ball rubs against my leg.

"Meow!"

Mr. Crazypants rises up on his back legs and paws me with his twelve front toes. Delaney was right—six-toed cats are the bomb. Even though his zealous cuddling is a pain in the neck, he's a badass dude otherwise. Delaney loves him, and he makes her happy, so that's a big win-win in my book.

"Be back soon, little dude," I say, then scratch him between the ears.

He rewards me with a loud rumble, and then I take off.

Fifteen minutes later, I reach the front door of Nirvana. Inside, Felipe greets me with a smile and a waggle of his fingers.

"Delaney is almost ready for you. Let me show you back. And I know you're still a no-robe man," he says as he escorts me to the Rainfall Room.

"No robes forever. That's my mantra."

Felipe opens the door, shoots me a smile, and shuts it as he leaves. I strip down to nothing, thinking back briefly to when I did this many months ago. I smile privately, loving that it set the two of us in motion.

I fold my clothes, place them on top of a stool, and climb onto the table. I know the routine well by now, since Delaney schedules regular massages for me.

We moved in together after a few months of dating. "The cat wants it, and so do I," she said one Sunday afternoon following another epic session of walking and kissing—in Greenwich Village that particular day, wandering in and out of shops and cafés.

"If Mr. Crazypants wants me full-time, then so be it," I'd said.

"And me," she'd reminded me.

We moved into my apartment, and she quickly added her feminine touches, including setting some lovely lilacs by the window. I did my part by making sure she had all the closet space she needed. For her clothes, and for all those new shoes.

As I linger on a recent memory of her wearing silver pumps while waiting for me in the kitchen, holding a glass of chardonnay, the door opens. I peer up from the face cradle to see a blond beauty wearing yoga pants and a sweet smile just for me.

"Hey, angel."

"Hey, handsome." She comes to my side and drops a soft kiss on my cheek. Her hair brushes against my skin.

"Mmm," I murmur, and I'm about to tug her onto the table with me, even though she has a strict no-screwing-at-work policy.

But then, she drops to her knees.

Startled, I prop myself up on my elbow. "What's up?"

She's not just on her knees. She's on one knee. She holds a black jewelry box. "This is where we started again. Where you showed up and made a grand gesture to win my heart. And you won it big time. Now I'm asking if you're ready for the next big gesture, because I know I am."

I blink as it registers. As the sheer enormity of this moment hits me. She's ready. She's fucking ready.

I part my lips to speak, but she's faster.

"Ask me again," she says, her voice soft but sure.

And I suppose it couldn't be more fitting that I'm naked. I slide out from under the sheet, yank her up to the table so she's perched right next to me on the edge, then take the box in my hand. "Will you marry me?"

She grins like the happiest person in the world, and she nods and nods and keeps on nodding. "Yes, yes, yes."

I slide the ring on her finger, where it belongs. She holds up her hand and the diamond sparkles in the dimly lit room.

At last.

It took me nearly a decade to find my way back to her. But when the love of your life slips through your fingers, then you're lucky enough to stumble into her life again, you do everything you can to win her back, even if you have to wait until she's ready.

I waited. I did it step by step. I didn't cut corners. I took my time.

She's no longer the one who got away.

She's the one I'm keeping close to my heart for all time.

THE END

Curious about Nicole? Find out who she falls
for in THE WILD ONE, releasing in summer 2017!

Sign up for my newsletter to receive an alert
when these sexy new books are available!

ACKNOWLEDGEMENTS

Thank you to Helen Williams for the amazing cover! Thank you to KP Simmon for everything. I am so grateful for the work that Kelley, Candi, Keyanna and Kara do for every book. Huge gratitude to my girls, Laurelin, CD and Kristy, and, of course, to Lili Valente. I'm indebted to the patient and fabulous feedback from Jen McCoy and Dena Marie when crafting these characters, and to Kim who watches over the finished book. Thank you to all my editors from Tiffany to Lauren to Janice and especially Karen on this one. Thank you to my family and my husband, and to my fabulous dogs! HUGE thank you to all the bloggers and reviewers who spread the word. Biggest thanks of all goes to my readers. I love you!

Xoxo
Lauren

Coming Soon!

My next all-guy POV romantic comedy is JOY STICK and it releases in May! Here's a sneak peek!

Prologue

Here's something I want to know. Why the fuck does the term *guilty pleasure* even exist? If something brings you pleasure, don't feel guilty.

Case closed.

But let's just be perfectly clear—I'm not talking about stuff a dude should feel ten tons of remorse about. Like, being a dick to your boss or cheating on your woman. If that kind of shit brings you pleasure, then may all the guilt from the skies rain down on you, along with golfball-sized hail and toads too.

What I don't get is why people feel bad about the good stuff in life they enjoy. Buying that pool table just because it looks fucking awesome in your living room. Or drinking the eighteen-year-old Scotch one night after a long day fixing an engine on a Mustang, instead of waiting for a special occasion to crack open the bottle.

Fuck that.

Life is short. Savor it now.

Hell, if it floats your boat to sink into a steaming hot bubble bath every so often, then, man, turn the water up high and toss a bath bomb into the claw-foot tub.

Not that I do *that.* Hell, I don't even know what a bath bomb is. And I absolutely, positively did not use the zingy lemongrass scented one the other night. The type that fizzes. I don't have a clue why it's missing from the cabinet.

Let's just talk about something else besides guilty pleasure bubble baths, OK?

In any case, I say *indulge.*

Yeah, my pool table rocks, and so does the Scotch. But hands down, my favorite indulgence happens to be the one-night stand.

What? Like that's such a crime? Nothing wrong with a night of round-the-clock fun of the X-rated variety. Besides, when I take a woman home for a one-and-done fiesta of five-star fucking, I'm honest about my intentions. I never promise more than I can deliver. But what I do serve up—in extra large quantities, thank you very much—is a fantastic time between the sheets with no strings attached when the sun comes up.

I've never felt guilty about this pleasure either, and that's because I maintain a few key guidelines when it comes to my favorite horizontal hobby.

Don't be an asshole.

Always be a gentleman.

And never sleep with the enemy.

Now, about that last rule . . . don't break it. Don't bend it. Don't even dip your toe on the other side.

Trust me on this.

As soon as I realized I wanted a whole helluva lot more than one night with a certain sexy brunette, I went on to shatter that last guideline in spectacular fashion. Now I've got the brand new tattoo, the wrecked electric blue roadster, and a pet monkey to show for it.

Yes, I said pet monkey.

And that's a big fucking problem for the King of Pleasure.

CHAPTER ONE

Cars are like ice cream.

There's a flavor for everyone.

Some auto enthusiasts opt for vanilla. For them, a basic sports car will do just fine.

Others want a sundae with everything on it, from the badass paint job to the jacked-up wheels to the sound system that registers on the Richter scale.

Then, you've got the car buffs who gravitate toward a dark chocolate gelato when they fork over big bucks for a sleek Aston Martin, outfitted with an engine that kills it on the Autobahn.

Every now and then though, you'll encounter the fellow who doesn't know what he likes, so he goes for rainbow sprinkles, bananas, chopped nuts, and a cherry on top. Like this guy I'm talking to right now at a custom car show just outside Manhattan.

The bespectacled man strokes his chin then asks in a smooth, sophisticated voice: "Could you make an armored car?"

That's the latest question from this thirtysomething guy in tailored slacks and a crisp white button-down. Wire-rimmed glasses slide to the bridge of his nose as he gestures to an emerald green, fully customized sports car that holds center stage.

"Armored cars are in my arsenal," I say, since I've made a few beasts designed to outlast the zombie apocalypse. Yeah, I've got some survivalist clients, and they order the bullet-proof glass too, I tell him.

He arches an eyebrow. "Could you add in some sleek tail fins?"

Ah, tail fins. I have a hunch where he's going now, and it's not to the land of the undead. "I can do that too."

"And maybe it can even ride low and respond to commands?"

I stifle a laugh since I have his number for sure now, and I fucking love the enthusiasm of the newbies. "Absolutely. I assume you'd want it in black?"

His blue eyes light up. "Yes. Black would be perfect."

For the Batmobile. Because that's what the dude just described. I'm not knocking him or the Batmobile. That vehicle is absolutely at the top of my bucket list too. What self-respecting gearhead wouldn't want to tool around town in a superhero's tricked-out ride?

This guy's nowhere near done though as he peppers me with a new set of questions. "Would you be able to make a car that—just for the sake of argument—can jump incredibly far distances?"

I don't need precognition to know where he's going with this new scenario. "Would you want it to play a little song when you hit the horn?" I ask.

His eyes twinkle. "Oh, that's a nice feature indeed."

I wonder where I came up with that idea. Could it be my vast knowledge of the *General Lee from Dukes of Hazard?*

The guy is rolling through the greatest hits of cars on TV or film.

And you know what? There's not a damn thing wrong with that. If he learns about cars from the tube or the screen, so be it. He knows his famous cars, after all. Maybe he'll ask me to make a VW Bug that talks. My sister has begged for that for years, and if I ever figure out how, I'm delivering it to her first.

"What about wings for doors?"

"Like a Delorean?"

He nods in excitement. "I love that car so much."

"I haven't met a Delorean I didn't want to marry either. That's the reason I got into this business in the first place."

"Are you a Back to the Future fan too?"

I hold up a fist for knocking. "You know it."

"Any chance you put a flux capacitor in it for me?"

"Absolutely. And I promise it'll hit 1.21 gigawatts when you crank the gas," I say, and as we laugh the click clack of high heels against asphalt grows louder. This show is swarming with women in heels, working the booths, posing seductively on hoods or beside doors. Can't say that bothers me. Nope, I definitely can't say I'm annoyed by the proliferation of female flesh one bit.

Cars and chicks—that's all I need for sustenance.

But now's not the time for checking out the scenery, because business always comes first. I extend a hand to the Back to the Future fan. "Max Summers of Summers Custom Autos."

He shakes. "David Winters. And I know this may shock you, but . . . *confession*—I know nothing about cars."

"Nothing wrong with that since I know a ton."

He smiles and shrugs sheepishly. "Excellent. I'm looking for a builder who can make the best. Total custom job. Like this one, I presume?" he asks, pointing to the sleek green beauty I'm keeping watch over at the show. I'm here with a client since I built this baby from the ground for Wagner Boost—an NFL lineman who's off signing autographs somewhere at this event. Wagner is a mammoth. At 6' 8" and 350 pounds—that's his morning weight, since he jokes that he shoots up to 360 after breakfast—he needed a car tailored to fit his frame. So I made it for him, and he loves it and likes to show it off.

"Let me tell you something," I say, patting the hood of Wagner's prized possession. "If you can dream it, I can damn near make it. If you want aftermarket tires, a brand new engine, custom upholstery, I'll take care of it. If you want to marry parts from a roadster you've see in a gangster flick into a futuristic prototype, I'll find a way. I'll deliver on your vision because that's what I do."

The tap tap of stiletto heels across the asphalt sounds closer now, as David fires off another question. "Can you—?"

A woman's voice interrupts. "Can you paint a badass tiger on the door?"

No. Fucking. Way.

That voice. That sexy purr. Like honey, like whiskey. Like dirty dreams.

Everything in me goes still. I haven't heard that voice in years. I don't even have to turn around because one more click, then another, and here she is, standing in front of me. Looking even hotter than she ever did before.

Long brown hair. Dark chocolate eyes. Legs than go on forever.

Henley Rose Marlowe.

Fuck me senseless.

It's her.

The woman who drove me crazy.

I'm momentarily speechless as I take her in because she's not twenty-one anymore. She's five years older and twenty-five times hotter. Yes, her hotness has squared with the years.

But I'm not about to let a potential deal slide through my fingers. I never let women get in the way of work, especially not one who's inserting herself into the middle of a conversation with a fucking *tiger* comment.

So I get around her interruption by going along with it.

"The tiger can even be roaring," I suggest, as if she's just some random car lover who's keen on chitchatting, not a girl who used to work under the hood in my shop.

"Maybe even breathing fire," Henley offers, like we've got this rapport down pat, *who's on first* style.

David gets into the action too, emitting a *rawr* as he holds up his hands like claws.

Henley flashes him the sexiest smile I've ever seen, and in less than a second, the fire-breathing tiger inhabits me. Because I'm jealous as hell. For no fucking reason.

David smiles back at her.

Okay, maybe for *that* reason.

Which is not an acceptable reason at all. I shake off the useless emotion as David speaks again. "That's it. I've officially decided I want a tiger on the door of a Delorean. Painted in green, like the color of money."

Yep, he's rainbow sprinkles all the way, and I focus on the sprinkles, not the flirty grins exchanged between this guy and a woman who was never mine.

"You can have it in royal purple, in emerald green, in sapphire blue," I tell him. "You can have it with a flag on the hood, a pinstripe on the door, and you can even have it with a monkey in the passenger seat."

"Purple, plus a monkey? I'm sold." He clasps my hand in a good-bye shake. "I'll be in touch." He takes a step to go then stops. "Is purple too crazy a color? What do you think?" he asks the woman who'd make any red-blooded man gawk. Perfect figure. Pouty lips. Tight waist. Gravity-defying tits.

When God made the ideal woman to sell a red-blooded man any bill of goods, he crafted Henley.

Not sure he intended her to have such a smartass mouth though.

She licks her lips. "Purple is hot as sin," she says to David, like the words are for his ears only. She presses her fingertip to her tongue then touches the hood of the car as if it burns her. She raises her hand, letting the imaginary flame fly high.

David eats up her show, laughing and grinning.

"That's an excellent selling point of purple. What about you, Max? Favorite color?" He holds up a hand as a stop sign. "Wait. Let me guess. Gold? Silver? Red? Blue?"

I shake my head. "Black."

Then David says good-bye and heads off, and I'm left with the vexing vixen who hates me.

She stares at me. Like a cat who won't look away. I don't break her showdown.

"*Black*," she repeats, tapping the toe of her red suede pump as she glares with dark brown eyes full of fury. "Like your heart."

Have I mentioned the last time I saw her she marched out of my shop in a blaze of glory and cursed me in what sounded like twelve different languages.

Might be because I fired her sexy ass five years ago.

Yeah, there's some bad blood between us.

CHAPTER TWO

Henley Rose and a hot car went together like peaches and cream, like fine Scotch and a long, dirty night.

Which meant working with her was like walking into the Garden of Eden every single day.

It was a test of willpower because the woman could craft a car like it was an erotic dance.

Not a strip tease.

Not an in-your-face pelvis thrust.

But a beautiful fucking ballet of woman seducing machine. Those hands, the way she wielded tools, the intensity in her focus. It was sensual, and it was sinful, and it was this man's fantasy made flesh.

Imagine what it was like working with her for one hard-on year.

I mean, hard year.

But I survived the challenge because she was the best in the class. And I never treated her differently because she was a woman, or because I thought about her naked an obscene amount of time. I treated her like anyone else—specifically, all the people I work with who I never ever imagine in anything less than full-on Siberian winter garb, complete with the thermals and Michelin Man coat.

"Black heart. That's an upgrade from cold, dead heart," I say coolly, reminding her of the words she uttered the day she stormed out.

"So you had the ticker replaced then?"

I tap my sternum. "All new model. But apparently, I'm still just the same cruel bastard," I say, using another favorite phrase of her from the last day I saw her.

She arches a brow. "Shame. You should have let me work on that part of you. I'm good at making all sorts of clunkers run better."

Jesus Christ. She still takes no prisoners. "I've no doubt you have all the tools to fix anything, and if you couldn't find the right one, you'd use a blowtorch."

She adopts an expression of indignation. "There's nothing wrong with using a *blowtorch*," she says, taking extra time on the first syllable.

How the fuck did I ever last with this woman? Before I can even fashion a comeback, she taps her toe against the tire on Wagner's car. "I see you still like to make your cars with such *big, manly* wheels."

I roll my eyes, then make a "give it to me now" motion with my hands. "All right, Henley. Deliver the punchline."

She bats her lashes. "What punchline?"

"*Big? Manly?* You're going to say it's some of substitution thing going on. That's what you always said about the guys who wanted the biggest cars, with the biggest wheels."

She smirks. "Was I wrong in my assessment?"

I laugh. "I don't know. I didn't check to see how that added up for them."

"Nor did I. My focus was *always* on the work."

"As well it should be."

"That's what you taught me."

"I'm glad you learned that lesson."

"I learned *so many* lessons from you."

I take a deep breath and change directions. "What was up with the badass tiger comment out of nowhere? Couldn't just wait till I was done to say hello?"

She winks. "C'mon. I was just having fun."

"Fun? More like trying to get involved in everything."

She feigns shocks, then dances her fingertips along the hood of Wagner's car. "I was merely being helpful and trying to land you a client. Don't you remember? I was always trying to help you."

I park my hands on my hips. "Why do I feel like you're here to taunt me rather than deliver your generous humanitarian aid?"

She clasps a hand to her chest. Her ample chest. "Taunt? Me? You? I was just excited to say hello to my former mentor. Forgive me for my exuberance," she says, in a too-sweet tone. "How are you these days?"

"I can't complain." I cross my arms. I don't know what to make of her, and I don't know that I want to let her in. "What about you? It's been a while."

"Five years. Three weeks. And two days. But who's counting?"

"Sounds like you're counting."

She shrugs like that's no big deal, then pops up on the hood and parks her sweet ass on Wagner's car. Wagner won't care. He likes pretty ladies, especially when they're on his prized ride. The problem is he'll probably want to bang Henley when he returns from signing autographs, and that's not going to fucking happen on my watch.

Not that I have any control over who she's banging.

But I'll do everything I can to make sure it's not a client of mine who gets his hands on her.

"What brings you to this neck of the woods?" Last I heard from her she'd gone back home to Northern California to work with a rival builder there.

She points her thumb in the general direction of Clint Savage, a burly bearded foul-mouthed motherfucker who kills it with some of the hottest custom rides on the planet. The bastard is talented and prolific. He pumps out kids as often as he makes cars. Well, his wife pumps out the kids. "I'm just booth bitching at Savage Rides," Henley says.

"Yeah?" That surprises me, but I don't let on. Henley was never a pretty set of legs and tits at a show. She was under the hood, working on the engine, getting her hands dirty.

She nods and smiles a yes. "He has me pose on top of the cars. We clean up like that." She snaps her fingers.

"Is that so?"

"Absolutely." She runs her eyes up and down my body. Lingers on my chest. Well, my T-shirt. I'm not some ass who parades shirtless at a car show. I save that for when I drive with the top down. No, seriously. Do I look like a douche? I don't drive shirtless either.

She straightens her spine and stands tall, hopping off the car. "*No.*" That's all she says, but that one word comes out exactly like "*No, you idiot.*"

She fucking hates me still. I sigh. "What are you doing here then at the show?"

She narrows her eyes. "I'm with a client too. You think you're the only game in town? I run a shop now. Here in New York too."

I never kept tabs on her since she walked away in a cloud of black smoke, and I figured it was best for me not to stalk her. I needed to stay away from the kind of temptation she brought to my shop every day. "Good for you."

She sets one hand on her hip and stares at me defiantly. "You really thought I was a booth babe?"

"You said you were here as one," I say, giving it back to her.

She huffs. "You never thought much of me, did you?"

You don't want to know the half of it. You don't want to know how much I thought of you and most of it was vastly inappropriate.

"Henley," I say, keeping my tone measured, "you were the most talented apprentice I ever worked with. I thought the world of your skills and you know it."

She sneers, then she pokes me. She stabs her index finger against my chest, her red polished nail scratching me, and instantly stirring up not-safe-for-work fantasies of her nails down my chest then my back. What can I say? I like it rough.

"Actions speak louder than words. And yours make it clear you never thought I was good enough," she says, and so much for playing it cool. She makes that impossible.

I give it right back to her, letting my gaze drift away from her eyes. Down to her neck then to her shoulder. She follows my path, then I say, "I see you haven't had that chip removed yet. I know a doctor who can take care of that for you."

Her eyebrows shoot into her hairline. But her voice is even. "Thanks for the tip. I'll be sure to think of you first when I'm ready to take it out, seeing as you're the reason I have one in the first place."

Let me revise my assessment. *A sexy chip on a fuckhot shoulder.* "Glad to know you're finally giving me credit for something."

She rolls her eyes. "I gave you all the credit, and you gave me nada." She curls her thumb and forefinger into an O. "Zilch. Zero."

"Don't forget goose egg while you're at it. Wouldn't want you to forget another way to describe how I robbed you of all opportunity."

She purses her lips and shakes her head. "I don't know why I came over here to talk to you."

"That's a fascinating question. One I'd love to know the answer to."

"I don't know. Call me crazy. But I thought maybe we could have a civilized conversation."

I laugh sharply. "You did? That's why you inserted yourself into a conversation with a potential client with your tiger comment?"

She wrenches back. "It was supposed to be funny." For once, her tone sounds hurt, like I've wounded her. "You used to tease me when I got all worked up about something. You called me tiger."

The memory smashes back into me. She's right. She's fucking right. I blink, remembering a time when she was pissed at herself over a struggle with a transmission tunnel that nicked her left hand, and I said, "Easy, tiger," before I moved in and helped her, showing her how to do it without slicing her finger off.

She thanked me in the sweetest voice, and then I put a Band-Aid on the cut.

She shrugs her shoulders in an *I-give-up* gesture, and I realize I'm letting her wind me up. This woman was the most fiery, spirited person I've ever worked with, but I can't let her get under my skin, or make me want to put Band-Aids on her when she can damn well do it herself. I need a new approach, especially if we're running in the same circles.

"See you later, Max."

She turns to go, but I grab her arm. "Wait." My voice is gentler now. "Tell me what you're up to now."

"Building cars."

"I figured that much from what you said. What's your specialty?"

The corner of her lips curve up in a smile as she moves closer. So damn close I can smell her sweet breath, and I'm half wondering how she smells so good at four in the afternoon, like cinnamon candy. But then, that was one of her many talents. Smelling good, looking good, working hard. "The kind I would have made with you if you'd have let me," she says and steps one inch closer. So close I could kiss her cinnamon lips. "They're called . . . *the best.*"

She spins on a heel and walks away.

I should call out after her. I should try harder to smooth over the past. But I'm better off letting her go. She's far too dangerous. Even though a part of me likes playing with fire.

And that part of me needs to stay the fuck away from a woman like her.

Also by Lauren Blakely

FULL PACKAGE, the #1 New York Times
Bestselling romantic comedy!

BIG ROCK, the hit New York Times
Bestselling standalone romantic comedy!

MISTER O, also a New York Times
Bestselling standalone romantic comedy!

WELL HUNG, a New York Times
Bestselling standalone romantic comedy!

THE SEXY ONE, a swoony New York Times
Bestselling standalone romance!

The New York Times and USA Today
Bestselling Seductive Nights series including
Night After Night, *After This Night*,
and *One More Night*

And the two standalone
romance novels, *Nights With Him* and *Forbidden Nights*,
both New York Times and USA Today Bestsellers!

Sweet Sinful Nights, *Sinful Desire*, *Sinful Longing*
and *Sinful Love*, the complete New York Times
Bestselling high-heat romantic suspense series
that spins off from Seductive Nights!

Playing With Her Heart, a USA Today bestseller, and a sexy Seductive Nights spin-off standalone! (Davis and Jill's romance)

21 Stolen Kisses, the USA Today Bestselling forbidden new adult romance!

Caught Up In Us, a New York Times and USA Today Bestseller! (Kat and Bryan's romance!)

Pretending He's Mine, a Barnes & Noble and iBooks Bestseller! (Reeve & Sutton's romance)

Trophy Husband, a New York Times and USA Today Bestseller! (Chris & McKenna's romance)

Far Too Tempting, the USA Today Bestselling standalone romance! (Matthew and Jane's romance)

Stars in Their Eyes, an iBooks bestseller! (William and Jess' romance)

My USA Today bestselling No Regrets series that includes

The Thrill of It
(Meet Harley and Trey)

and its sequel

Every Second With You

My New York Times and USA Today
Bestselling Fighting Fire series that includes

Burn For Me
(Smith and Jamie's romance!)

Melt for Him
(Megan and Becker's romance!)

and *Consumed by You*
(Travis and Cara's romance!)

The Sapphire Affair series…
The Sapphire Affair
The Sapphire Heist

CONTACT

I love hearing from readers! You can find me on Twitter at LaurenBlakely3, or Facebook at LaurenBlakelyBooks, or online at LaurenBlakely.com. You can also email me at laurenblakelybooks@gmail.com

Made in the USA
San Bernardino, CA
19 March 2017